I0595421

Felix Rabbe

Shelley

the man and the poet - From the French of Félix Rabbe - Vol. 2

Felix Rabbe

Shelley
the man and the poet - From the French of Félix Rabbe - Vol. 2

ISBN/EAN: 9783337387204

Printed in Europe, USA, Canada, Australia, Japan

Cover: Foto ©Andreas Hilbeck / pixelio.de

More available books at **www.hansebooks.com**

SHELLEY:

THE MAN AND THE POET.

FROM THE FRENCH OF FELIX RABBE.

In Two Volumes.

VOL. II.

WARD AND DOWNEY,

12, YORK STREET, COVENT GARDEN, LONDON.

1888.

[All rights reserved.]

CONTENTS.

CHAPTER V.

CHAPTER VI.

CHAPTER VII.

CHAPTER VIII.

CHAPTER IX.

CHAPTER X.

APPENDIX.

SHELLEY:

THE MAN AND THE POET.

CHAPTER I.

"HISTORY OF A SIX WEEKS' TOUR"—JOURNAL OF SHELLEY AND MARY—1814.

AT four o'clock on the morning of July 28th, the fugitives, accompanied by Jane Clairmont, who was to act as interpreter, left Skinner Street for Dover. But Shelley shall tell the story himself: *

* We owe to Mr. Dowden the very interesting extracts from Shelley's Journal, from which the account published by Mary in 1817 was compiled, under the following title : " History of a Six Weeks' Tour through a part of France, Switzerland, Germany, and Holland; with Letters descriptive of a Sail round the Lake of Geneva, and of the Glaciers of Chamouni." We have completed Shelley's Journal by the printed narrative, all passages from the former being enclosed in brackets [   ], thus.

[*July* 28.—The night preceding this morning, all being decided, I ordered a chaise to be ready by four o'clock. I watched until the lightning and the stars became pale. At length it was four,   I believed it not possible that we should succeed ; still there appeared to lurk some danger even in certainty.   I went ; I saw her ; she came to me.   Yet one quarter of an hour remained.   Still some arrangement must be made ; and she left me for a short time.   How dreadful did this time appear !   It seemed that we trifled with life and hope.   A few minutes passed.   She was in my arms—— we were safe.   We were on our road to Dover.

Mary was ill as we travelled ; yet in that illness what pleasure and security did we not share !   The heat made her faint ; it was necessary at every stage that we should repose. I was divided between anxiety for her health and terror lest our pursuers should arrive.   I reproached myself with not allowing her sufficient time to rest, with conceiving any evil so great that the slightest portion of her comfort might be sacrificed to avoid it.

At Dartford we took four horses, that we might outstrip pursuit.   We arrived at Dover before four o'clock (where Mary was refreshed by a sea-bath).   Some time was necessarily expended in consideration, in dinner, in bar- gaining with sailors and Custom-house officers.   At length we engaged a small boat to convey us to Calais ; it was ready by six o'clock.   The evening was most beautiful ; the sands slowly receded ; we felt safe.   There was little wind, the sails flapped in the flagging breeze.

The moon rose, the night came on, and with the night a slow heavy swell, and a fresher breeze which soon became so violent as to toss the boat very much.   Mary was much affected by the sea ; she could scarcely move.   She lay in my arms through the night ; the little strength which re- mained in my own exhausted frame was all expended in keeping her head at rest on my bosom.   The wind was violent and contrary. If we could not reach Calais, the sailors proposed making for Boulogne. They promised only two hours' sail from the shore; yet hour after hour passed, and we were still far distant, when the moon sank in the red and stormy horizon, and the fast-flashing lightning became pale in the breaking day. We were proceeding slowly against the wind, when suddenly a thunder-squall struck the sail, and the waves rushed into the boat. Even the sailors believed that our situation was perilous. The wind had now changed, and we drove before a wind that came in violent gusts, directly to Calais.

Mary did not know our danger; she was resting between my knees, that were unable to support her. She did not speak or look, but I felt that she was there. I had time in that moment to reflect and even to reason upon death; it was rather a thing of discomfort and of disappointment than horror to me. We should never be separated, but in death we might not know and feel our union as now. I hope, but my hopes are not unmixed with fear for what will befall this inestimable spirit when we appear to die.

The morning broke, the lightning died away, the violence of the wind abated. We arrived at Calais whilst Mary still slept; we drove upon the sands. Suddenly the broad sun rose over France.

Friday, July 29.—I said: "Mary, look; the sun rises over France." We walked over the sands to the inn; we were shown into an apartment that answered the purpose both of a sitting and sleeping-room.]

I heard for the first time the confused buzz of voices speaking a different language from that to which I had been accustomed, and saw a costume very unlike that worn on the opposite side of the Channel; the women with high caps and short jackets; the men with ear-rings; ladies walking about with high bonnets or *coiffures* lodged on the top of the head, the hair dragged up underneath, without any stray curls to decorate the temples or cheeks. There is, however, something very pleasing in the manners and appearance of the people of Calais that prepossesses you in their favour. A national reflection might occur that when Edward III. took Calais, he turned out the old inhabitants, and peopled it almost entirely with our own countrymen ; but unfortunately the manners are not English.

We remained that day and the greater part of the next at Calais ; we had been obliged to leave our boxes the night before at the English Custom-house, and it was arranged that they should go by the packet of the following day, which, detained by the contrary wind, did not arrive until night.

[In the evening Captain Davison came and told us that a fat lady had arrived, who had said that I had run away with her daughter ; it was Mrs. Godwin. Jane spent the night with her mother.

Saturday, July 30.—Jane informs us that she is unable to withstand the pathos of Mrs. Godwin's appeal. She appealed to the municipality of Paris—to past slavery and to future freedom. I counselled her to take at least an hour for consideration. She returned to Mrs. Godwin and informed her that she resolved to continue with us.

I met Mrs. Godwin in the street apparently proceeding to embark for Dover. I walked alone with Mary to the field beyond the gate (a field among the fortifications—haymakers at work in it). At six in the evening we left Calais and arrived at Boulogne at ten.]

We left Calais in a cabriolet drawn by three horses. To persons who had never before seen anything but a spruce English chaise and post-boy, there was something irresistibly ludicrous in our equipage. Our cabriolet was shaped something like a post-chaise, except that it had only two wheels, and consequently there were no doors at the sides ; the front was let down to admit passengers. The three horses were placed abreast, the tallest in the middle, who was rendered more formidable by the addition of an unintelligible article of harness, resembling a pair of wooden wings fastened to his shoulders ; the harness was of rope ; and the postillion, a queer, upright little fellow, with a long pigtail, *craquéed* his whip, and clattered on ; while an old forlorn shepherd with a cocked hat gazed on us as we passed.

The roads are excellent, but the heat was intense, and Mary suffered greatly from it. We slept at Boulogne the first night, where there was an ugly, but remarkably good-tempered *femme de chambre*. This made us for the first time remark the difference which exists between this class of persons in France and in England. In the latter country they are prudish, and if they become in the least degree familiar they are impudent. The lower orders in France have the easiness and politeness of the most well-bred English ; they treat you unaffectedly as their equal, and consequently there is no scope for insolence.

We had ordered horses to be ready during the night, but were too fatigued to make use of them. The man insisted on being paid for the whole post. "Ah, madame," said the *femme de chambre*, "pensez-y ; c'est pour dédommager les pauvres chevaux d'avoir perdu leur doux sommeil." A joke from an English chambermaid would have been quite another thing.

In order to hasten the journey as much as possible, on account of Mary's health, we did not rest the following night, and the next day about two, arrived in Paris.

[*Tuesday, August* 2.— We engaged lodgings at the Hôtel de Vienne. Mary looked over, with me, the papers contained in her box. They consisted of her own writings, letters from her father and her friends, and my letters. She promised me that I should be permitted to read and study these productions of her mind that preceded our intercourse. I shall claim this promise at Uri. In the evening we walked to the gardens of the Tuilleries; they are very formal and uninteresting, without any grass. Mary was not well; we returned, and were too happy to sleep.*

Wednesday, August 3.— Received a cold and stupid letter from Hookham. He said that Mrs. Boinville's family were reduced to the utmost misery by the distant chance of their being called upon in the course of a year to pay forty pounds for me. He did not send the money. Wrote to Tavernier. Mary read to me some passages from Lord Byron's poems. I was not before so clearly aware how much colouring our own feelings throw upon the liveliest delineations of other minds. Our own perceptions are the world to us.

---

* The "History of a Six Weeks' Tour" adds the following details about Paris : " In this city there are no hotels where you can reside as long or as short a time as you please, and we were obliged to engage apartments at an hotel for a week. They were dear and not very pleasant. As usual in France, the principal apartment was a bedchamber ; there was another closet with a bed, and an ante-chamber which we used as a sitting-room. . . . I think the Boulevards infinitely pleasanter than the Tuilleries. This street nearly surrounds Paris, and is eight miles in extent ; it is very wide, and planted on either side with trees. At one end is a superb cascade which refreshes the senses by its continual splashing ; near this stands the gate of St. Denis, a beautiful piece of sculpture. I do not know how it may at present be disfigured by the Gothic barbarism of the conquerors of France, who were not contented with retaking the spoils of Napoleon, but with impotent malice destroyed the monuments of their own defeat. When I saw this gate it was in its splendour, and made you imagine that the days of Roman greatness were transported to Paris."

Thursday, August 4.—Mary told me that this was my birthday; I thought it had been the 27th June. Tavernier breakfasted; he is an idiot. I sold my watch, chain, etc., which brought eight napoleons five francs.* Tavernier dined; the fool infinitely more insupportable. He walked with us in the evening to the Boulevard; he walked with Jane.

Friday, August 5.—Breakfasted with some friends of Tavernier. I committed the mistake of imagining a married woman to be a little baby of nine years old, and if her child (whom I imagined to be her sister) had not possessed a more prepossessing countenance, I should have taken her in my lap and offered her a lump of sugar. The ladies talked of dress and eating. We went with Tavernier to the police and the church of Notre Dame, the interior of which much disappointed our expectations. At the Louvre we saw one picture apparently of the Deluge, which was terribly impressive. It was the only remarkable picture which we had time to observe. There was Heaven and Hell also; the Blessed looked too stupid. In the evening we sallied forth in search of H. M. (Helen Marie) Williams. After numerous unavailing inquiries, we met at the Place Vendôme a Frenchman who could speak English. He offered us his services in the necessary inquiries. He took us out of our way for the pleasure of hearing himself talk; he told us that he had assisted in bribing the mob to overthrow the statue of Napoleon; that he was a Royalist, and had been in the English army during the reign of Bonaparte; he was the first Royalist who had entered Paris. He made us sit down in the garden of the Tuilleries, and there with a smile of abundant and overflowing vanity, confessed that he was

---

* It has been stated that Shelley sent this money to Harriet.

an author and a poet.   We invited him to breakfast, hoping to derive from his officiousness a relief from our embarrassments.

Saturday, August 6.—M. R. de Savi (the "author and poet") breakfasted with us ; we go with him to M. Peregaux the banker, who refuses to advance money.   I learn from Tavernier the direction of H. M. Williams.   Secure that my statement of our history and situation cannot fail to interest, I hasten hither.   She is absent in the country ; the time of her return is uncertain.   On my return to the hotel we go to Tavernier's office to seek for letters ; we hear that Tavernier has letters for us, and is gone to our hotel.   We return.   We had appointed to dine with M. R. de Savi at six ; we keep the appointment at eight, leaving Jane to wait for Tavernier. M. R. de Savi had relinquished all hope.   We return. Tavernier brings a dull and insolent letter from Hookham.

Sunday, August 7.—Tavernier breakfasts.   Promises money.   The morning passes in delightful converse.   We almost forget that we are prisoners in Paris ; Mary especially seems insensible to all future evil.   She feels as if our love would alone suffice to resist the invasions of calamity.   She rested on my bosom and seemed even indifferent to take sufficient food for the sustenance of life.   We went to Tavernier and received a remittance of sixty pounds.   We talk over our plans and determine to walk to Uri.   We went to sleep early on the sofa.]

In England we could not have put our plan in execution without sustaining continual insult and impertinence ; the French are far more tolerant of the vagaries of their neighbours.   We resolved to walk through France, and with this design we determined to purchase an ass, to carry our portmanteau and one of us by turns.

Early therefore on Monday, August 8th, Shelley and Claire went to the ass market and purchased an ass, and the rest of the day until four in the afternoon, was spent in preparations for our departure; during which, Madame l'hôtesse paid us a visit, and attempted to dissuade us from our design. She represented to us that a large army had been recently disbanded, that the soldiers and officers wandered idle about the country, and that *les dames seraient certainement enlevées*. But we were proof against her arguments, and packing up a few necessaries, leaving the rest to go by the diligence, we departed in a *fiacre* from the door of the hotel, our little ass following.

We dismissed the coach at the barrier. It was dusk, and the ass seemed totally unable to bear one of us, appearing to sink under the portmanteau, although it was small and light. We were, however, merry enough, and thought the leagues short. We arrived at Charenton about ten.

Charenton is prettily situated in a valley, through which the Seine flows, winding among banks variegated with trees. On looking at this scene Claire exclaimed, "Oh! this is beautiful enough; let us live here." This was her exclamation on every new scene, and as each surpassed the one before, she cried, "I am glad we did not stay at Charenton, but let us live here."

Finding our ass useless, we sold it before we proceeded on our journey, and bought a mule for ten napoleons. About nine o'clock we departed. We were clad in black silk. I rode on the mule, which carried also our portmanteau; Shelley and Claire followed, bringing a small basket of provisions. About one o'clock we arrived at Gros-Bois, where under the shade of trees we ate our bread and fruit, and drank our wine, thinking of Don Quixote and Sancho.

This night we slept at Guignes, in the same room and beds in which Napoleon and some of his generals had rested during the late war. The little old woman of the place was highly gratified in having this story to tell, and spoke in warm praise of the Empress Josephine and Marie Louise, who had at different times passed on that road.

After having admired the picturesque situation of Provins, which "formed a scene for painting," our travellers reached that part of the country that had been most devastated during the war, and where smoking ruins still marked the passage of the Cossack. Throughout their journey from Nogent to Troyes, there were but ruined villages, houses burned down, blackened beams, broken walls, devastated gardens, deplorable ruins, and inhabitants still more wretched and deplorable. They can procure no milk, the cows had been taken by the Cossacks; they think themselves fortunate when they find shelter in a poor inn where they are offered rancid bacon, sour bread, and impossible beds. At Echemine the inhabitants, as if belonging to another world, are ignorant that Napoleon has been deposed, and when Shelley asked why they did not rebuild their cottages, replied, they were afraid of the Cossacks. On approaching Troyes, a little green vineyard seems to them like an oasis in the Libyan desert.

On August 13th they reached that "dirty and uninviting town," and there, owing to Shelley having sprained an ankle, and walking being impossible, the mule was sold and an open carriage bought for five napoleons; a driver also was engaged, who undertook for the sum of eight napoleons to convey the travellers to Neufchâtel in six days. The simple vanity of their muleteer amused our travellers. He pointed out a plain as the scene of a battle between the Russians and the French—"where the Russians gained the victory?" interrupted Mary. "Oh, no, madame," he replied, "the French are never beaten." "But how was it, then, that the Russians entered Troyes?" "Oh, after being beaten, they took a circuitous route, and thus entered the town."

Shelley made use of his short sojourn at Troyes to write a long letter to Harriet, in which he proposed she should join their travelling party, and requested her to address her reply to the Post Office, Neufchâtel. He ends his description of the terrible state of France with the following singular remark: ". . . dreadful as these calamities are, I can scarcely pity the inhabitants; they are the most unamiable, inhospitable, and unaccommodating of the human race."

At Besançon, their proximity to the mountains

delighted them; but the roads became difficult, and the driver refused to proceed. They were obliged to pass the night in the miserable inn of a miserable village called Mort; after a delightful evening spent in climbing rocks, and reading a tale by Mary Wollstonecraft, also Shakespeare's *As You Like It,* they determined on sleeping by the kitchen fire, as an alternative to sharing a bedroom with the driver; " Shelley much disturbed by the creaking door, the screams of a poor smothered child, and the girl who washed the glasses."

The driver, still scared at the mountains, halted at the little village of Noé. Our travellers took advantage of the delay to wander in a wood, where they entered into serious converse on the perfectibility and future destiny of the world.*

---

* Claire records this conversation in her journal: " Shelley said there would come a time when nowhere on the earth would there be a dirty cottage to be found. Mary asked what time would elapse before that time would come; he said, ' Perhaps a thousand years.' We said, ' Perhaps it would never come, as it was so difficult to persuade the poor to be clean.' But he said it must infallibly arrive, for Society was progressive, and was evidently moving forwards towards perfectibility; and then he described the career made by man. I wish I could remember the whole,

This was their farewell to France. As they approached Switzerland, after leaving Saint Sulpice, the picturesque beauties of the Alpine scenery made them forget all their previous misadventures. On the 19th August, when two leagues from Neufchâtel, they had their first view of the Alps. "How great is my rapture!" cried Shelley. "I a fiery man, with my heart full of

but half has slipped out of my memory—only I recollect that men were first savages ; then nomadic tribes wandering from place to place with their flocks ; then they formed into villages; then into towns ; and then improvement in mind, morals, comfort, etc., set in ; and then next came the Arts, and then the Sciences ; and from this point Society would go on step by step to almost perfection. In the meanwhile the *voiturier*, grown tired of waiting, had gone on alone. We found him again at Pontarlier. He was very impertinent ; asked why we had stayed so long in the woods, there was nothing to see in the woods ; said he had waited two hours at Noé expecting us to return, and then had driven on ; it was all our faults, he said ; and after thinking awhile, Shelley remarked that the driver was right, and it was his dissertation upon the perfectibility of Man that had put us into such difficulties. Mary laughed and said : 'Men always were the source of a thousand difficulties.' Then Shelley asked her why she of a sudden looked so sad, and she answered : 'I was thinking of my father, and wondering what he was now feeling.' He then said : 'Do you mean that as a reproach to me ?' and she answered : 'Oh, no ! don't let us think more about it.'"

youth, and with my beloved by my side, I behold those lordly, immeasurable Alps. They look like a second world gleaming on one; they look like dreams more than realities, they are so heavenly pure and white."

The sum of sixty pounds they had brought from Paris was expended. No letters for them at Neufchâtel. Fortunately, a banker is found who consents to advance Shelley the sum of thirty-eight pounds, sufficient to take them to Uri, the intended close of their journey, and to establish them quietly in some lonely cottage. Two days' driving brought them to Lucerne, and its long imagined delights. Brünnen, with the sight of William Tell's Chapel, fascinated them; "this lovely lake, these sublime mountains and wild forests seemed a fit cradle for a mind aspiring to high adventure and heroic deeds." They could not weary of contemplating "the divine objects that surrounded" them.

The romance-writer and poet, full of dreams of a golden age and terrestrial paradise, was then meditating his romance of "The Assassins," *

* This was a Christian tribe, who at the very beginning of Christianity had withdrawn into the valleys of the

of which, unfortunately, only a short fragment remains. The story opens with the siege of Jerusalem. He purposed that Uri should be for him the solitary vale of Bethzatanai, where those other exiles from the holy city had sought peace, love, and God, far from the civilised world, " learning to identify this mysterious friend and benefactor with the delight that is bred among the solitary rocks, and has its dwelling alike in the changing colours of the clouds, and the inmost recesses of the caverns."

But, in the season of its utmost prosperity and magnificence, Art might not aspire to vie with Nature in the valley of Bethzatanai. All that was wonderful and lovely was collected in this deep seclusion. The fluctuating elements seemed to have been rendered everlastingly permanent in forms of wonder and delight. The mountains of Lebanon had been divided to their base to form this happy valley ; on every side their icy summits darted their white pinnacles into the clear blue sky, imaging, in their grotesque outline, minarets, and ruined domes, and columns worn with time. Far below, the silver clouds rolled their bright volumes in many beautiful shapes, and fed the eternal springs that, quitting the dark chasms like a thousand radiant rainbows, leaped into the quiet vale, then, lingering in many a dark

---

Lebanon, and became the origin of the famous Assassins, who fought against the Crusaders under the Old Man of the Mountain.

glade among the groves of cypress and of palm, lost themselves in the lake. The immensity of these precipitous mountains, with their starry pyramids of snow, excluded the sun,
which overtopped not, even in its meridian, their overhanging rocks. But a more heavenly and serener light was
reflected from their icy mirrors, which, piercing through the
many-tinted clouds, produced lights and colours of inexhaustible variety. The herbage was perpetually verdant, and
clothed the darkest recesses of the caverns and the woods.
Nature, undisturbed, had become an enchantress in these
solitudes ; she had collected here all that was wonderful and
divine from the armoury of her omnipotence. The very
winds breathed health and renovation, and the joyousness of
youthful courage. Fountains of crystalline water played perpetually among the aromatic flowers, and mingled a freshness
with their odour. The pine-boughs became instruments of
exquisite contrivance, among which every varying breeze
waked music of new and more delightful melody. Meteoric
shapes, more effulgent than the moonlight, hung on the
wandering clouds, and mixed in discordant dance around
the spiral fountains. Blue vapours assumed strange lineaments under the rocks and among the ruins, lingering like
ghosts with slow and solemn step. Through a dark chasm
to the east, in the long perspective of a portal glittering with
the unnumbered riches of a subterranean world, shone the
broad moon, pouring, in one yellow and unbroken stream,
her horizontal beams. Nearer the icy region, autumn and
spring held an alternate reign. The sere leaves fell and
choked the sluggish brooks, the chilling fogs hung diamonds
on every spray, and in the dark, cold evening the howling
winds made melancholy music in the trees. Far above shone
the bright throne of winter, clear, cold, and dazzling. Sometimes there were seen the snowflakes to fall before the sinking
orb of the beamless sun, like a shower of fiery sulphur. The
cataracts, arrested in their course, seemed, with their trans-

parent columns, to support the dark-browed rocks. Sometimes the icy whirlwind scooped the powdery snow aloft, to mingle with the hissing meteors, and scatter spangles through the rare and rayless atmosphere. . . .

To the Arabians, constant spectators of so sublime a scene:

Thus securely excluded from an abhorred world, all thought of its judgment was cancelled by the rapidity of their fervid imaginations. They ceased to acknowledge, or deigned not to advert to, the distinctions with which the majority of base and vulgar minds control the longings and struggles of the soul towards its place of rest. A new and sacred fire was kindled in their hearts and sparkled in their eyes. Every gesture, every feature, the minutest action, was modelled to beneficence and beauty, by the holy inspiration that had descended on their searching spirits. The epidemic transport communicated itself through every heart, with the rapidity of a blast from heaven. They were already disembodied spirits ; they were already the inhabitants of paradise. To live, to breathe, to move, was itself a sensation of immeasurable transport. Every new contemplation of the condition of his nature brought to the happy enthusiast an added measure of delight, and impelled to every organ where mind is united to external things, a keener and more exquisite perception of all that they contain of lovely and divine. To love, to be beloved, suddenly became an insatiable famine of his nature, which the wide circle of the universe, comprehending beings of such inexhaustible variety and stupendous magnitude of excellence, appeared too narrow and confined to satiate.

Alas that these visitings of the spirit of life should fluctuate and pass away ! That the moments when the human mind is commensurate with all that it can conceive of excellent and powerful, should not endure with its existence, and survive its most momentous change ! But the beauty of a vernal sunset, with its overhanging curtains of empurpled cloud, is rapidly dissolved, to return at some unexpected period, and spread an alleviating melancholy over the dark vigils of despair.

Uri, however, was the dream of one day only. The six months' intended residence in the hideous Brünnen house called the Château, dwindled to one of forty-eight hours. Only twenty-eight pounds remained in the travellers' purse, and they must at once return to London. On August 28th they reached Lucerne, where Shelley read *King Lear* aloud,* and worked at his novel of " The Assassins." From motives of economy, they decided on travelling by water, taking the *diligence par eau* from Reuss to Lauffenburg ; the passengers, " uncleanly," disgusting smokers, and altogether so uncivil and rude, that Shelley was obliged to strike one of them.

The Reuss is exceedingly rapid, and we descended several falls, one of them more than eight feet. . . . There is some-

---

* Claire, who was highly impressionable, was struck with so much horror at *King Lear* that Shelley was obliged to discontinue reading it aloud.

thing very delicious in the sensation, when at one moment you are at the top of a fall of water, and before the second has expired you are at the bottom, still rushing on with the impulse which the descent has given.

We shall frequently meet with a recollection of this sensation in the recital of the fantastic voyages made by the heroes of Shelley's poems.

From Basle to Mayence our travellers descended the Rhine on a boat laden with goods.

Tuesday, August 30.—The Rhine is violently rapid to-day, and although interrupted by no rocks is swollen with high waves ; it is full of little islands, green and beautiful. Before we arrived at Shaufane the river became suddenly narrow, and the boat dashed with inconceivable rapidity round the base of a rocky hill covered with pines.

A ruined tower, with its desolated windows, stood on the summit of another hill that jutted into the river ; beyond, the sunset was illuminating the mountains and the clouds. and casting the reflection of its hues on the agitated river . . . Here we had no fellow-passengers to disturb our tranquillity by their vulgarity and rudeness. . . . Shelley read aloud to us Mary Wollstonecraft's " Letters from Norway," * and we passed our time delightfully.

The next morning a light skiff took the place of the boat, and, on leaving Strasbourg, our travellers once more took their places in the *diligence par eau*

---

* Letters written during a short residence in Sweden, Norway, and Denmark, 1796.

in company of University students and of one terrible* Republican who talked of nothing but cutting off kings' heads. At one of the most dangerous passes of the Rhine they came on a boat that had foundered the same morning, and whose entire crew had perished. Their own boat-man, proud to show off his few words of French, consoled them by saying "que c'est seulement un bâteau qui était subitement renversé, et tous les peuples sont seulement noyés."

From Mayence to Cologne—that part of the Rhine which is so marvellously described in the third canto of " Childe Harold "—they were again in company with the terrible Germans—smoking, shouting, and (worst of all to English eyes) kissing each other.

---

* Jane, in her journal, speaks of two other passengers— one a man "that pretended to something," and the other a schoolmaster who spoke a little English, and who sang German songs that she much admired. "As we were just passing the dangerous defile" (of the Rhine), she says, "the man of pretensions turned to us, and said : 'Allons! il faut prier le bon Dieu.' We laughed ; he answered, 'Eh bien ! donc il faut chanter.' The schoolmaster immediately began, and they sang an animated German song, which had a much finer effect when seconded by the breaking of the waves over the rocks."

Before their delighted eyes pass visions of "hills covered with vines and trees, craggy cliffs crowned by desolate towers, and wooded islands where picturesque ruins peepec from behind the foliage and cast the shadows of their forms on the troubled waters which disturbed without deforming them." They left Bonn, that "loveliest paradise on earth," although unfortunately inhabited by such wretched specimens of the human race, and reached Cologne by road. From Cologne to Cleves they drove in a post-chaise behind the diligence, and accomplished three leagues in seven or eight hours; then continued their journey by posting across the monotonous plains of Holland, whose sole beauty—a delightful verdure—reminded them of the green fields of England. They embarked at Rotterdam, and then ensued a delay of two days at Marsluys through stress of weather, during which Shelley worked at his romance of "The Assassins," while Mary began a tale entitled "Hate," and Jane a kind of philosophical novel called "The Idiot." On September 10th they had travelled eight hundred miles for less than thirty pounds. But they had only one guinea left in their possession.

At last, under the guidance of an English captain, their vessel crossed the bar at the mouth of the Rhine, and on September 13th lay at Gravesend in sight of the Kentish hills.

This rapid journey, amid scenes so various, and seen as it were in a fantastic mirage, left an indelible impression on the mind of the poet. He recurs to it with beautifying and idealising touches in all his great compositions. The living memory of Nature's scenes, troubled and calm, serene and terrible by turns, evoked in Shelley marvellous visions which followed him ceaselessly, and were depicted whenever the framework of his poetical creations permitted. In the preface to "Laon and Cythna" he declares, with little or no exaggeration:

I have been a wanderer among distant fields. I have sailed down mighty rivers, and seen the sun rise and set, and the stars come forth, whilst I have sailed night and day down a rapid stream among mountains.

But, although he was struck by the grandiose aspect of Nature, he was equally impressed with the desolation and ruin wrought by man; with the fatal effects of war and invasion; and these he is to depict with terrible strength in "Laon and Cythna."

I have seen the theatre of the more visible ravages of tyranny and war, cities and villages reduced to scattered groups of black and roofless houses, and the naked inhabitants sitting famished upon their desolated thresholds.

This six weeks' journey was not lost to posterity; to it was due in great measure "Alastor" and the "Revolt of Islam."

CHAPTER II.

SHELLEY IN LONDON AND AT BISHOPSGATE—
"ALASTOR"—1814–1816.

ON his return to London, in the winter of 1814–15, Shelley found himself materially and morally in a critical position. Debts had accumulated, and his father was less than ever inclined to pay them. His creditors were clamorous, and each day brought fresh difficulties. Still more painful was the alienation of the greater number of his London friends, Maimouna included. Godwin's door was closed against him; yet the sage of Skinner Street did not refuse to be under pecuniary obligations to him whose conduct he considered unpardonable.*

* This strange attitude of Godwin ended by exasperating Shelley, and in his correspondence with the philosopher of Skinner Street he cannot conceal his bitterness. He writes under date March 6th, 1816 : "My astonishment, and I will confess when I have been treated with most harshness and

Hogg and Peacock alone remained true to him. His relations with Harriet had been complicated by the birth of a second child named Charles Bysshe, and were only a source of trouble and annoyance.

Reading, writing, conversation, discussion with Hogg or Peacock, and Latin and Greek lessons to Mary, were pleasant diversions of his daily recurring vexations. After a long day of business and fatigue Shelley would return to the Margaret Street lodgings with some new volume of poetry, Wordsworth's " Excursion," * or Byron's " Lara,"

cruelty by you, my indignation has been extreme, that, knowing as you do my nature, any considerations should have prevailed on you to be thus harsh and cruel. I lamented also over my ruined hopes, of all that your genius once taught me to expect from your virtue, when I found that for yourself, your family, and your creditors, you would submit to that communication with me, which you once rejected and abhorred, and which no pity for my poverty or sufferings, assumed willingly for you, could avail to extort. Do not talk of *forgiveness* again to me, for my blood boils in my veins, and my gall rises against all that bears the human form, when I think of what I, their benefactor and ardent lover, have endured of enmity and contempt from you and from all mankind."

* Mary's Journal : " Shelley brings home Wordsworth's 'Excursion,' of which we read a part ; much disappointed. He is a slave."

and the evening was spent in reading aloud ancient and modern prose and poetry. Coleridge, Spenser, Milton, or Seneca were followed by Godwin and Lewis's tales, or the stories of a German disciple of Godwin, Charles Brockden Brown.* Four of these stories, according to Peacock, were works that, together with Schiller's "Brigands" and Goethe's "Faust," exercised a powerful influence on Shelley's mind and character. Some evenings were devoted to "Garnerin's Lectures on Electricity, the Gases, and the Phantasmagoria," or to the theatre. In 1814 Edmund Kean appeared for the first time on the boards of Drury Lane. On October 13th Shelley was present at his representation of *Hamlet*. His first impression of this great actor, to whom he subsequently thought of entrusting the character of Count Cenci, was unfavourable; at the end of the second act he left the theatre.

* These four novels of Brown's are, "Wieland," "Ormond," "Edgar Huntley," and "Arthur Mervyn."

† Mary's Journal: "The extreme depravity and disgusting nature of the stage, the inefficacy of acting to encourage or maintain the delusion. The loathsome sight of men personating characters which do not and cannot belong to them. Shelley displeased with what he saw of Kean."

To these intellectual pastimes were added other forms of recreation: visits to Exeter 'Change, to Covent Garden Market, to Lucien Bonaparte's collection of pictures,* to walks by the Serpentine or the Surrey Canal, and often to a pond near Primrose Hill, where Shelley delightedly sailed his paper boats.

There remained little leisure for composition, yet Shelley continued to work at his novel, and contributed to the December number of the *Critical Review* an article on Hogg's philosophical novel, "Memoirs of Prince Alexis Haimatoff." He bitterly regretted the literary impotence to which he was reduced by pecuniary embarrassments and their attendant cares :

"One day," writes Peacock, "as we were walking together on the banks of the Surrey Canal, and discoursing of Wordsworth and quoting some of his verses, Shelley suddenly said to me : " Do you think Wordsworth could have written such poetry if he ever had dealings with money-lenders ? "

---

* Mary mentions, among these pictures, in her journal, a "Magdalen," by Greuze, and Carlo Dolci's "Four Evangelists," and in Newman Street there was a statue of Theoclea, "a divinity," exclaims Mary, "that raises your mind to all virtue and excellence ; I never beheld anything half so wonderfully beautiful."

At one period (from October 23rd to November 9th) the danger from the money-lenders became so pressing, that Shelley, having been warned in time of his impending arrest, was forced to leave the St. Pancras lodgings and part for a while from his beloved one. Bailiffs, however, were on his track, and he took refuge sometimes with his friend Peacock, at others in various hotels, where he contrived, with every imaginable precaution, to receive short visits from Mary, with whom he was in close correspondence in order to keep her informed of daily events, and to arrange places and times of meeting. These letters, which have been published for the first time by Mr. Dowden, while revealing Shelley's state of agitation and perplexity, depict still more vividly his ardent love in that time of bitter trial. We give a few extracts full of passionate adoration :

This separation is a calamity not to be endured patiently ; I cannot support your absence. I thought that it would be less painful to me. . . . But, my beloved, this will not last. . . . We shall soon be restored to each other. The wretchedness of our separation, I am convinced, will endow me with eloquence and energies adequate to the peril. . . . Light of my life, my very spirit of hope . . . when, when

shall I meet you? . . . Give my love to Jane. I think she
has a sincere affection for you.

Εμον κριτεριον των αγαθων τοδε.

. . . I wander restlessly about. I cannot read or even
write ; but this will soon pass. I should not inflict my own
Mary with my dejection ; she has sufficient cause for disturb-
ance to need consolation from me. Well, we shall meet
to-day. I cannot write, but I love you with so unalterable a
love that the contemplation of me will serve for a letter . . .
My dearest, best Mary, let me see your sweet eyes full of
happiness when we meet. All will be well. I hope to have
deserved many kisses. . . . Know you, my best Mary, that I
feel myself, in your absence, almost degraded to the level of
the vulgar and impure. I feel their vacant stiff eyeballs
fixed upon me, until I seem to have been infected with their
loathsome meaning—to inhale a sickness that subdues me to
languor. Oh ! those redeeming eyes of Mary, that they
might beam upon me before I sleep ! Praise my forbearance,
oh ! beloved one—that I do not rashly fly to you, and at
least secure a moment's bliss. Wherefore should I delay ?
Do you not long to meet me ? All that is exalted and
buoyant in my nature urges me towards you, reproaches me
with cold delay, laughs at all fear, and spurns to dream of
prudence. Why am I not with you ?

Alas ! we must not meet.

. . . How hard and stubborn must be the spirit that
does not confess you to be the subtlest and most exquisitely
fashioned intelligence ; that among women there is no equal
mind to yours ! And I possess this treasure ! How beyond
all estimate is my felicity ! Yes ! I am encouraged ; I care
not what happens ; I am most happy.

My beloved Mary, I know not whether these transient
meetings produce not as much pain as pleasure. What have
I said ? I do not mean it. I will not forget the sweet

moments when I saw your eyes—the divine rapture of the few and fleeting kisses.

... Mary, love, we must be reunited. ... Your thoughts alone can waken mine to energy ; my mind without yours is dead and cold, as the dark midnight river when the moon is down. It seems as if you alone could shield me from impurity and vice. If I was absent from you long, I should shudder with horror at myself; my understanding becomes undisciplined without you. ... Evidently you surpass me in originality and simplicity of mind. How divinely sweet a task it is to imitate each other's excellences, and each moment to become wiser in this surpassing love, so that constituting but on being, all real knowledge may be comprised in the maxim γνῶθι σεαυτον (Know thyself) with infinite more justice than in its narrow and common application.

How terrible if month after month I should pass without you, or only to see you by snatches and moments. ... Love me, my dearest, best Mary, love me in confidence and security ; do not think of me as one in danger, or even as one in sorrow. The remembrance and expectation of such sweet moments as we experienced last night, consoles, strengthens, and redeems me from despondency. There is eternity in those moments ; they contain the true elixir of immortal life.

My own beloved Mary, do I not love you? Is not your image the only consolation to my lonely and benighted condition ? Do I not love you with a most unextinguishable love ; a feeling that well compensates for the altered looks of those who love none but themselves ? What sentiment but disgust and indignation is excited by the desertion of those who fly because they think constancy imprudent !

The feeling is sweet, most ennobling, and producing a most celestial balm, with which the sick and weary spirit eposes upon one who may not be doubted ; to whom the slightest taint of suspicion is death—irrevocable annihilation. To-morrow, blest creature, I shall clasp you again —*for ever.* Shall it be so? This is the ancient language, that love alone can translate.

So my beloved boasts that she is more perfect in the practice than I in the theory of love. Is it thus? No, sweet Mary, you only meant that you loved me more than you could express; that reasoning was too cold and slow for the rapid fervour of your conceptions. Perhaps, in truth, Peacock had infected me; my disquisitions were cold—my subtleties unmeaningly refined; and I am a harp responsive to every wind—the scented gale of summer can wake it to a sweet melody, but rough cold blasts draw forth discordance and jarring sounds.

My own love, did I not appear happy to-day? For a few moments I was entranced in most delicious pleasure; yet I was absent and dejected. I knew not when we might meet again, when I might hold you in my arms and gaze on your dear eyes at will, and snatch momentary kisses in the midst of one happy hour, and sport in security with my entire and unbroken bliss. . . . There are moments in your absence, my love, when the bitterness with which I· regret the unrecoverable time wasted in unprofitable solitude and worldly cares is a most painful weight; you alone reconcile me to myself and to my beloved hopes.*

---

* Mary's own letters are no less passionate and tender. The following extract will be read with interest ;

> " *Tuesday, October 25th,* 1814.

" For what a minute did I see you yesterday ! Is this the way, my beloved, we are to live till the 6th? In the morning when I wake I turn to look for you. Dearest Shelley, you are solitary and uncomfortable. Why cannot I

On November 9th, all danger being over, through arrangements entered into by Shelley the lovers were once more united, and, leaving the St. Pancras lodgings, removed their household goods to Nelson Square.

The early months of the year 1815 showed a somewhat clearer horizon. Old Sir Bysshe died on January 6th, and, after long and tedious negotiations between Shelley and his father, an arrangement was made by which he agreed to cede certain inherited rights, and in return was to receive an annual income of £1000.* He at

be with you to cheer you and to press you to my heart? Ah! my love, you have no friends; why then should you be torn from the only one who has affection for you? But I shall see you to-night, and this is the hope I shall live on through the day. Be happy, dear Shelley, and think of me. Why do I say this, dearest, and only one? I know how tenderly you love me, and how you repine at your absence from me. When shall we be free from fear of treachery? ... I was so dreadfully tired yesterday that I was obliged to take a coach home. Forgive this extravagance, but I am so very weak at present. ... A morning's rest, however, will set me quite right again; I shall be well when I meet you this evening. I send you 'Diogenes' [probably a translation of Wieland's 'Diogenes'], as you have no books."

* Mary relates in her journal how Shelley, on hearing of his grandfather's death, went down to Field Place to attempt a reconciliation with his father. He was refused admittance,

once appropriated a proportion of that sum to a provision for Harriet, allowing her an annuity of two hundred pounds, and in April he handed over one thousand pounds to Godwin.

Meanwhile, the excitement, privations, and anxiety of the closing months of 1814, had seriously affected his health ; he believed himself to be attacked by pulmonary consumption, but happily the danger passed away. It is probable that in the state of melancholy induced by ill-health he composed the "Stanzas on Death," and conceived the first idea of "Alastor." Another poignant trouble also tried his weakened constitution. On February 22nd, a seven-months babe, a delicate little girl, was born to Mary; but notwithstanding the tenderest care, the infant died on March 6th. In order to give any idea of the parents' agonising grief, it would be needful to transcribe their journal, from which Mr. Dowden has quoted portions dating from February 22nd to March 20th. All Europe was ringing with Napoleon's return to France, but scarcely an echo is found in their journal :

so sat himself down outside the door of his former home, and consoled himself with reading "Comus" from a pocket edition of Milton.

"March 1.—Bonaparte invades France." All their thoughts, their souls, are centred on a cradle that will soon be empty. Books, and an occasional visit from Hogg and Peacock, constitute their only diversion from that absorbing anxiety. After the babe's death, the journal contains but a funereal chant. "March 9.—Still think about my little dead baby." "March 19.—Dream that my little baby came to life again, that it had only been cold, and that we rubbed it before the fire and it lived. Awake and find no baby. I think about the little thing all day. Not in good spirits. Shelley is very unwell." That Mary's feelings were shared by Shelley we cannot doubt, and we possess indisputable. proof in that passage of "Laon and Cythna," wherein he describes so exquisitely the birth and death of the babe, and Mary's dream. Such emotions could not be so touchingly described unless they had been experienced.

However perfect the union of mind and heart between Shelley and Mary, a slight cloud nevertheless obscured their happiness, caused by the abiding presence of Jane Clairmont (Claire) in their home. Shelley's attentions to her, their frequent walks together when Mary was unable to accompany them, their reading " Pastor Fido " and " Orlando Furioso " together, soon awoke a very natural jealousy in Mary's sensitive heart. Yet it was difficult to get rid of a friend who had been so true under trial, who was so devoted to Shelley's interests, and who was so attractive by her talents, her qualities, and even her faults. Mrs. Godwin, who thought her an objectionable companion for Fanny, was unwilling to receive her in Skinner Street ; Shelley's house seemed to be her only resource. But Mary felt too keenly on the subject to bear long delay ; and after much discussion . and hesitation, it was agreed that Claire should take up her abode with Mrs. Bicknall, who owned a charming cottage at Lynmouth. The departure of Shelley's friend is chronicled in Mary's journal with a satisfaction and joy she does not attempt to conceal :

Friday, May 12.—Shelley and his friend (Claire) have a last conversation.

May 13.—Claire goes ; Shelley walks with her. Charles Clairmont comes to breakfast—talk. Shelley goes out with him. . . . Jefferson (Hogg) does not come till five. Get very anxious about Shelley ; go out to meet him. . . .

Shelley returns at half-past six ; *the business is finished.*
After dinner Shelley is very tired. . . . *I begin a new journal
with our regeneration.*

Shelley, while estimating Claire at her true
worth, was nevertheless attached to her, and
must have regretted the necessity of the sacrifice he had made for the sake of peace. The
passing cloud between the two women, and
their subsequent early reconciliation, form the
ground-work of his domestic idyll, " Rosalind
and Helen."

During their sad separation of the preceding
year, Mary on one occasion wrote to Shelley :

Oh ! how I long to be at our dear home, where nothing
can trouble us, neither friends nor enemies ! . . . Nantgwilt !
do you not wish to be settled there, in a house you know,
love, with your own Mary, nothing to disturb you, studying,
walking ?

Shelley, too, was anxious to fulfil Mary's wish.
He was as impatiently desirous as herself to
escape from London. Part of the summer was
passed by him in a tour along the south coast
of Devon in search of a retired and picturesque
retreat. Meanwhile Mary was staying at Clifton,
and besought him not to prolong his absence.

"To-morrow," she writes, "is the 28th of July" (the anniversary of their flight to Dover). "Dearest, ought we not to be together on that day? Indeed we ought, my love, as I shall shed some tears to think we are not. Do not be angry, dear love ; your Pecksie is a good girl, and is quite well now again, except a headache when she waits so anxiously for her love's letters. . . .

"My dear, dear love, I most earnestly and with tearful eyes beg that I may come to you, if you do not like to leave the searches after a house."

At last, in the month of August, he found a suitable house at Bishopsgate, on the borders of Windsor Park, not far from the Thames, and in that house they immediately established their home, and there remained until late spring in 1816. The period of their sojourn at Bishopsgate is one of the most tranquil and happy in Shelley's life. At the end of August, in company with Mary, Peacock,* and Charles Clairmont,† Shelley

---

* Five years before, Peacock had sung the glories of the Thames in verse.

† Charles Clairmont gave a detailed account of this excursion in a letter to his sister Claire, to be found in Mr. Dowden's work. He thus describes their visit to Oxford : "We arrived (at Oxford) about seven in the evening, and stopped till four the next day. . . . We saw the Bodleian Library, the Clarendon Press, and walked through the quadrangles of the different colleges. We visited the very rooms where the two noted infidels, Shelley and Hogg, pored,

boated up the river as far as Lechlade and Cricklade (Gloucestershire), and to that excursion we owe the lines on the churchyard in Lechlade, " A Summer Evening Churchyard," which, although still melancholy in sentiment, are sweeter and calmer, as was the poet's own spirit at that epoch Death to him is no longer terrible; no longer is the stroke of death frightful to one whose brain is not encircled by nerves of steel; he hears the dead " sleeping in their sepulchres and moulder-ing as they sleep—a thrilling sound."   " Thus solemnised and softened, death is mild, and terrorless as this serenest night," and " loveliest dreams " keep " perpetual watch " on its " breath-less sleep."   Already we hear the accents of " Alastor."

A few days after his return to Bishopsgate, Shelley wrote to Hogg:

I found your letter on my return from a water ex-cursion on the Thames, the particulars of which will be recounted in another letter. The exercise and dissipation of mind attached to such an expedition have produced so favourable an effect upon my health, that my habitual dejection

with the incessant and the unwearied application of the alchymist, over the certified and natural boundaries of human knowledge.'

and irritability have almost deserted me, and I can devote six hours of the day to study without difficulty. I have been engaged lately in the commencement of several literary plans, which, if my present temper of mind endures, I shall probably complete in the winter. I have consequently deserted Cicero, or proceed but slowly with his philosophic dialogues. . . . I have been induced by one of the subjects I am now pursuing to consult Bayle. I think he betrays great obliquity of understanding and coarseness of feeling. . . . No events, as you know, disturb our tranquillity.

Of the various works planned by Shelley in the happy retirement of Bishopsgate only " Alastor " was completed. " Now. at last," exclaim the critics, " we have the real, the immortal Shelley ! " Mr. Rossetti, indeed, justly compares it with " Prometheus Unbound," and " The Cenci." It is certain that between " Alastor " and " Queen Mab " there is an abyss. It has been said of Châteaubriand, " What remains to us of him ? "— " René." Did " Alastor " alone remain to us, it would be sufficient to rank its author among the very greatest poets who have sung and wept for us. Its dominant tone is not to be found in " Queen Mab "—a tone of dreamy and almost despairing sadness, which is the more poignant and penetrating for being mingled with the most brilliant and lifelike descriptions of Nature.

"Alastor" is the first idealised autobiography of Shelley; the outcome of a psychological moment in which the discouragement engendered by the disenchanting contact of a real and an ideal world takes complete hold of the soul, and includes the whole universe in its own melancholy. Alastor* is the embodiment of the "Spirit of Solitude," of that evil genius which separates a soul from its fellows; the demon from whom Shelley suffered so much from the moment when, declaring war against every superstition, prejudice, and hypocrisy, he saw the world turn its back upon him and reply to his words of blessing and salvation by its anathema and hate. Mingled with the bitterness of disillusion was his presentiment of approaching death; and with his heart still bleeding at the terrible separation exacted of him by his ideal, the poet journeys through the half-seen marvels of the world towards his grave—a supreme intellect whose loss is "too deep for tears," and who will leave a void in the senseless universe. Shelley would not have belonged to his epoch had he not experienced that moral unrest, born of the eighteenth century and of the Revolution,

* The word is taken from Æschylus.

which had already been diversely expressed in "Werther," in "René," and in "Oberman." If there be any resemblance to these, it is assuredly to Senancour's hero. Alastor is not embittered like Werther; he is altogether unlike the "beau ténébreux" of Châteaubriand; nor has he the fatuity of "Childe Harold." He is the poet-Oberman.

In Senancour's "Rêveries" (1798) there is a similar yearning for the regeneration of mankind.

The misfortune of Shelley's hero, Shelley's own misfortune, and the misfortune, we will add, of every poet worthy of the name, is the inability to find in any created being the realisation of their sublime ideal. "Alastor" has been rightly compared with the "Endymion" of Keats. Endymion also personifies a soul in search of its ideal, but unlike the hero of "Alastor" it succeeds in finding the object of its search.* The spirit of Alastor is quite opposite. Though Shelley may condemn the

* "Alastor" was published at the beginning of 1816, with "Stanzas to Coleridge," Stanzas, April, 1814, "Mutability," "Death," "A Summer Evening Churchyard," "Lines to

egoism of the solitary idealist, he nevertheless prefers the fate of the poet dying a victim to his quenchless thirst, but purified and redeemed by death, to the mournful destiny of those cold and impassive souls who, "deluded by no generous error, instigated by no sacred thirst of doubtful knowledge, duped by no illustrious superstition, loving nothing on this earth, and cherishing no hopes beyond, yet keep aloof from sympathies with their kind."

The winter at Bishopsgate was to the poet a season of self-communion, and of melancholy tempered by love, that is marvellously reproduced in his poem. His solitude was occasionally broken by visits from such friends as Hogg, Peacock, and a Quaker physician, Dr. Pope, with whom Shelley discussed theology in amicable fashion. "I like to hear thee talk, friend Shelley; I see thou art very deep." We catch an echo of those serene discussions in the dialogue published by Shelley in 1814, "A Refutation of Deism," which we have already mentioned.

Wordsworth," the translation of "A Sonnet by Dante," a translation of some lines from "Moschus," and the "Demon of the World," from "Queen Mab."

Meanwhile he was reading Greek authors with Hogg and Peacock, and teaching Mary Latin.

"Mary," he wrote to Hogg in September, 1815, "has finished the fifth book of the 'Æneid,'* and her progress in Latin is such as to satisfy my best expectations."

In her Biographical and Critical Notes on Shelley, Mary informs us that the poet felt within himself an equal inclination for "poetry and metaphysical discussions," and that "resolving on the former," he engaged "in the study of the poets of Greece, Italy, and England," without neglecting the "constant perusal of portions of the Old Testament — the Psalms, the Book of Job, the Prophet Isaiah, and others—the sublime poetry of which filled him with delight."

There remains to us only a fragment which can be referred to Shelley's passion for metaphysics, but it is sufficient almost to cause regret that poetry should have suddenly stayed his hand. His philosophical essays belong to that year (1815), and treat of his favourite subjects

* Shelley himself at this time was reading Lucan's "Pharsalia," "a poem, as it appears to me," he says, "of wonderful genius, and transcending Virgil."

of meditation, *i.e.* Life, Death, a Future State, Love, the Human Mind, the Phenomena of Dreams, etc. It is evident throughout that Berkeley's idealism has prevailed over the materialistic tendencies contracted by Shelley when studying the French philosophers of the eighteenth century; he is a convinced upholder of the " Intellectual System." No philosopher has so loudly condemned the enervating doctrines of materialism, or exalted so enthusiastically the only reality which in his eyes is deserving of the name, Spirit; the reality of external things being of " such stuff as dreams are made of."

· The shocking absurdities of the popular philosophy of mind and matter, its fatal consequences in morals, and their violent dogmatism concerning the source of all things, had early conducted me to materialism. This materialism is a seducing system to young and superficial minds. It allows its disciples to talk, and dispenses them from thinking. But I was discontented with such a view of life as it afforded ; man is a being of high aspirations " looking both before and after," whose " thoughts wander through eternity," disclaiming alliance with transience and decay ; incapable of imagining to himself annihilation ; existing but in the future and the past ; being not what he is, but what he has been and shall be. Whatever may be his true and final destination, there is a spirit within him at enmity with nothingness and dissolution. This is the character of all life and being. Each is at once the centre and the circumference ; the point to which all things are referred, and the line in which all things are contained. . . .

The spiritual chain which links all creatures together, and which places each individual soul in actual contact with the soul of the universe, is Love.

In the motion of the very leaves of spring, in the blue air, there is then found a secret correspondence with our heart. There is eloquence in the tongueless wind, and a melody in the flowing brooks, and the rustling of the reeds beside them, which, by their inconceivable relation to something within the soul, awaken the spirits to a dance of breathless rapture, and bring tears of mysterious tenderness to the eyes, like the enthusiasm of patriotic success, or the voice of one beloved singing to you alone.

Metaphysics such as these stand very near to poetry, and Shelley did well in abandoning deduction and dogmatism, to clothe his idealism in the lyrical language that alone was worthy of it. What are Plato, Berkeley, and Malebranche but poets; and what are metaphysics themselves but poetry and dreams ?

CHAPTER III.

JOURNEY TO AND SOJOURN IN SWITZERLAND—
SHELLEY AND BYRON.

ON January 24th, 1816, at the very time that Byron's separation from his wife was the scandal of the day, a child was born to gladden the quiet home at Bishopsgate. He received the name of William, after Mary's father.

There was so much resemblance between the lives and circumstances of the two poets that it was fitting they should meet. Both, too, were under the ban of public opinion.

Shelley was only waiting for an opportunity to make the acquaintance of an author of whom he had never lost sight since the time when he had quoted the "Hours of Idleness" in "St. Irvyne." He had sent him a copy of "Queen

Mab," and Byron was said to admire the poem, while he disclaimed the authorship of the Notes.

An entirely fortuitous circumstance brought them together.

At that time Byron was on the Committee of Management of Drury Lane Theatre, endeavouring to infuse fresh life into the drama by new masterpieces that neither Walter Scott, Mathurin, Coleridge, nor any one else would write for him; offering plays by Sotheby or Burgess which the Committee enthusiastically refused; harassed by authors and authoresses, milliners and Irish adventurers, by dancing masters and actors, "ungovernable people"; quarrelling over ballet-girls, and dining and drinking with Sheridan, Kinnaird, and others.

One morning an elegant girl, rather small, but with marvellous shoulders and arms, lovely hands and feet, with the voice of a siren, and with dark hair and passionate dark eyes, introduced herself to Byron. She was Jane Clairmont, or "Claire." She had come to solicit the poet's interest in order to obtain an engagement at the theatre, and Byron interested himself so much, that he immediately made her his mistress and arranged to meet her at Geneva. While Byron, who set out on April 25th, was travelling in princely fashion towards Geneva, by way of Flanders and the Rhine, Shelley, who left England early in May, accompanied by Claire, Mary, and the little William and his nurse, was journeying for the second time to Paris.

We must now record the commencement of a most romantic and mysterious occurrence in our poet's romantic life.

The night before Shelley's departure from London (the story was related to Byron and Medwin by him, shortly before his death), he received a visit from a married lady, "young, handsome, and of noble connections," who confessed to him that she, although he was personally unknown to her, had long adored him in her secret soul, and had resolved to belong to, and follow him to the ends of the world. Shelley explained to her that he was not free to dispose of himself, softening his refusal as far as possible, and received the adieux of his beautiful and interesting visitor. Thenceforth, she followed in his footsteps, traced him to Switzerland, back to England, then to Italy, and died at Naples, to Shelley's inconsolable grief. Most of his friends and biographers are inclined to look upon this sad and gentle lady who follows the loved footsteps, as an imaginary incarnation of the ideal woman whom he vainly sought in flesh and blood ; in one word, as a poetic hallucination. But although we are ready to acknowledge, as we have already stated in our notice of Shelley's novels, that he was apt to introduce the creatures of his imagination into the realities of life, and that in particular, certain passages in his poems, even those which, like " Alastor," * were written before the journey to Switzerland, contain striking allusions to the mysterious sympathies which attract "the young maidens " to Shelley ; still it is difficult to accept hallucination as an explanation of incidents so prolonged, so precise, and so extraordinary. Moreover, as we shall see, there are mysterious allusions in the poems written while at Naples, that can hardly be explained except by accepting the truth of Medwin's narrative. That the sceptical Byron

* Vol. I., p. 84.

did not so accept it, is not surprising, and no more convinces us than do the gratuitous assurances of Mr. Jeaffreson.*

Unprovided with letters of introduction, and without acquaintances in Paris, the travellers were compelled to wait at their hotel until the French officials, who had become suspicious since the escape of La Valette, should please to counter-sign their passports. They found the French less courteous to English folk than before the last invasion of the Allies; ill-humour and discontent were visible on every countenance.

Nor is it wonderful that they should regard the subjects of a Government which fills their country with hostile garrisons, and sustains a detested dynasty on the throne, with an acrimony and indignation of which that Government alone is the proper object. This feeling is honourable to the French, and encouraging to all those of every nation in Europe who have a fellow-feeling with the oppressed, and who cherish an unconquerable hope that the cause of liberty must at length prevail.

Four days later they reached Champagnolles, a little village situated in the depths of the mountains, and the awful desolation of the

* Mr. Rossetti, without coming to a positive conclusion, admits the great probability of the truth of the story. Mr. Dowden is of the same opinion.

Rousses and Nion passes was presently exchanged for one of the most smiling of landscapes. In the Hôtel Sécheron at Geneva, the travellers awoke next morning to a view of the lake and the Alps.

To what a different scene are we now arrived! To the warm sunshine, and to the humming of sun-loving insects! From the windows of our hotel we see the lovely lake, blue as the heavens which it reflects, and sparkling with golden beams. The opposite shore is sloping and covered with vines. . . . Gentlemen's seats are scattered over these banks, behind which rise the various ridges of black mountains, and towering far above in the midst of its snowy Alps, the majestic Mont Blanc, highest and queen of all. Such is the view reflected by the lake; it is a bright summer scene, without any of that sacred solitude and deep seclusion that delighted us at Lucerne.—(*May* 17, 1816.)

Their first proceeding at Geneva was to hire a boat, and every evening at about six o'clock they sailed on the lake, sometimes gliding over its glassy surface, at others speeded along by a strong wind. They seldom returned until ten o'clock, and then, as they approached the shore they were "saluted by the delightful scent of flowers and new-mown grass, and the chirp of the grasshoppers and the song of the evening birds."

The first few days at Geneva were passed thus in a most delightful solitude:

We do not enter into society here, yet our time passes swiftly and delightfully. We read Latin and Italian during the heats of noon, and when the sun declines we walk in the garden of the hotel, looking at the rabbits, relieving fallen cockchafers, and watching the motions of a myriad of lizards, who inhabit a southern wall of the garden.

The lucky trio, "escaped from the gloom of winter and of London," inhale happiness at every pore:

I feel as happy as a new-fledged bird [it is Mary who still writes], and hardly care to what twig I fly, so that I may try my new-fledged wings. A more experienced bird may be more difficult in its choice of a bower; but in my present temper of mind the budding flowers, the fresh grass of spring, and the happy creatures about me, that live and enjoy these pleasures, are quite enough to afford me exquisite delight, even though clouds should shut out Mont Blanc from my sight.

Ten days after their arrival, Lord Byron, with his inseparable companion Polidori, came to the Sécheron Hotel, where he remained for a few days in the company of his new friends. Soon, however, the two parties separated, outwardly at least, Byron removing to the Villa Diodati,* and the

* It was at Geneva that Milton, on his return from Italy in 1639, had paid a visit to his friend Dr. John Diodati, a Geneva Professor of Theology.

Shelleys settling towards the end of May in a cottage known as Campagne Chapuis, or Campagne Mont Alègre, turning its back on Mont Blanc, and facing the sombre view of the Jura, behind which they nightly watched the setting of the sun. At their feet lay the lake, and their boat was moored in a little creek. The clear splendid weather of their early stay broke up, rain and storm detained our travellers within doors. All seemed to them grand and majestic; amid the wild scenery, storms were more terrible and grandiose; and in the intervals of fine weather the sun shone with a brightness and warmth unknown in England. They were deeply interested in the phenomena of Nature, and watched them with a patience worthy of professional astronomers. Shelley, who is, beyond all others, the painter of storm and tempest, garnered up colours and pictures for future description.

"We watch them," writes Mary, June 1st, 1816, "as they approach from the opposite side of the lake, observing the lightning play among the clouds in various parts of the heavens, and dart in jagged figures upon the piny heights of Jura, dark with the shadow of the overhanging cloud, while perhaps the sun is shining cheerily upon us. One night we *enjoyed* a finer storm than I had ever before beheld. The lake was lit up, the pines on Jura made visible, and all the scene illuminated for an instant, when a pitchy blackness succeeded, and the thunder came in frightful bursts over our heads amid the darkness.

Compared with such splendid spectacles the narrow and ill-paved streets, and the meaningless and unbeautiful buildings of Geneva, offered few attractions to the lovers of Nature.

But they gazed with interest on Rousseau's obelisk standing in the Promenade of Plain-Palais, where the people took vengeance, during the Revolution, on the magistrates of Geneva for having banished the great philosopher, " and where," says Mary, " from respect to the memory of their predecessors none of the present magistrates ever walk."

The most striking characteristic of the people of Geneva, besides their Puritanism, is the equality between the various classes of citizens, which is due to the greater liberty and the higher culture of the working classes :

" Nevertheless," continues Mary, "the peasants of Switzerland may not emulate the vivacity and grace of the French. . . . Nothing is more pleasant than to listen to the evening song of the vine-dressers. They are all women,

and most of them have harmonious although masculine
voices. The theme of their ballads consists of shepherds,
love, flocks, and the sons of kings who fall in love with
beautiful shepherdesses. Their tunes are monotonous, but
it is sweet to hear them in the stillness of the evening, while
we are enjoying the sight of the setting sun, either from the
hill behind the house or from the lake."

On the 23rd of June, Shelley and Byron made
an excursion round the lake together. We will
leave Shelley to tell the story himself:

Montalègre, near Coligni, Geneva, *July* 12.

It is nearly a fortnight since I have returned from Vevey.
This journey has been on every account delightful, but most
especially because I then first knew the divine beauty of
Rousseau's imagination as it exhibits itself in "Julie." It is
inconceivable what an enchantment the scene itself lends,
to those delineations from which its own most touching
charm arises. But I will give you an abstract of our voyage,
which lasted eight days, and if you have a map of Switzerland
you can follow me.

We left Montalègre at half-past two on the 23rd of June.
The lake was calm, and after three hours of rowing, we
arrived at Hermance, a beautiful little village containing a
ruined tower, built, the villagers say, by Julius Cæsar. . . .

Leaving Hermance, we arrived at sunset at the village of
Nerni. After looking at our lodgings, which were gloomy
and dirty, we walked out by the side of the lake. It was
beautiful to see the vast expanse of these purple and misty
waters, broken by the craggy islets near to its slant and
"beached margin." There were many fish sporting in the

lake, and multitudes were collected close to the rocks to catch the flies which inhabited them.

On returning to the village we sat on a wall beside the lake, looking at some children who were playing a game like ninepins. The children here appeared in an extraordinary way deformed and diseased. Most of them were crooked, and with enlarged throats; but one little boy had such exquisite grace in his mien and motions as I never before saw equalled in a child. His countenance was beautiful for the expression with which it overflowed. There was a mixture of pride and gentleness in his eyes and lips—the indications of sensibility, which his education will probably pervert to misery, or seduce to crime; but there was more of gentleness than of pride, and it seemed that the pride was tamed from its original wildness by the habitual exercise of milder feelings. My companion gave him a piece of money which he took without speaking, with a sweet smile of easy thankfulness, and then with an unembarrassed air turned to his play. All this might scarcely be; but the imagination surely could not forbear to breathe into the most inanimate forms some likeness of its own visions, on such a serene and glowing evening, in this remote and romantic village, beside the calm lake that bore us hither.

On returning to our inn, we found that the servant had arranged our rooms, and deprived them of the greater portion of their former disconsolate appearance. They reminded my companion of Greece; it was five years, he said, since he had slept in such beds. The influence of the recollections excited by this circumstance on our conversation gradually faded, and I retired to rest. . . .

The next morning we passed Yvoire, a scattered village with an ancient castle, whose houses are interspersed with trees, and which stands at a little distance from Nerni on the promontory which bounds a deep bay, some miles in extent. So soon as we arrived at this promontory, the lake began to assume an aspect of wilder magnificence. The mountains of Savoy, whose summits were bright with snow, descended in broken slopes to the lake ; on high, the rocks were dark with pine forests, which become deeper and more immense, until the ice and snow mingle with the points of naked rock that pierce the blue air; but below, groves of walnut, chestnut, and oak, with openings of lawny fields, attested the milder climate.

As soon as we had passed the opposite promontory, we saw the river Drance, which descends from between a chasm in the mountains, and makes a plain near the lake, intersected by its divided streams. Thousands of *besolets*, beautiful water-birds, like sea-gulls, but smaller, with purple on their backs, take their station on the shallows, where its waters mingle with the lake. As we approached Evian, the mountains descended more precipitously to the lake, and masses of intermingled wood and rock overhung its shining spire. . . .

About half-an-hour after we arrived at Evian, a few flashes of lightning came from a dark cloud, directly overhead, and continued after the cloud had dispersed. "Diespiter per pura tonantes egit equos," a phenomenon which certainly had no influence on me, corresponding with that which it produced on Horace. *

The appearance of the inhabitants of Evian is more wretched, diseased, and poor, than I ever recollect to have seen. The contrast, indeed, between the subjects of the King of Sardinia, and the citizens of the independent republics of Switzerland, affords a powerful illustration of the blighting effects of despotism, within the space of a few miles. They have mineral waters here, *eaux savonneuses* they call them. In the evening we had some difficulty about our passports, but so soon as the syndic heard my companion's rank and name, he apologised for the circumstance. . . .

We here heard (Meillerie) that the Empress Maria

Louisa had slept at Meillerie . . . in remembrance of Saint-Preux. How beautiful it is to find that the common sentiments of human nature can attach themselves to those who are most removed from its duties and its enjoyments, when Genius pleads for their admission at the gate of Power. . . . We dined there, and had some honey, the best I have ever tasted, the very essence of the mountain flowers, and as fragrant. Probably the village derives its name from this production. Meillerie is the well-known scene of Saint-Preux's visionary exile ; but Meillerie is indeed enchanted ground, were Rousseau no magician. . . .

The lake appeared somewhat calmer as we left Meillerie, sailing close to the banks, whose magnificence augmented with the turn of every promontory. But we congratulated ourselves too soon. The wind gradually increased in violence until it blew tremendously ; and as it came from the remotest extremity of the lake, produced waves of a frightful height, and covered the whole surface with a chaos of foam. One of our boatmen, who was a dreadfully stupid fellow, persisted in holding the sail at a time when the boat was on the point of being driven under water by the hurricane. On discovering his error, he let it entirely go, and the boat for a moment refused to obey the helm ; in addition, the rudder was so broken as to render the management of it very difficult ; one wave fell in, and then another. My companion, an excellent swimmer, took off his coat. I did the same, and we sat with our arms crossed, every instant expecting to be swamped. The sail was, however, again held, the boat obeyed the helm ; and, still in imminent peril from the immensity of the waves, we arrived in a few minutes at a sheltered port in the village of St. Gingoux.

I felt at this near prospect of death a mixture of sensations, among which terror entered, though but subordinately. My feelings would have been less painful had I been alone ; but I knew that my companion would have attempted to save me, and I was overcome with humiliation when I thought that his life might have been risked to preserve mine. When we arrived at St. Gingoux, the inhabitants who stood on the shore, unaccustomed to see a vessel as frail as ours, and fearing to venture at all on such a sea, exchanged looks of wonder and congratulation with our boatmen, who, as well as ourselves, were well pleased to set foot on shore.

St. Gingoux is even more beautiful than Meillerie. The mountains are higher, and their loftiest points of elevation descend more abruptly to the lake. On high the aërial summits still cherish great depths of snow in their ravines, and in the paths of their unseen torrents. One of the highest of these is called Roche de St. Julien, beneath whose pinnacles the forests become deeper and more extensive. The chestnut gives a peculiarity to the scene, which is most beautiful, and will make a picture in my memory, distinct from all other mountain scenes which I have ever before visited.

As we arrived here early, we took a *voiture* to visit the mouths of the Rhone. We went between the mountains and the lake, under groves of mighty chestnut-trees, beside perpetual streams, which are nourished by the snows above, and form stalactites on the rocks over which they fall. We saw an immense chestnut-tree which had been overthrown by the hurricane of the morning. The place where the Rhone joins the lake was marked by a line of tremendous breakers; the river is as rapid as when it leaves the lake, but is muddy and dark. . . . We returned to St. Gingoux before sunset, and I passed the evening in reading " Julie."

As my companion rises late, I had time before breakfast on the ensuing morning to hunt the waterfalls of the river that fall into the lake at St. Gingoux. The stream is indeed, from the declivity over which it falls, only a succession of waterfalls, which roar over the rocks with a perpetual sound, and suspend their unceasing spray on the leaves and flowers that overhang and adorn its savage banks. The path that conducted along this river sometimes avoided the precipices of its shores by leading through meadows, sometimes threaded the base of the perpendicular and caverned rocks. I gathered in these meadows a nosegay of such flowers as I never saw in England, and which I thought more beautiful for that rarity.

On my return, after breakfast we sailed for Clarens, determining first to see the three mouths of the Rhone, and then the Castle of Chillon. The day was fine and the water calm. We passed from the blue waters of the lake over the stream of the Rhone, which is rapid even at a great distance from its confluence with the lake; the turbid waters mixed with those of the lake, but mixed with them unwillingly. (See " Nouvelle Héloïse," Letter 17, part 4.) I read " Julie " all day ; an overflowing, as it now seems, surrounded by the scenes which it has so wonderfully peopled, of sublimest genius,and more than human sensibility. Meillerie, the Castle of Chillon, Clarens, the mountains of La Valais and Savoy present themselves to the imagination as monuments of things that were once familiar, and of beings that were once dear to it. They were created, indeed, by one mind, but a mind so powerfully bright as to cast a shade of false-hood on the records that are called reality.

We passed on to the Castle of Chillon,* and visited its dungeons and towers. These prisons are excavated below the lake ; the principal dungeon is supported by seven columns, whose branching capitals support the roof. Close to the very walls the lake is 8oo feet deep ; iron rings are fastened to these columns, and on them were engraven a

---

* Reminiscences of the Castle of Chillon occur in many places in " The Revolt of Islam."

multitude of names, partly those of visitors, and partly doubt-less those of the prisoners, of whom now no memory remains, and who thus beguiled a solitude which they have long ceased to feel. One date was as ancient as 1670. At the commencement of the Reformation, and, indeed, long after that period, this dungeon was the receptacle of those who shook or who denied the system of idolatry from the effects of which mankind is even now slowly emerging.

Close to this long and lofty dungeon was a narrow cell, and beyond it one larger and far more lofty and dark, sup-ported upon two unornamented arches. Across one of these arches was a beam, now black and rotten, on which prisoners were hung in secret. I never saw a monument more terrible, of that cold and inhuman tyranny which it has been the delight of man to exercise over man. It was indeed one of those many tremendous fulfilments which render the "per-nicies humani generis" of the great Tacitus so solemn and irrefragable a prophecy. . . .

We proceeded with a contrary wind to Clarens against a heavy swell. I never felt more strongly than on landing at Clarens, that the spirit of old times had deserted its once cherished habitation. A thousand times, thought I, have Julia and St.-Preux walked on this terraced road, looking towards these mountains which I now behold ; nay, treading on the ground where I now tread. From the window of our lodging our landlady pointed out " le bosquet de Julie." At least the inhabitants of this village are impressed with an idea that the persons of that romance had actual existence. In the evening we walked thither. It is indeed Julia's wood. The hay was making under the trees ; the trees themselves were aged, but vigorous, and interspersed with younger ones, which are destined to be their successors, and in future years when we are dead, to afford a shade to future worshippers of Nature, who love the memory of that tenderness and peace of which this was the imaginary abode. We walked forward among the vineyards, whose narrow terraces overlook this affecting scene. Why did the cold maxims of the world compel me at this moment to repress the tears of melancholy transport which it would have been so sweet to indulge immeasurably, even until the darkness of night had swallowed up the objects which excited them ?

I forgot to remark, what indeed my companion remarked to me,* that our danger from the storm took place precisely in the spot where Julie and her lover were nearly overset, and where St.-Preux was tempted to plunge with her into the lake.

On the following day we went to see the Castle of Clarens, a strong, square house, with very few windows, surrounded by a double terrace that overlooks the valley, or rather the plain of Clarens. The road which conducted to it wound up the steep ascent through woods of walnut and chestnut. We gathered roses on the terrace in the feeling that they might be the posterity of some planted by Julie's hand. We sent their dead and withered leaves to the absent.

We went again to the " bosquet de Julie," and found that the precise spot was now utterly obliterated, and a heap of stones marked the place where the little chapel had once stood. Whilst we were execrating the author of this brutal folly, our guide informed us that the land belonged to the Convent of St. Bernard, and that this outrage had been committed by their orders. I knew before that if avarice could harden the hearts of men, a system of prescriptive religion has an influence far more inimical to natural sensibility. I know that an isolated man is sometimes

---

* At a later period Byron remarked to Medwin : " It would have been a more classical end, to have perished there, but a less pleasant one."

restrained by shame from outraging the venerable feelings arising out of the memory of genius, which once made Nature even lovelier than itself ; but associated man holds it as the very sacrament of his union to forswear all delicacy, all benevolence, all remorse ; all that is true, or tender, or sublime.

We sailed from Clarens to Vevey. . . .

It was at Vevey that Rousseau conceived the design of "Julia." . . .

The rain detained us two days at Ouchy. We, however, visited Lausanne, and saw Gibbon's house. We were shown the decayed summer-house where he finished his History, and the old acacias on the terrace from which he saw Mont Blanc, after having written the last sentence. There is something grand and even touching in the regret which he expresses at the completion of his task. It was conceived amid the ruins of the Capitol. The sudden departure of his accustomed and cherished toil must have left him like the death of a dear friend, sad and solitary.

My companion gathered some acacia leaves to preserve in remembrance of him.* I refrained from doing so, fearing to outrage the greater and more sacred name of Rousseau, the contemplation of whose imperishable creations had left no vacancy in my heart for mortal things. Gibbon had a cold and unimpassioned spirit. I never felt more inclination to rail at the prejudices which cling to such a thing, than now that Julie and Clarens, Lausanne and the Roman Empire, compelled me to a contrast between Rousseau and Gibbon.

This animated narrative of Shelley's should be compared with Byron's stanzas in the third

---

* Byron wrote to Murray after the visit to Ouchy on the 27th June, 1816.

canto of " Childe Harold," of which, as his friend says, Shelley speaks in terms of rapturous praise.

These stanzas begin with the lines :

Clarens ! sweet Clarens, birthplace of deep Love !
Thine air is the young breath of passionate thought ;
Thy trees take root in Love ; the snows above .   .
The very glaciers have his colours caught,
And sunset into rose-hues sees them wrought
By rays which sleep there lovingly ; the rocks,
The permanent crags, tell here of Love, who sought
In them a refuge from the worldly shocks,
Which stir and sting the soul with hope that woos, then mocks.

These scenes profoundly impressed Shelley's imagination also, and transformed themselves there into new creations, keeping only that amount of reality which creative genius retains when idealising Nature.

Shelley's landscapes resemble those of Leonardo da Vinci, or other old Italian masters.

Anything we could say of Shelley's* enthusiasm

* Shelley seems to have taken great interest from an early age in all that concerned Rousseau. Hogg quotes an anecdote of Jean-Jacques that appealed to the poet's imagination, and will be appreciated by Rousseau's admirers. It is strange to find a hitherto unpublished anecdote in Hogg's book :

" Our kind friend J. F. N. informed us that some old

at this epoch for Rousseau, would pale beside his enthusiastic expressions of admiration for the "Nouvelle Héloïse" in the passage we have quoted, but, although Shelley was powerfully attracted by Rousseau's admirable portrayal of Nature, and his incomparable interpretation of the purest and sweetest feelings of love, he was not blind to the errors of the thinker and the

gentleman of his acquaintance, whose name I have forgotten, came over from France in the packet with Rousseau and David Hume. The Scotch philosopher was sick, and kept below, but the citizen of Geneva was quite well and lively, and remained on deck. He was sociable, talkative, and inquisitive, and asked many questions. Observing this gentleman writing upon a substance that was new to him, he begged to know what it might be. It was ass's skin, a substance much used formerly in pocket-books, but now seldom to be seen. The nature of the tablet was explained to him ; how well it received and retained the marks of a black-lead pencil, and how readily the characters were effaced when it was wetted. Rousseau was much surprised at the novelty, upon which the gentleman presented him with the pocket-book, and it was accepted with great and almost childish eagerness. During the remainder of the voyage, with the infantine simplicity of genius, the most eloquent of philosophers was. constantly playing with his new toy ; busily writing upon the ass's skin, wiping out and writing again. Nevertheless, it is by no means impossible that the fanciful, capricious, suspicious man soon afterwards might take offence at the gift, imagine that some treachery lurked in it ;

philosopher; and although, like him, Shelley taught men to return to the truth and simplicity of Nature, and was like him the irreconcilable foe of all social conventions, he strenuously opposed Rousseau's interpretation of the word "Nature," and nothing seemed to him more false than the wish that mankind should revert to the state of savages and of brutes. Uncivilised man seemed to him the most pernicious and miserable of beings.

"Man," he said, "was once a wild beast, who has become, through civilisation, a moralist, a metaphysician, an astronomer, and a poet. Lucretius and Virgil, in order to prove the progress of human nature, had but to compare themselves with the cannibals of Scythia. Where justice increases, so does equality; and there is more justice now, because civilisation is more widely distributed."

---

that there was a snake in the grass; that the smooth tablet was contrived purposely to betray and ruin him, poisoned by the deceitful David, and thereupon it might be committed to the flames. A subtle poison infused by the envenomed malice of the jealous, insidious Hume into the ass's skin, gradually ascending up the pencil into the fingers, and proceeding thence along the arm, and finally arriving at the heart, and thereupon instantaneous death; the bare idea of such an incident was charming to Shelley, and every tablet of ass's skin was a page of romance."

He severely condemned the part taken by Rousseau in the eighteenth century, as an instigation to the Revolution:

Rousseau gave license by his writings to passions that only incapacitate and contract the human heart.

But with this exception, his admiration for Rousseau grew with his years. In. his "Essay on Christianity," he goes so far as to compare him to Christ:

He is perhaps the philosopher among the moderns who, in the structure of his feelings and understanding, resembles most nearly the mysterious sage of Judea. It is impossible to read those passionate words in which Jesus Christ upbraids the pusillanimity and sensuality of mankind without being strongly reminded of the more connected and systematic enthusiasm of Rousseau.

In this respect Shelley is the true son of both; but Rousseau had so entirely captivated his heart and his imagination, that in the last and uncompleted poem, in which he endeavoured to sum up all his metaphysical and moral teaching on life and human destiny, he invokes the spirit of Rousseau to lead him through the Hell of this world, just as Dante took Virgil, the mild prophet-poet, for his guide in the infernal regions.

One week spent in intimacy with Byron sufficed for Shelley to discover the real Byron beneath the fantastic appearances that concealed him from the vulgar gaze. On July 17th, in a letter to Peacock, he pronounces the following categorical opinion:

Lord Byron is an exceedingly interesting person ; and as such, is it not to be regretted that he is a slave to the vilest and most vulgar prejudices, and as mad as the winds?

His opinion of his noble friend hardly varied after this. He continued to admire his genius, which he regarded as "capable of rendering him the redeemer of his degraded country, if he would but direct it to that end."

In society there is no more agreeable or unassuming being ; as a companion he is good-humoured, candid, and witty ; but Byron's qualities are tarnished by pride. He compares his extraordinary faculties with the little minds about him, and conceives an intense conviction of the nothingness of life, and is consumed by impatience and self-concentration that degenerate into scepticism. Shelley could not pardon his immoral life, and endeavoured more than once to raise him from the slough; their intimacy in

Switzerland produced the happiest effect on Byron, whose mind was elevated and enlarged by contact with that of his friend. The reader must be blind indeed who cannot see traces of Shelley's influence in the third canto of "Childe Harold," and the accompanying notes. Moore* mentions and deplores that influence. He says:

On philosophy and poetry the conversation of the two poets generally turned, and as might be expected from Lord Byron's facility in receiving new impressions, the opinions of his companion were not altogether without some influence on his mind. Here and there among those fine bursts of passion and description that abound in the third canto of "Childe Harold," may be discovered traces of that mysticism of meaning, that sublimity losing itself in its own vagueness, which so much characterised the writings of his extraordinary friend, and in one of the notes we find Shelley's favourite Pantheism of Love thus glanced at.†

It is probable that Byron read some portions of the third canto to his friends, during the evenings at Diodati,‡ although they were mostly

* Moore's "Life of Byron," Vol. III., p. 65.

† See note beginning : "But this is not all ; the feeling with which all around Clarens," etc.

‡ On May 28th of the following year, Mary writes in her journal : "Do you not remember, Shelley, when you first read it to me? One evening after returning from Diodati.

spent in animated conversation between Byron and Shelley, to which Mary listened with passionate attention; Byron's voice touched her to the heart.

"I do not think," she writes in her journal, "that any person's voice has the same power of awakening melancholy in me as Albè's. I have been accustomed, when hearing it, to listen and speak little; another's voice, not mine, ever replied—a voice whose strings are broken. When Albè ceases to speak, I expect to hear *that other* voice, and when I hear another instead, it jars strangely with every association . . . and thus . . . when Albè speaks, and Shelley does not answer, it is as thunder without rain—the form of the sun without heat or light."

One evening (it was June 18th), after a conversation on apparitions and ghosts, Byron recited

It was in our little room at Chapuis. The lake was before us, and the mighty Jura. That time is past, and this will also pass, when I may weep to read these words, and again moralise on the flight of time. . . . I think of our excursions on the lake. How we saw him when he came down to us, or welcomed our arrival with a good-humoured smile. How vividly does each verse of his poem recall some scene of this kind to my memory! This time will soon also be a recollection. We may see him again, and again enjoy his society; but the time will also arrive when that which is now an anticipation will be only in the memory. Death will at length come, and in the last moment all will be a dream.

some lines from Coleridge's " Christabel," which had just been published :

<blockquote>
She unbound
The cincture from beneath her breast :
Her silken robe, and inner vest,
Dropt to her feet, and full in view,
Behold ! her bosom and half her side—
Hideous, deformed, and pale of hue,
A sight to dream of, not to tell !
And she is to sleep by Christabel.
</blockquote>

Seized with horror, Shelley uttered a piercing cry; he suddenly thought of a woman he had heard of, who had eyes instead of nipples. When he had recovered and calm was restored, Byron proposed that each one should write a ghost story. Shelley began one, which, as usual, he soon abandoned. Byron began his celebrated tale of the " Vampire," which Polidori finished and published three years later, while Mary wrote her " Frankenstein ; or, the Modern Prometheus."

A few days afterwards Shelley made another Alpine excursion, but this time he was accompanied by Mary and Claire. They left Geneva on July 20th, and passing through Bonneville, Cluses, Sallanches, and Servoz, they reached the valley of Chamouni; Shelley was much impressed with a waterfall near Maglans, at least twelve hundred feet high, dashing from "the overhanging brow of a black precipice, imitating a veil of the most exquisite woof." At Servoz, Mont Blanc was before them.

"Mont Blanc was before us," writes Shelley, "but it was covered with cloud; its base, furrowed with dreadful gaps, was seen above. Pinnacles of snow intolerably bright, part of the chain connected with Mont Blanc, shone through the clouds at intervals on high. I never knew—I never imagined what mountains were before. The immensity of these aërial summits excited, when they suddenly burst upon the sight, a sentiment of ecstatic wonder not unallied to madness. And, remember, this was all one scene; it all pressed home to our regard and imagination. Though it embraced a vast extent of space, the snowy pyramids which shot into the bright blue sky seemed to overhang our path; the ravine, clothed with gigantic pines, and black with its depth below, so deep that the very roaring of the untameable Arve, which rolled through it, could not be heard above—all was as much our own as if we had been the creators of such impressions in the minds of others as now occupied our own. Nature was the poet whose harmony held our spirits more breathless than that of the divinest."

The sight of the Montanvert and Les Bossons glaciers caused him unspeakable rapture; the dazzling white of precipice and pinnacles—the latter resembling so many glass needles beneath

a net of frosted silver; the masses of ice slipping
down and breaking into powder as they struck
the rocks beneath, the slow but incessant movement of the glaciers encroaching in their irresistible march on the surrounding pasture lands
and forests,' accomplishing in the course of
centuries the destruction that would be completed
in one hour by a torrent of lava, and bearing
with them huge rocks and piled-up heaps of
sand and stones from their mountain sources;
all these wondrous sights moved him to admiration and to philosophical reflection on the destiny
of our globe; on the sublime but sombre theory
of Buffon, that the earth, at a certain period,
will become a frozen mass, by reason of the
spread of the ice from the Polar regions and
higher points of the earth's surface.

"Do you who assert the supremacy of Ahriman," he
wrote, in a moment of poetical exaltation, "imagine him
throned among these desolating snows, among these palaces
of death and frost, so sculptured in this their terrible
magnificence by the adamantine hand of necessity, and that
he casts around him, as the first essays of his final usurpa-
tions, avalanches, torrents, rocks, and thunders, and, above
all, these deadly glaciers, at once the proof and symbols of
his reign;—add to this the degradation of the human species,
who in these regions are half-deformed or idiotic, and most

of whom are deprived of anything that can excite admiration. This is part of the subject more mournful and less sublime, but such as neither the poet nor the philosopher should disdain to regard."

He afterwards compares Mont Blanc to the god of the Stoics, a vast animal whose frozen blood for ever circulated within his stony veins.

It was at the foot of the giant mountain that Shelley composed his poem of " Mont Blanc," " under the immediate impression," he says himself, " of the deep and powerful feelings excited by the objects which it attempts to describe; and as an undisciplined overflowing of the soul, rests its claim to approbation on an attempt to imitate the untameable wildness and inaccessible solemnity from which those feelings sprang."

In this admirable poem, wherein Shelley truly tries to vie with the horror and beauty of Nature, we find his ideal Ahriman, transformed into the personification of the " old Earthquake demon," teaching

> . . . her young
> Ruin. Were these their toys? . . .

He interrogates the wilderness—the splendid and funereal chaos; to others they reply with Doubt and Death; to Shelley the mysterious tongue teaches a

> . . . faith so mild,
> So solemn, so serene, that man may be
> But for such faith with nature reconciled;

and by that reconciliation, that union of the spirit of man with the great spirit of Nature, he finds a means of raising himself above all mortal passions, and all the sorrows of humanity.

> Thou hast a voice, great Mountain, to repeal
> Large codes of fraud and woe.

Shelley gazes on Mont Blanc piercing the infinite sky, still, snowy, and serene, towering far above the unearthly shapes, scarred, ghastly, and riven, that are piled around; the image of Nature's spirit, of the secret strength of things which govern thought, without which Mont Blanc itself, and earth, and stars, and sea would be but silence, solitude, and vacancy.*

* On leaving Montanvert, Shelley had written in the Travellers' Album the two beautiful lines—

> "God! let the torrents, like a shout of nations,
> Answer, and let the ice-plains echo God!"

In another inn Album, in the same handwriting, was written—

> Εἰμὶ φιλάνδρωπος, δημοχράτιχος τ' ἄθεος τε.

Lord Byron is said to have effaced the latter inscription.

It is clear, from the thought expressed at the close of the poem—a thought which is frequently repeated in Shelley's works—that Pantheism with him was pure idealism. And it becomes still more incontrovertible on perusal of his "Hymn to Intellectual Beauty," which was also written while in Switzerland, and for progress of thought and beauty of form is one of the culminating points in Shelley's poetry; it is an invocation of his real Muse—that "unseen Power," that "Spirit of Beauty" called "Demon, Ghost, or Heaven," whose "light alone" "gives grace and truth to life's unquiet dream."

All Shelley is in that exquisite Hymn.

Another remarkable personage, much esteemed by our poet, was at this epoch introduced to Shelley: Matthew Gregory Lewis, author of "The Monk." It was now that Lewis added a codicil to his will, witnessed by the three friends (Byron, Shelley, and Polidori), requiring the heir of his Jamaica estates to visit the property every three years in order to maintain the privileges and rights of the slaves who should belong to the then proprietor.*

* Forgues' "Originaux et beaux Esprits de l'Angleterre:"

Yet amid all the enjoyment of travel and the pecuniary anxieties it entails, Shelley looked wistfully towards England, where he had passed many happy moments, and longed to return thither as soon as possible. On May 15th, 1816, he wrote to Peacock :

You live by the shores of a tranquil stream, among low and woody hills. You live in a free country, where you may act without restraint, and possess that which you possess in security ; and so long as the name of country and the selfish conceptions it includes shall subsist, England, I am persuaded, is the most free and the most refined. . . .

So long as man is such as he now is, the experience of which I speak will never teach him to despise the country of his birth ; far otherwise, like Wordsworth, he will never know what love subsists between that and him until absence shall have made its beauty more heartfelt ; our poets and our philosophers, our mountains and our lakes, the rural lanes and fields which are so especially our own, are ties which, until I become utterly senseless, can never be broken asunder.

These, and the memory of them, if I never should return, these and the affections of the mind, with which having been once united, are inseparable (*sic*), will make the name of England dear to me for ever, even if I should permanently return to it no more. . . . My present intention is to return to England, and to make that most excellent of nations my perpetual resting-place.

M. G. Lewis. Lewis had just returned from Jamaica, where he had been securing the welfare of the numerous negroes on his plantations. . . .

Yet before returning to England for ever, he wished to see more of the world.

"If possible," he wrote on July 17th, "we think of descending the Danube in a boat, of visiting Constantinople and Athens, then Rome and the Tuscan cities, and returning by the South of France, always following great rivers—the Danube, the Po, the Rhone, and the Garonne. Rivers are not like roads, the work of the hands of man; they imitate mind, which wanders at will over pathless deserts, and flows through Nature's loveliest recesses, which are inaccessible to anything besides. . . . This Eastern scheme is one which has just seized on our imaginations. I fear that the detail of execution will destroy it, as all other wild and beautiful visions. . . . Tell me, in return, all English news. What has become of my poem ["Alastor"]? I hope it has already sheltered itself in the bosom of its mother, Oblivion, from whose embraces no one could have been so barbarous as to tear it except me.

"Tell me of the political state of England; its literature, of which when I speak, Coleridge is in my thoughts; yourself, lastly your own employments, your historical labours. . . .

"You must shelter my roofless Penates, dedicate some new temple to them, and perform the functions of a priest in my absence. They are innocent deities, and their worship neither sanguinary nor absurd.

"Leave Mammon and Jehovah to those who delight in wickedness and slavery; their altars are stained with blood, or polluted with gold, the price of blood. But the shrines of the Penates are good wood fires, or window-frames intertwined with creeping plants; their hymns are the purring of kittens, the hissing of kettles, the long talks over the past and the dead, the laugh of children, the warm wind of summer filling the quiet house, and the pelting storm of winter struggling in vain for entrance. . . .

"I trust entirely to your discretion on the subject of a house. Certainly the Forest engages my preference, because of the sylvan nature of the place and the beasts with which it is filled. But I am not insensible to the beauties of the Thames. . . .

"Recollect, however, we are now choosing a fixed, settled, eternal home, and as such its internal qualities will affect us more constantly than those which consist in the surrounding scenery, which, whatever it may be at first, will shortly be no more than the colours with which our own habits shall invest it."

The fixed, settled, and lasting home for which Shelley was seeking, was destined to endure barely two years.

CHAPTER IV.

SHELLEY AT BATH—SUICIDE OF HARRIET AND MARRIAGE OF SHELLEY—THE HERMIT OF MARLOW—"LAON AND CYTHNA"—"PRINCE ATHANASIUS"—ADDRESS TO THE ENGLISH PEOPLE—1816-1818.

ON returning to London, September 7th, 1816, Shelley hastened to join his friend Peacock, and stayed a fortnight with him at Marlow, where he determined to settle, and while the temple of his Penates was being prepared, he removed for a time to Bath.

On October 9th, Mary received an alarming letter ; and Shelley immediately set off for Bristol and Swansea. But the day preceding that of his arrival, October 10th, poor Fanny Imlay had committed suicide in the bedroom of an inn ; a bottle of laudanum lay upon the table by her side, with a note which ran thus: " I have long determined that the best thing I could do was to put an end to the existence of a being whose birth was unfortunate, and whose life has only been a series of pain to those persons who have hurt their health in endeavouring to promote her welfare. Perhaps to hear of my death will give you pain; but you will soon have the blessing of forgetting that such a creature ever existed as . . ."

As Shelley read this touching farewell, he recalled his last hurried interview with Fanny in London, and penned the mournful stanza:

> Her voice did quiver as we parted;
>   Yet knew I not that heart was broken
> From whence it came, and I departed
>   Heeding not the words then spoken.
>   Misery, O Misery!
>   This world is all too wide for thee! *

---

* Mr. Dowden proves satisfactorily that Fanny's death cannot be attributed to an unfortunate attachment for Shelley, as Claire asserts. Her letters, collected by Mr. Dowden, sufficiently explain her suicide as being merely the natural result of the excessive melancholy inherent in her disposition and increased by the nature of her surroundings at Skinner Street.

This tragic event was soon succeeded by another still more painful to Shelley. On December 14th a letter from Hookham acquainted him with the death of Harriet Westbrook, whose body had been found in the Serpentine. She was twenty-two years of age. Her life from the date of her separation from Shelley, is somewhat obscure to us. Thornton Hunt asserts that having been deserted by her lover (a captain in the army according to Trelawney), she was thrown on the streets, repudiated by her father and sister, driven from their house, and finally, feeling deserted by the whole universe, her thoughts reverted to the idea of voluntary death, which from childhood had been cherished by her.

Shelley, who had always been mindful of her since their separation, and had provided for her maintenance, had for a few weeks lost sight of her, and was vainly inquiring for her address.

On receiving the fatal news Shelley hastened to London to claim his children, and nothing can give a clearer idea of his state of mind than the letter he wrote on the following day to Mary :

I have spent a day, my beloved, of somewhat agonising sensations, such as the contemplation of vice, and folly, and hard-heartedness exceeding all conception must produce. Leigh Hunt has been with me all day, and his delicate and tender attentions to me, his kind speeches of you, have sustained me against the weight of the horror of this event.

The children I have not got. I have seen Longdill, who recommends proceeding with the utmost caution and resoluteness ; he seems interested. I told him I was under contract of marriage to you, and he said that in such an event all pretence to detain the children would cease. Hunt said very delicately that this would be soothing intelligence to you. Yes, my only hope, my darling love, this will be one among the innumerable benefits which you will have bestowed upon me, and which will still be inferior in value to the greatest of benefits—yourself. It is through you that ·I can entertain without despair the recollection of the horrors of unutterable villainy that led to this dark, dreadful death. . . . Everything tends to prove, however, that beyond the shock of so hideous a catastrophe having fallen on a human being once so nearly connected with me, there would, in any case, be little to regret. Hookham, Longdill, every one does me full justice ; bears testimony to the upright spirit and liberality of my conduct to her. There is but one voice in condemnation of the detestable Westbrooks. If they should dare to bring it before Chancery, a scene of such fearful horror would be unfolded as would cover them with scorn and shame. . . . Do you, dearest and best, seek happiness—where it ought to reside—in your own pure and perfect bosom ; in the thoughts of how dear and how good you are to me ; how wise and how extensively beneficial you are perhaps now destined to become. Remember my poor babes, Ianthe and Charles. How tender and dear a mother they will find in you—darling William, too ! My eyes overflow with tears. To-morrow I will write again.

Nothing can be more tender and loving than

Mary's reply to this letter; her hand trembles as she thinks of poor Fanny's sad fate :

> · Poor dear Fanny ! If she had lived until this moment she would have been saved, for my house would then have been a proper asylum for her. ... How very happy shall I be to possess those darling treasures of yours ! [Ianthe and Charles] . . . There will be a sweet brother and sister for my William, who will lose his pre-eminence as eldest. . . .

Harriet's suicide, following on that of Fanny, was a frightful blow to Shelley; his character was altered by it, and the remembrance haunted him to his last hour. Thornton Hunt writes :

> I am well aware that he *had* suffered severely, and that he continued to be haunted by certain recollections, partly real and partly imaginative, which pursued him like an Orestes. If exteriorly he appeared to bear this blow philosophically, the reason is he was as undemonstrative as he was profound, and at all times of his life was remarkably free, as De Quincey observes, from "sickly sentimentalism."

From a feeling of delicacy and a regard for appearances, Shelley hesitated as to an immediate marriage with Mary. But on the advice of Peacock and that of Sir Lumley Skeffington, author of a play called "The Word of Honour," and considered to be an infallible judge in such delicate matters, the formal ceremony was gone through without delay.

He needed no hints from Godwin; still less was it, as Mr. Jeaffreson implies, a wish to annoy his father. On December 30th, 1816, the marriage was celebrated at St. Mildred's in presence of Godwin and his wife.

During this time of trial Shelley found some consolation in a new friendship which proved enduring. Until the autumn of 1816, he had no close relations with Leigh Hunt, in whom, however, he had been deeply interested as a victim of intolerance and tyranny.*

Hunt had at first contemned the productions of the young poet. It was not until he had

* Shelley had expressed his sympathy at the time of Hunt's imprisonment, and it was probably on the occasion of his liberation that he wrote the following sonnet :

For me, my friend, if not that tears did tremble
   In my faint eyes, or that my heart beat fast
With feelings that make rapture pain resemble,
   Yet from thy voice that falsehood starts aghast.
I thank thee! Let the tyrant keep
His chains and tears—yea, let him weep
With rage to see thee freshly risen,
Like strength from slumber, from the prison
In which he vainly hoped the soul to bind,
Which on the chains must prey that fetter humankind.

read "Alastor" and the "Hymn to Intellectual Beauty," that he made reparation in the columns of the *Examiner* by an article in which he mentions Shelley as "one of the young poets who promises to shed lustre on the new school." "If the rest answer," he added, "to what we have seen, we shall have no hesitation in announcing him for a very striking and original thinker." The ice was now broken.

Early in November Shelley was at Marlow, and took the opportunity of visiting his new friend at his pretty Hampstead home, in the neighbourhood of Marlow. In January, 1817, the Chancery suit concerning his children by Harriet brought Shelley up to London. The Westbrooks denounced him as author of "Queen Mab," Atheist, and Republican, and he must prepare his defence. Shelley might well fear that the reactionary and intolerant spirit of the times, which had driven Cobbett to America, might visit on him the severe penalties of the law of libel, and that, like Eaton, he might be punished with imprisonment and the stocks. Mary, ever anxious and loving, soon joined him in London.

His literary connection with Hunt and his circle, of which the *Examiner* was the centre and mainspring, was fortunate for Shelley, in diverting his mind from his fears and anxieties; and Mary became intimate with Hunt's wife, the Marianne whose name lives for ever in the poet's verse.

"That was a memorable evening" (February 5th, 1817), writes Mr. Dowden, "when the three 'Young Poets' of his *Examiner* article of three months since—Reynolds, Keats, and Shelley—supped together at Hampstead with their generous critic. 'Keats,' we are told by Leigh Hunt, 'did not take to Shelley as kindly as Shelley did to him. . . . Keats being a little too sensitive on the score of his origin, felt inclined to see in every man of birth a sort of natural enemy.'" At Hunt's table Shelley also became acquainted with Charles Lamb—but the latter, to Shelley's regret, drew away from him—and Hazlitt, with whom he discussed politics until three in the morning. With Brougham, also, the great and terrible editor of the *Edinburgh Review*, the advocate of the *Examiner* in Government prosecutions, and his own adviser in the Chancery suit, Shelley now became acquainted, and in Horace Smith he found a true and devoted friend, who, to the ardour of a poet and the zeal of a political reformer, added the sound judgment of a man of business. Shelley himself has sketched him for us. "Is it not odd, that the only truly generous person I ever knew, who had money to be generous with, should be a stockbroker? And he writes poetry, too, and pastoral dramas, and yet knows how to make money, and does make it, and is still generous." And later, in a letter to Mrs. Gisborne, he says:

> Wit and sense,
> Virtue and human knowledge—all that might
> Make this dull world a business of delight—
> Are all combined in Horace Smith.

In March, Shelley set up his peaceful Penates in a spacious cottage (Albion House) at Marlow, not far from the Thames. It was surrounded by a large garden, beyond which lay open meadows leading towards undulating wooded slopes. Eight dormer windows gave a Gothic appearance to the front of the house. The largest room, large enough for a ballroom, but damp and cold, was fitted up by Shelley as a library. His writing-table stood between two life-sized casts of Apollo and Urania.* The household consisted of Shelley, his wife, little William, Claire and little Alba,† Elise, a Swiss nurse, and Harry, the gardener and man-of-all-work.

The happiness of Shelley and Mary was now complete ; Mary spent her time in reading, studying, and writing "Frankenstein"; ‡ Claire also wrote, but her special delight was music ; she accompanied herself on the piano, to which she sang in a voice compared by her former music-master, Corri, to a string of pearls, giving the most exquisite delight to Shelley, whose soul was "dissolved" in "consuming ecstasies." §

If the hermitage of Marlow were a temple of poetry, it was also one of friendship. Shelley's

---

* Mr. Dowden says *Venus*.

† Alba or Allegra, the child of Byron and Claire, was born at Bath on January 12th, 1817. At Marlow she passed for the daughter of a friend in London, sent into the country for her health.

‡ "Frankenstein; or, the Modern Prometheus," 1813 (3 vols.). The most remarkable of Mary's works; the preface was written by Shelley.

§ "To Constantia Singing." A poem addressed to Claire under that name.

friends enjoyed without scruple the generous hospitality he offered them. They were Godwin, Peacock, Hogg, the Hunts, and Horace Smith. But the poet made no acquaintance among the neighbouring commonplace gentry, whom he held in horror.

One of his greatest amusements at Marlow was boating on the river. His little mimic fleets of paper boats no longer sufficed him; he owned a boat, made for both oars and sail, which he had christened the *Vaga* (to which his friends would playfully add the syllable "bond"). Leigh Hunt gives the following account of the daily life of the Hermit of Marlow :

He rose early in the morning, walked and read before breakfast, took that meal sparingly, wrote and studied the greater part of the morning, walked and read again, dined on vegetables (for he took neither meat nor wine), conversed with his friends (to whom his house was ever open), again walked out, and usually finished with reading to his wife till ten o'clock, when he went to bed. His book was generally Plato or Homer, or one of the Greek tragedians, and the Bible, in which he took a great, though peculiar, and often admiring interest.

While in the enjoyment of these peaceful days consecrated to study and friendship, a blow was

struck which was terrible to his feelings as a
father, and decisive of the future course of his
life.

"Jew" Westbrook's petition to the Court of
Chancery, praying that all control over the education of his children should be taken from Shelley,
came before the Court in March, 1817, and on
the 27th of that month the High Chancellor,
Lord Eldon, pronounced judgment in favour
of the petitioner. Harriet's children were placed
under the guardianship of their grandfather, and
that of Dr. Hume, a clergyman of the Anglican
Church.

The considerations alleged by Mr. Westbrook
were that Shelley had deserted his wife, and that
he was an avowed Atheist, who would educate his
children in his own principles; "Queen Mab"
was quoted to prove his opinions concerning
God and marriage, as also his Letter to Lord
Ellenborough.

Notwithstanding the skilful defence set up by
Shelley, Lord Eldon, who had taken time to
consider his judgment, pronounced against him.
Purposely leaving aside the accusation of Atheism,
he dwelt principally on the immorality of Shelley's

opinions on marriage, and on his conduct as influenced by these.

" There is nothing in evidence before me," said his Lordship, "sufficient to authorise me in thinking that this gentleman has changed, before he arrived at the age of twenty-five, the principles he avowed at nineteen. I think there is ample evidence in the papers, and in his conduct, that no such change has taken place. . . . This is a case in which, as the matter appears to me, the father's principles cannot be misunderstood; in which his conduct, which I cannot but consider as highly immoral, has been established in proof, and established as the effect of those principles; conduct, nevertheless, which he represents to himself and others not as conduct to be considered as immoral, but to be recommended and observed in practice, and as worthy of approbation . . . conduct which the law animadverts upon as inconsistent with the duties of such persons and those of the community."

Shelley was consequently restrained " from intermeddling with the children until the further order of the Court."

Although Shelley did not appeal from this judgment to the House of Lords, yet he did not despair of obtaining justice and a reversal of the odious sentence, in the event of a change in the political situation. In a letter to Peacock, written at Naples in 1819, he says: " We have reports here of a change in the English Ministry—to what does it amount? for, besides my national interest in it, I am on the watch to vindicate my most sacred rights, invaded by the Chancery Court."

Meanwhile, the poet vindicated the father, and Lord Eldon acquired in Shelley's indignant verse an immortality he would have sought in vain from his own judicial prose.

Among the poems of 1817, we may read the terrible curse invoked by an outraged father on him whom he calls the

> . . . darkest crest
> Of that foul, knotted, many-headed worm
> Which rends our mother's bosom—priestly pest!
>
> By those unpractised accents of young speech,
> Which he who is a father thought to frame
> To gentlest lore such as the wisest teach.
> *Thou* strike the lyre of mind! oh, grief and shame! . . .
> I curse thee . . .

Nor does Shelley miss a later opportunity of branding him who had torn away his children; in the " Mask of Anarchy" (1819), he depicts Lord Eldon under the name of Fraud:

> Next came Fraud, and he had on,
> Like Lord Eldon, an ermine gown.
> His big tears, for he wept well,
> Turned to millstones as they fell;

> And the little children who
> Round his feet played to and fro,
> Thinking every tear a gem,
> Had their brains knocked out by them.

The weeping Eldon in " Œdipus Tyrannus " will appear again as " Dakry, the Wizard Minister of Swellfoot."

Thus bereft of two children, Shelley turned an anxious gaze on his little William, lest, in the name of religion and morality, a sacrilegious hand should claim that child too from his father's care. He conceived the project of removing him from his ungrateful country, and seeking beyond the sea the sunny shores of Italy or Greece.

His dream of a lasting abode in free England had vanished; his health was terribly affected by the successive shocks he had undergone, and required a warmer climate ; it was his duty to live for those who remained to him, those to whom his life might be a source of happiness, usefulness, safety, and honour, while his death would deprive them of all these things.*

It might be expected that under repeated

* Letter to Godwin, Dec. 7, 1817.

strokes of misfortune, the poet would bend and sink. But on the contrary, he seemed to acquire new strength and spirit. While anxiously awaiting the decision of the Court, he wrote his longest poem. While the law was branding him as unfit "for the most rudimentary duties of social life," he was preparing to protest more strongly than ever against those principles in the name of which he was condemned; and he pursued with confidence and enthusiasm the moral and social ideal which he had proclaimed, and for which he had already suffered martyrdom. He composed "Laon and Cythna."

"The poem was written," says Mary, " in his boat as it floated under the beech-groves of Bisham, or during wanderings in the neighbouring country, which is distinguished for peculiar beauty. The chalk hills break into cliffs that overhang the Thames, or form valleys clothed with beech ; the wilder portion of the country is rendered beautiful by exuberant vegetation ; and the cultivated part is peculiarly fertile. With all this wealth of nature which, either in the form of gentlemen's parks or soil dedicated to agriculture, flourished around, Marlow was inhabited (I hope it is altered now) by a very poor population. The women are lace-makers, and lose their health by sedentary labour, for which they were very ill paid. The poor-laws ground to the dust not only the paupers, but those who had risen just above that state, and were obliged to pay poor-rates. . . .

Shelley afforded what alleviation he could.* In the winter, while bringing out his poem, he had a severe attack of ophthalmia, caught while visiting the poor cottages. I mention these things—for this minute and active sympathy with his fellow creatures gives a thousandfold interest to his speculations, and stamps with reality his pleadings for the human race."

And, in fact, if there is one distinctive mark amid its exuberance of moral, political, and religious teaching in the poem, it is the ardent love of mankind burning, from beginning to end, with irresistible and contagious fire. We find in it

* His sojourn at Marlow was one continual exercise of benevolence ; many long pages might be filled with the narration of his charitable deeds, as told by his biographers. This period of his life resembles the lives of the Saints. One of his neighbours and friends, Mrs. Madocks, who acted as his almoner during the absence of the Hermit of Marlow, gives the following testimony in 1859 : "Every spot is sacred that he visited ; he was a gentleman that seldom took money about with him, and we received numerous little billets, written sometimes on the leaf of a book, to pay the bearer the sum he specified, sometimes as much as half-a-crown ; and one day he came home without shoes, saying that he had no paper, so he gave the poor man his shoes. Like St. Francis, his charity was extended to the dumb creation. He would buy cray-fish of the men who brought them through the streets, and would order his servant to bear them back to their lurking-places in the Thames."

precisely the same creed as in "Queen Mab"; hatred of tyranny and custom, condemnation of selfishness and cupidity that darken the heart and destroy the energies of man, intense longing to rescue the human race from the ignominious yoke of religion, and woman from the degrading slavery that lowers and corrupts her. But these doctrines are set forth with such passionate conviction, with such forcible and burning eloquence, they are so full of sympathy, love, and hope, that we are carried away, in spite of ourselves, by the deep and rushing stream; we forget to admire the eloquent poetry, because we are bewildered by the magical descriptions, and filled with the strange charm of the marvellous and divine evocations of this new Apocalypse. Shelley himself called his poem a "Vision of the Nineteenth Century." He no longer gives us the melancholy despair of Alastor who, in his disillusion, seeks rest and oblivion in death; but, revived by love, Shelley, in the person of Laon, his hero, who is the embodiment of ideal devotion to the regeneration and happiness of mankind, combats all the sad realities which oppose that regeneration, and delay the coming of that happiness to which he calls poor erring humanity.

This is the dominant idea of the poem, and Shelley opens the subject by an allegorical myth, in which he depicts, under striking imagery, the history of the old strife between good and evil in the world, such as he conceived it. To the reader it is a somewhat confusing assemblage of the traditions of India and those of Greece, of Manichæism, and of Christianity. Good and evil are twin geniuses—equal gods ; in the formidable strife that is waged between them, evil is represented by the eagle, the bird of Jupiter, who was afterwards depicted in the " Prometheus " as personifying the principle of evil; and the serpent is the incarnation of the Morning Star or principle of good, the Avatar of human genius, the Prometheus of the Greeks, the Lucifer or Satan of the Bible.

The fair, mysterious woman who receives the wounded Serpent in her bosom is, in this poem, the incarnation of the Spirit of Nature ; assuming the rôle that in " Prometheus " is to be played by Asia—the personification of Divine love, the new Eve, the lover of the Morning Star, of Prometheus—Lucifer.

The whole of this allegory is embodied in human forms in "Laon and Cythna."

The principal rôle is given to the woman, Cythna.

Shelley, who became a more and more devoted follower of Mary Wollstonecraft since his union with her daughter, created Cythna to be the prophetess and apostle of the regeneration of her sex. If Laon awakes in Cythna the love of freedom, Cythna awakes in Laon the love of purity; she instinctively loathes the joy-less sensuality of which women are the victims, which flings their grace and beauty as a prey to the hyena—lust. She desires for woman equality, liberty, justice, and dignity. She would avenge the outrage and insult woman has too long endured; and her gentle martyrdom is more potent against tyranny than the armed resistance of Laon; her torturers are converted.

All these thoughts are in Mary Wollstone-craft's book, the "Rights of Women," but the suavity, the passion, the divine music are Shelley's.*

* In proof of this the reader is referred to Shelley's enthusiastic panegyric of Mary Wollstonecraft, in the Dedication to his wife, stanza xii. He also alludes, later, to Mary's revolutionary enthusiasm, and to her sojourn in Paris during the early years of the Revolution.

If ever a poet has existed worthy of the French Revolution, he is certainly the author of the "Revolt of Islam." The subject, whatever may be said of it, is as full of inspiration to a poet as the rescue of the Saviour's tomb, or the discovery of a new World.

Michelet, after narrating the stirring episode of the Federation in his "History of the Revolution," exclaims : "I have held in my hands for a moment, on the altar of Federation, the uncovered heart of France; I saw the beating of that heroic heart at the first ray of the faith of the future. How then should I worship the little gods of this world? I had caught a glimpse of God. May the sublime vision, that for an instant was ours during the solemn act of French fraternity, lift us above all the moral misery of our times, and give us back a spark of the heroic fire that burned in the hearts of our fathers ! "

Shelley's great soul divined that which drew from Michelet tears of admiration and love, and it is difficult to read the episode of the Federation in canto v., without feeling the glow of that heroic fire of which Michelet speaks.

Shelley's ideas upon the essence of the moral laws, and the arbitrariness of human institutions, brought him to the logical conclusion that the impediments to marriage, invented by man and sanctioned by religion, are as artificial and as immoral as the law of its indissolubility. To make this conclusion distinctly evident, he placed his hero and heroine, Laon and Cythna, in the relationship of brother and sister—joined together in the most perfect union by the double ties of consanguinity and love.

But it required all Shelley's ingenuousness to believe that such doctrines could be printed and published in prudish England. Nevertheless, they were published; a few copies of a first edition were circulated; but so unfavourable an impression was produced that the publishers became alarmed, stopped further publication, and requested Shelley to revise his poem. He was forced, therefore, to abolish all trace of fraternal relationship between Laon and Cythna, and likewise to soften several passages in which Atheism and the stake were too perceptible. "Laon and Cythna," revised, corrected, and purified, reappeared under the title of the "Revolt of Islam."

But these concessions to public opinion failed to disarm criticism. Shelley was mistaken when he believed the public would receive his amended work favourably, and without prejudice. Reviled, derided, and stigmatised, "Laon and Cythna" only strengthened the existing prejudice against the author of "Queen Mab."

The faithful portrayal of his own mind, which Shelley regards as one of the principal merits of "Laon and Cythna," he had previously attempted that same year in "Prince Athanasius," a poem still more personal to himself, and which has remained merely a sketch or fragment. In the whole of Shelley's works there is not one more psychological, profound, or subtle, and if we wish to know the very finest mood of the poet's mind, self-analysed in its most fugitive phases and in its most delicate shades, it is there we must seek it. It is pure spirit analysing and dissecting itself in order to discover the undiscoverable cause of the infinite uneasiness with which it is devoured. But at last Shelley feared to lose his foothold in a world of such subtlety, and forbore to complete the study lest his analysis might become morbid and beyond the

comprehension of the most attentive reader. Such
as it is, the fragment of "Prince Athanasius"
is of the highest importance for what I may
designate as the psychological autobiography of
the poet. Athanasius, like the youth in "Alastor,"
seeks throughout the world a human being to love.
On the vessel on which he embarks, a lady comes
to him in whom he thinks he sees the realisation
of his ideal of love and beauty. But soon he
perceives that she is but *Pandemos,* or the
earthly and unworthy Venus, who, after casting
her spell over him, deserts him. Athanasius, beaten
down by sorrow, dies. To his death-bed comes
Urania, she who alone can fill and satisfy his
soul, and kisses his lips. Of this great conception there remain but a few lines of the final
fragment, in which Shelley depicts Mary as
Urania, and the admirable address to Uranian love,

> Thou art the wine whose drunkenness is all
> We can desire, O Love !

with which Shelley longs to inebriate the human
race.

After the composition of "Laon and Cythna,"
projects of very various kinds occupied Shelley's
imagination; he read the pages of Tacitus on

Otho, and contemplated writing a poem on the great and melancholy emperor, " who, both tyrant and tyrannicide, hallowed the Roman sword by bathing it in his own blood." But amidst his various projects, his imagination turns towards one object, one type, the incarnation of his own spirit and his own love; a type that since " Queen Mab " has been constantly rising higher and higher, becoming more and more pure and ideal as it passed through Alastor, Prince Athanasius, Laon in the " Revolt of Islam," and culminated at last in the final conception of Prometheus.

The laborious inception of the great idea with which this work is penetrated, its continuing and (to his mind) imperfect progress, and his despair at finding the world deaf to the voice of truth and love, overwhelm his soul, much more than any exterior trials can, with an incurable sadness which he expressed in heart-broken words ; he bitterly deplores the impotence of · his thoughts which rise and fall in solitude, the vain efforts of his imagination which succeeds only in possessing " one-half of the shadow which it creates."

Once more descend

The shadows of my soul upon mankind ;
For to those hearts with which they never blend,

Thoughts are but shadows which the flashing mind,
From the swift clouds which track its flight of fire,
Casts on the gloomy world it leaves behind.

He longs for "a chariot of cloud":

Oh, that a chariot of cloud were mine!
I would sail on the waves of the billowy wind
To the mountain peak and the rocky lake,"

in regions inaccessible to common mortals, and to which he showed the author of " Childe Harold " the path, for Byron echoed Shelley in the beautiful stanza, that the latter loved to apply to himself:

On the sea,
The boldest steer but where their ports invite ;
But there are wanderers o'er eternity,
Whose bark drives on and on, and ne'er shall anchored be.

This hopeless quest of the ideal did not, however, prevent Shelley from eagerly watching the course of political events in his native land, and from making use of events which stirred the mind of the people, to set forth his own ideas, express his views, and explain the lessons of contemporary history by the light of his own theories.

The great question of Parliamentary Reform was agitated in England in 1817, and Shelley, ever eager for the rights of the people, published a political pamphlet on the subject, named: " A Proposal for putting Reform to the Vote throughout the Country, by the Hermit of Marlow."

The whole question, in his opinion, was this: Should the people legislate for themselves, or should they be governed by laws made by an assembly which does not even represent even one thousandth part of the community? We may find his reply in his Irish pamphlets: " No, the people may not be thus governed." The actual constitution of Parliament appears to him a spectacle to arouse indignation and horror:

> An hospital for lunatics is the only theatre where we can conceive so mournful a comedy to be exhibited as this mighty nation now exhibits. . . . The prerogatives of Parliament constitute a sovereignty which is exercised in contempt of the people . . . for its misery and ruin. . . . It is the object of the Reformers to restore the people to a sovereignty thus held in their contempt, by making the House of Commons a complete representative of the will of the people.

In order to attain this end, Shelley advised the holding of a permanent meeting " to take into consideration the most effectual measures for ascertaining the will " of the people, and put his name down on the subscription-list for

necessary expenses, for a sum of £100, being a
tenth part of his income. As to the requisite
reforms, Shelley thought with Cobbett that annual
parliaments ought to be adopted, but he considered the English nation as yet insufficiently
prepared for universal suffrage—

The consequence of the immediate extension of the
elective franchise to every male adult, would be to place
power in the hands of men who have been rendered brutal,
and torpid, and ferocious, by ages of slavery. . . . I allow
Major Cartwright's arguments to be unanswerable; ab-
stractedly it is the right of every human being to have a
share in the Government. But Mr. Paine's arguments are
also unanswerable; a pure republic may be shown . . . to
be that system of social order, the fittest to produce the
happiness and promote the genuine eminence of man.
Yet nothing can less consist with reason, or afford smaller
hopes of any beneficial issue, than the plan which should
abolish the regal and the aristocratical branches of our
constitution, before the public mind, through many grada-
tions of improvement, shall have arrived at the maturity
which can disregard these symbols of its childhood.

The moderate reform desired by Shelley was
accomplished, more than half a century later, by
Mr. Gladstone.

On Nov. 6th, 1817, occurred the premature death
of the young Princess Charlotte, daughter of
George IV. and Caroline of Brunswick, the idol

of the English people. Suddenly snatched from domestic joys that had consoled her for an unhappy childhood, the "fair and innocent princess" carried with her to the grave the lamentations of all England.

Shelley was shocked at the national mourning for a woman, who, although interesting from her misfortunes and her premature death, was yet chiefly so as a Princess and future Queen of England. In grief so solemn and ostentatious he detected signs of servility and baseness, and "the Hermit of Marlow" wrote an "Address to the People" with the following motto: "We pity the plumage, but forget the dying bird."

The dying bird thus forgotten by the English people in their pity for its bright plumage, represented the common and hidden miseries of suffering humanity, the sorrows of the people, of which poor Charlotte's destiny formed a very small part.

Shelley understands the public mourning of the Athenians for the death of those whose valour, intelligence, or genius had illumined the Republic; he would have thought it well that, when Milton died, "the universal English nation had been clothed in solemn black," that "the French nation should have enjoined a public mourning at the death of Rousseau and Voltaire." "It were well done also," he says, " that men should mourn for any public calamity which has befallen their country or the world, though it be not death. This helps to maintain that connection between one man and another, and all men considered as a whole, which is the bond of social life. There should be public mourning when those events take place which make all good men mourn in their hearts— the rule of foreign or domestic tyrants, the abuse of public faith, the wresting of old and venerable laws to the murder of the innocent, the established insecurity of all those . . . who cherish an unconquerable enthusiasm for public good. . . When the French Republic was extinguished the world ought to have mourned." In an eloquent parallel he compares the death of the young, amiable, and interesting Princess, "the last and the best of her race," with that of the three men who were executed for political offences on the same day—Brandreth, Ludlam, and Turner— whose frightful death by hanging and decapita-tion constitutes a calamity that the English na-

tion should lament with inconsolable grief.* He
ends with an eloquent peroration which we must
quote in its entirety :

Mourn, then, People of England !   Clothe yourselves
in solemn black. Let the bells be tolled. Think of mortality
and change. Shroud yourselves in solitude and the gloom
of sacred sorrow. Spare no symbol of universal grief. Weep
—mourn—lament. Fill the great City—fill the boundless
fields with lamentation and the echo of groans. A beautiful
Princess is dead—she who should have been the Queen of
her beloved nation, and whose posterity should have ruled it
for ever. She loved the domestic affections, and cherished
arts which adorn, and valour which defends. She was
amiable, and would have become wise, but she was young,
and in the flower of youth the despoiler came. LIBERTY is
dead ! Slave ! I charge thee, disturb not the depth and
solemnity of our grief by any meaner sorrow. If one has
died who was like her that should have ruled over this land,
like Liberty, young, innocent, and lovely, know that the
power through which that one perished was God, and that it
was a private grief. But *man* has murdered Liberty ; and
whilst the life was ebbing from its wound, there descended
on the heads and on the hearts of every human thing the
sympathy of an universal blast and curse. Fetters heavier
than iron weigh upon us, because they bind our souls. We
move about in a dungeon more pestilential than damp and
narrow walls, because the earth is its floor and the heavens
are its roof. Let us follow the corpse of British Liberty

---

* Shelley lifts up his voice in strong reprobation of the
penalty of death : " Nothing is more horrible than that man
should for any cause take the life of man."

slowly and reverentially to its tomb ; and if some glorious
Phantom should appear, and make its throne of broken
swords and sceptres and royal crowns trampled in the dust,
let us say that the Spirit of Liberty has arisen from its
grave, and left all that was gross and mortal there, and kneel
down to worship it as our Queen.

The foregoing lines became subsequently the
theme of Shelley's version of " God save the King "
—God save Liberty ! ·

CHAPTER V.

SHELLEY IN ITALY—MILAN, LEGHORN, LUCCA, VENICE, THE CAPUCHINS, FLORENCE, AND PADUA — "ROSALIND AND HELEN," AND "JULIAN AND MADDALO"—1818.

EARLY in February, 1818, Shelley, who was impatient to get into a milder climate, on account of the increasing delicacy of his health, bade adieu to Marlow. It was with profound regret that he left the scenes associated with the intellectual pleasure which he had enjoyed in the composition of "Laon and Cythna."

On the 9th March, William Shelley, Clara Everina Shelley (born on the 3rd September, 1817, at Marlow), and Clara Allegra, Byron's daughter, were duly baptized at St. Giles's-in-the-Fields, and on the 11th Shelley took his last look at the shores of England.

A new life was about to begin for him under the sunny sky of Italy, "that paradise of exiles and pariahs," as he calls it. His genius, freed from all enmities and resentments, was about to soar boldly into the serene spheres of the purely ideal. On losing sight of England, Shelley seemed to lose sight of earth altogether; by daily contact with the masterpieces of Italian Art and Nature his taste was refined, his conceptions were elevated and purified; he became invested with the beauty and grandeur of the antique, through his absorbed contemplation of its ruins, his assiduous study of sculpture, his researches into Plato and Æschylus, in short, his loving worship of all the arts. His faculties expanded, together with his senses and his frame, under these favourable physical conditions; and to this epoch we owe the incomparable poet of the "Prometheus," the "Epipsychidion," the "Adonaïs," and the "Hellas."

We have the history of this transformation, this full bloom of his poetic genius, in his "Letters from Italy." These letters are held by the best judges to occupy an exceptional place in the epistolary literature of the century.

If they do not possess the brilliancy, the humour, the petulance, and the wonderful "go" of Byron's letters, they possess greater solidity and seriousness, a deeper passion, a more sincere enthusiasm, and absolute frankness of thought and feeling. Mr. Garnett has justly remarked that Shelley's letters represent exactly the way in which the poet, as a poet, contemplates life and Nature. A great deal of the pleasure which they produce proceeds from their close agreement with the poetical works upon which they are the involuntary commentary. They prove that the ideal world of Shelley was to him a real world, and that the habitual level of the life of the man was not lower than that of the poet.

On the 12th of March, 1818, Shelley embarked on the *Lady Castlereagh* for Calais. He was accompanied by his wife, Miss Clairmont, Elise (the Swiss girl), Milly (a young maid-servant from Marlow), his own two children, and the little Allegra, who was only fourteen months old. He hoped to bring about a reconciliation between Byron and the mother, through the medium of this child. The party travelled through France by way of Calais, Rheims,

Langres, Dijon, and Lyons, Shelley reading aloud Schlegel's work, and a new poem by Hunt, called "Foliage."

On the 26th of March, Shelley crossed the Pass of the Échelles, and entered the valleys of the Alps. The winding road, cut in the rock on the face of the mountain, which leads to Chambéry, produced a vivid impression upon him. He declares that the site resembles that described in the "Prometheus" of Æschylus, and proceeds to draw an exquisite word-picture of it. But although the poet, whose mind is already full of his "Prometheus," seeks for images in proportion with his subject amid the grand natural scenery of the Alpine ranges, the humanitarian philosopher is moved to the deepest pity by the poverty and wretchedness of the inhabitants of those fertile valleys. Shelley remarks continually upon this contrast between man and Nature while he journeys into Italy, and he is disposed to exaggerate it ingenuously, in order to stigmatise the tyranny of Governments, which he regards as its sole true cause, with greater truth and liberty. These melancholy impressions are, however, speedily dispelled by the charms of Alpine Nature; while the carriages are climbing the ascent of Mont Cenis, Shelley becomes intoxicated with delight, he sings as he goes. While descending the Alps, his chest expands, his sensations become more acute and vivid under the influence of the beauty of the country and the serenity of the sky; he feels more keenly than ever that he depends upon these things for life. With what delight he hears for the first time at Susa a pretty Italian woman speaking "the clear, the perfect language of Italy, after the nasal, clipped cacophony of the French"! The first objects which he meets in that favoured land delight and enchant him; those objects are, firstly, the Arch of Augustus at Susa, which is like the gate of Italy, and a fair woman whose graceful mien and blonde beauty recalled Fuseli's Eve.

Shelley arrived at Milan on the 4th of April, and remained there for a month. He was particularly struck by two things, the Duomo and the Opera. But the lake of Como had a far greater attraction for the poet. The beauty of its shores, and its lovely villas, Tanzi, Tremezzina, Sommariva, Pliniana, is, according to him, to be surpassed only by that of the Lakes of Killarney. He would have liked to settle down permanently in one of those enchanting places, Pliniana, a half-ruined villa, with great laurel hedges, overlooking the finest landscape in the world. He had, however, to relinquish his own wishes in deference to those of Mary, who did not relish "that divine solitude of Como" so keenly as he did, and he bent his steps towards Pisa, being attracted thither by the vicinity of the sea.

He left Milan with great regret and crossed the Apennines, which he considered much less beautiful than the Alps : "An immense and indeterminate scene, in which the imagination cannot find a shelter." On the other hand, the plains of Parma had the aspect of a garden in his eyes. He remained only three or four days at Pisa, "a large and disagreeable town almost without inhabitants," and arrived on the 10th of May at Leghorn, where he was detained a full month by the pleasure which he derived from the society of the Gisbornes, new friends to whom he was introduced by Godwin. Mrs. Gisborne, who from her childhood had led an adventurous life, was peculiarly calculated to attract and fascinate Shelley. She was the daughter of an English merchant settled at Constantinople, and, at the age of eight years, she was separated from her mother. Her father brought her up with the greatest care in the free society of the English merchants and diplomatists. In 1785, Jeremy Bentham, then visiting the Bosphorus, had remarked the young girl, who, at fifteen, was quite womanly, and exhibited extraordinary capacity for the arts. He played Eichner's sonatas for the piano and the violin with her. Shortly afterwards we find her at Rome with her father, taking lessons in painting from Angelica Kaufmann. The English painter, Barry, was so much struck by some of her sketches that he strongly urged her to devote herself exclusively to painting. At Rome she married Mr. William Reveley, an architect, who brought her to London, where she formed a social alliance with all the advanced intellects of the time—for she fully shared the Liberal convictions of her husband—and placed herself under the philosophic guidance of Godwin and Mary Wollstonecraft. When Mary was born she took her to her own house, and tended her with maternal solicitude. She became a widow early, and, having refused Godwin, she married Mr. John Gisborne in 1800, and retired to Italy with her new husband and her son by her first marriage. Mr. Gisborne gave his wife's son a sound scientific education. When Shelley found the Gisborne family installed at Leghorn, Henry Reveley was an engineer of great promise, with a pronounced taste for mechanics and the new applications of science.

The story of Maria Gisborne, her relations with Mary Wollstonecraft, her beauty, her character, and, above all, her freedom from religious or social prejudices, could not fail to captivate the inflammable soul of the poet. As for the husband, he was an excellent man — placidity itself—with but little capacity for business, in which he had never succeeded ; erudite, well-read, not without interest in poetry in general, and enthusiastic about Calderon. He had initiated his wife into the beauties of the *Magico Prodigioso* and the *Autos*, and in their school Shelley learned to love that other Shakespeare whom he had met more than once unconsciously, and who was thenceforth to share the poet's devotion to the author of *Macbeth* and *King Lear.*

These agreeable relations, which speedily developed into a warm and close friendship, diverted Shelley's thoughts from the unpleasantness of that great commercial town, which is the most untaught and unattractive of the Italian cities, and he bade farewell with sincere regret to the accomplished woman who was destined to inspire one of his most original poems, a masterpiece of humour and grace, the " Letter to Maria Gisborne." At the Baths of Lucca, where there were English people only, Shelley was free to give himself up entirely to his studious tastes and the carrying out of his poetic plans. He rejoiced in being restored to silence, and that chosen society of all the ages, his books, which he had carefully packed before leaving England, and found again at Lucca, and in his picturesque walks in the chestnut woods, on the banks of the river, or across the mountains. His dwelling was a restored and repainted cottage in the midst of grand scenery, surrounded by wooded mountains, surmounted here and there by the bare crest of some far-distant Apennine. The house stood in a little garden, with a laurel grove at the end of it so thick that the sun could not pierce it with his rays. The poet's happy days at Lucca were passed in walks with Mary in the neighbourhood, long excursions on horseback to the *Prato fiorito*, a field of flowers on the summit of one of the Apennines, or to the sanctuary of the *Monte Pelerino*, the loftiest of those mountains; attentive observation of the slightest perturbations of the atmosphere, which he studied in order to paint it; contemplation of the beautiful Italian evenings; study of the great Italian poets, Ariosto, Petrarch, and Tasso; and in reading and translating Plato.

The admirable translation of the "Banquet of Plato," which dates from this epoch, was the work of ten mornings. Although this translation seemed to him very insufficient to convey in English the inimitable graces of the original, it may safely be affirmed that, not since the Renaissance, has Plato found so enthusiastic an interpreter, one so apt to comprehend and to embody all the charm and poetry of his language. Mrs. Shelley is justified in her claim for this translation, that it presents the great Athenian to English readers in a style worthy of him.

In translating Plato's " Banquet," Shelley also purposed to give Mary an idea of the sentiments and manners (*mœurs*) of the Athenians. With this object he began an essay which was to form a preface to his translation, upon the literature, the arts, and the manners of the Athenians. We have only a fragment of this essay, entitled, " A Discourse upon the Manners of the Ancients in relation to the subject of Love." Shelley's mind was deeply impressed with the unrivalled grandeur of that unique epoch in the history of the human mind; and as he held that no person had hitherto depicted the life of the ancient Greeks with exactitude and fidelity, he designed to supply the deficiency. To do this it was necessary, in his belief, to divest himself of all modern prejudices and considerations, to become altogether pagan, entirely Greek. In his praiseworthy work, " Le Voyage du Jeune Anacharsis," the Abbé Barthélemy commits the fault of never forgetting that he is a Christian and a Frenchman; and although Wieland makes a tolerable pagan, he still has too much political prejudice. He is too much afraid of diminishing the interest of his recital by depicting sentiments with which a modern European could not sympathise. All books written upon the Greeks seemed to Shelley to have been written for children, and on principles of timid prudery incompatible with truth.

To begin the work by an explanation of the Greek ideas upon the subject of love, was to take the bull by the horns, and no one could realise more fully than Shelley the conditions imposed upon any writer who should try to restore to life the true traditions of Greek antiquity upon this obscure and delicate subject. It is deeply to be regretted that he did no more than sketch the outline of the picture, perhaps because he was deterred by the very delicacy of the subject; but, such as it is, his sketch is rich in fruitful ideas and original views. No more just idea of the position of woman in ancient times, and the causes of her inferiority and degradation, could be given. While doing justice to the progress in the relations of the two sexes accomplished by Christianity and Chivalry, Shelley objected with justice to the exaggeration of the merit of that revolution, and would not admit the pretension that the Greeks knew nothing of sentimental or ideal love, and the claim of that passion to be the exclusive product of Christian or chivalrous ideas.

Amid the charms of solitude, and the calm of his mind, which was refreshed by the living spring of Nature and Plato, Shelley once more found inspiration. In the middle of August (1818), upon the entreaty of Mary, he finished his poem of "Rosalind and Helen," * which he had begun at Marlow, one of those rare works in which Shelley, coming down from his dreamy heights, touches ordinary life, and consents to depict purely human passions.

"Rosalind and Helen" possessed a special interest for Mary. It is easy for any reader who has even a superficial knowledge of Shelley's history to discover Claire and Mary, separated for awhile, and at enmity, under the names of Rosalind and Helen, and to find Shelley himself in Lionel. He wrote this narrative in the hopes of cementing the friendship of the two young women who were now reunited under his roof,

* "Rosalind and Helen" was published by Ollier in the spring of 1819, together with "Verses written in the Euganean Mountains," the "Hymn to Intellectual Beauty," and the sonnet "Ozymandias."

and, in fact, from thenceforth (1818) their mutual attachment was undisturbed.

On the 17th of August Shelley went to Venice, accompanied by Claire, to visit Lord Byron. The poor mother hoped that Shelley would procure permission for her to see her daughter again. At Padua Shelley took a gondola, and, by a strange chance, he selected a gondolier who had formerly been in Byron's service. This man talked incessantly of the *Giovanotto Inglese,* who bore an outlandish name, lived sumptuously, and spent money lavishly. Venice was reached at midnight, and the gondola sustained a tempest of wind, rain, and lightning in the lagoon.

On the day after his arrival, Shelley, leaving Claire with the Hoppners,* went to Byron's dwelling. The conversation between the friends soon turned upon the delicate matter that Shelley had so much at heart, and the latter believed that he had gained some points. Byron seemed even disposed to give up the child to her mother. Their interview, which was full of kindliness and good-humour, was prolonged by an excursion in

* Mr. Hoppner was British Consul at Venice, and Mrs. Hoppner had taken charge of the little Allegra.

a gondola, and the two poets indulged in the latter diversion several times during Shelley's stay at Venice. To that sojourn we owe the poem of " Julian and Maddalo," so eloquently eulogised by Mr. Rossetti, who declares that it alone would suffice to justify the poet's deathless fame, and holds that, together with the " Prometheus " and " The Cenci," it completes the supreme trinity of Shelley's genius.

The reader will easily recognise the two friends under the names of Julian and Maddalo. It would be difficult to depict two such different natures better than Shelley depicts them in his preface, and to tell the whole truth with greater tact and delicacy. In his letters to his friends he is sharper and more caustic; it is in them that we must seek for his real views of the genius and the character of the author of " Don Juan."

Byron, who was anxious to have Shelley near him, offered him the use of his villa, called dei Cappucini, near Este. Shelley accepted this proposal, and pressed his wife to join him there. During his absence he had been very anxious about her, and had written several letters to her, full of the tenderness of his loving heart, and of truly paternal solicitude. He had also addressed some pretty verses to her. His instructions for the journey, which she was to make under the guidance of the accomplished Paolo, were of the most minute and thoughtful kind.

Mary, who was longing to rejoin her husband came with all haste to Este. The Villa dei Cappucini, an ancient residence of the Medici, was situated in the neighbourhood of that city, on the summit of a little hill surrounded by several loftier ones. The house was pleasant and commodious; a wall enclosed between trellised vines, or *Pergola*, as the Italians call it, led from the house to the bottom of the garden, where there was a summer-house. This was used by Shelley as his study, and there he wrote "Julian and Maddalo," and began the "Prometheus." The praises of the villa, the views from it, and the great plain of Lombardy which stretched below are sung in many of the poet's letters of this peaceful epoch.

A melancholy event darkened the fair days of the Villa dei Cappucini; this was the death of the little Clara, who had been taken ill with dysentery during the journey. The child was taken from Este to Venice for medical advice, but she died almost immediately upon arriving there, and the sorrowing parents returned to mourn her in their saddened home.

. To Shelley, beautiful Venice, with "its silent streets paved with water," was a bitter and lugubrious spectacle.. He saw nothing there save the dungeons, the *piombi*, and the *oubliettes*, a city enslaved from the day on which the rights of the people had been usurped, but more degraded still since its subjection to the Austrian yoke. "I had no idea," he writes, "of the excess to which avarice, cowardice, superstition, ignorance, passionless debauchery, and all the unspeakable brutalities which degrade human nature, may be carried, until I had seen Venice!"

No traveller in Italy has felt the misfortune of that fair land become the prey of the foreigner, so keenly as Shelley; no poet has so bitterly deplored the shame and misery of her servitude, or sung so nobly her hopes of a national resurrection; none has associated himself so enthusiastically with her every attempt to accomplish her freedom.

Petrarch's house and tomb, sacredly preserved at Arqua, attracted him to the Euganean Mountains, but the deeper feeling for liberty mingles with that for Nature, in the emotions of the disciple of Laura's lover, when he contemplates Padua, "where the lamp of learning burns no longer, or is only a mocking meteor." In the ruins of Florence, he beholds the chastisement of an inexpiable crime, the attempt against the liberty of Pisa, and, on rising from the perusal of Sismondi's "Italian Republics," he utters in song the heroic legend of Marenghi, who avenged his banishment from Florence by burning a Pisan ship.

Winter was approaching, and Shelley left the Villa dei Cappucini on the 5th November, 1818, for the South of Italy. After two days' journey by very bad roads, he arrived at Ferrara, and recorded his admiration of the "true country of Pasiphaë," through which he had passed. He afterwards remembered the little white oxen of the plain of Ferrara, when he wrote his satirical drama *Œdipus*, in which he places the English Royal Pasiphaë upon the stage. Ferrara, at the time of Shelley's visit, was no longer the adventurous city of Ariosto ; but, although deserted and melancholy, it had still preserved an air of grandeur and magnificence, something fanciful, too, which recalled its poetic memories. Shelley visited the Cathedral, but was driven from it by the importunity of the beggars, before he had time to discover whether the fresco of the Last Judgment is a copy or an original by Michael Angelo;* and the famous Public Library, containing 160,000 volumes, and immensely rich in manuscripts and miniatures, "whose colours are as fresh as though they dated from yesterday." The great attraction of Ferrara for Shelley lay in the recollections of his brother poets, Ariosto and Tasso. He pauses in deeply-moved contemplation before the tomb of Ariosto, in one of the great halls of the Library, surmounted by an expressive bust of the poet, or before his arm-chair, a common piece of furniture enough in walnut-wood, picturing to himself Ariosto still sitting there, the open book of " Satires " close at hand, and the old inkstand aiding the living poet's fancy. But nothing interests him so deeply as the autograph manuscripts of the two poets; the Satires of Ariosto, and a manuscript of the Geru-

* A superb inspiration of Bastianino after Michael Angelo.

salemme Liberata, also some sonnets of Tasso's
to his persecutor. Shelley's mind, always in quest
of some manifestation beyond the present and
tangible object, seeks to divine the symbol of
their soul and their genius in these mute characters,
subjecting them to close examination and analysis.
He peruses those sonnets which Tasso wrote in
his prison—they are in praise of his tormentor,
and, moved by profound pity for the weakness
of the noble victim, he comprehends and pardons.
Shelley does not fail to visit the Hospital of
Saint Anne, in which is the prison "which for
seven years and three months shut out that
glorious being from the air and the light, where
those poetic influences which he has communicated
to thousands of readers, were nurtured." In its
darkest corner he saw the mark of the chains,
fastened to the wall, by which his hands and feet
were bound. There, in his mind's eye, he beheld
the unfortunate poet; his eyes fixed upon the
barred window, following with his despairing gaze
the beloved shadow of Leonora, towards the
tower of the palace, which is to be seen in the
distance. He piously detaches a morsel of the
wood of the real door of this dark and baneful

prison, to be sent to his friend Peacock. Not an instant's doubt has Shelley of the authenticity of the hateful place; he is not a critical and sceptical traveller like Goethe, who saw nothing in Tasso's prison but an ordinary coal-cellar, in which he was assuredly never incarcerated, and quotes on the occasion, Luther's famous inkstain, which is renewed from time to time, for the satisfaction of credulous tourists.

From Ferrara, Shelley proceeded to Bologna, where he arrived on the 8th November. Here, Shelley ventured on the yet untrodden ground of art-criticism. Until the period of his travels in Italy, he had been indifferent to the Fine Arts, with the exception of Sculpture; but his mind was too ardently fixed upon the search after the Beautiful, to admit of his neglecting to pursue it under all its forms. The Italian Museums had awakened in him that insatiable curiosity which made him observe in painting as well as in statuary, "the laws according to which that ideal beauty, of which we have in ourselves a perception so intense and yet so obscure, is realised in outward forms." He was not an amateur by profession; he was not a learned connoisseur;

but he possessed what is worth more than erudition and technical knowledge, that is to say, natural taste and love of the beautiful, which is its principle and its rule. He felt strongly and keenly, and he expressed ardently what he felt; in his descriptions of pictures there is freshness and grace of sentiment, sincerity and truth of impressions, which render marvellously the effect of the work, and place it, so to speak, before our eyes. In the tone, the keenness, and the originality of his criticisms, he approaches the great master of this kind of writing, our own Diderot.

The two painters who strike him most in that wonderful Bologna gallery, are Correggio and Guido. He admires a picture representing "Four Saints," by the former, "of exquisite execution," and especially a "Beatified Christ, of inexpressible beauty," which gives him the highest idea of the painter's genius. Above all, he admires the vaporous and fluid light with which each seems to be penetrated. Like Goethe, he is enamoured of the divine genius of Guido, "who ought never to have painted," he says, "anything but that which is most perfect to behold, instead of those dreadfully stupid subjects which no amount of abuse can sufficiently stigmatise. On this point Shelley thinks with Goethe, and would willingly have endorsed the saying of the great German pagan : "Faith has resuscitated the arts, Superstition has laid hold on them and killed them afresh." His favourites among the masterpieces of Italian Art are heathen or allegorical subjects. He remembers with delight Guido's "Rape of Proserpine," "in which Proserpine casts a languishing, half-resigned look upon the flowers which she leaves behind her in the fields of Enna." He endeavours to convey this tender impression in verse. Guido's "Victorious Samson" has, to his mind, something of "the strength and elegance" of the Apollo; the picture of "Fortune" he regards as "a work of true beauty." He also admires the "Massacre of the Innocents" and "The Dying Christ," but the first of these pictures strikes him as a feeble rendering of so horrible a subject; and apropos of the second, although "very fine," he says : "One grows tired, whatever may be the conception and the execution of the subject, of seeing that agonised and monotonous figure eternally stereotyped in a prescribed attitude of torture." He experiences a similar feeling on contemplating Guercino's "St. Bruno," which represents to him the sublime of mystical horror. He could not admire the mannered and forced method of Guercino.

Amid all these masterpieces, Raffaelle's "Saint Cecilia" delighted Shelley most :

You forget that it is a picture as you look at it ; and yet it is most unlike any of those things which we call reality, It is of the inspired and ideal kind, and seems to have been conceived and executed in a similar state of feeling to that which produced among the ancients those perfect specimens of poetry and sculpture which are the baffling models of succeeding generations. There is a unity and a perfection in it of an incommunicable kind. The central figure, St. Cecilia, seems rapt in such inspiration as produced her image in the poet's mind ; her deep, dark, eloquent eyes lifted up her chestnut hair flung back from her forehead—she holds an organ in her hands—her countenance as it were calmed by the depth of its passion and rapture, and penetrated throughout with the warm and radiant light of life. She is listening to the music of heaven, and, as I imagine, has just ceased to sing, for the four figures that surround her evidently point, by their attitudes, towards her ; particularly St. John, who with a tender yet impassioned gesture, bends his countenance towards her, languid with the depth of his emotion. At her feet lie various instruments of music, broken and unstrung. Of the colouring I do not speak ; it eclipses Nature, yet it has all her charm and softness.

Remembering Shelley's extreme admiration of the grace and charm of Raffaelle, Correggio, and Guido, we cannot feel surprise at his verdict on the grand, masculine, and severe style of Michael Angelo, which he criticises, with reference to his "Last Judgment," and estimates the painter as the "Titus Andronicus" of his art :

With respect to Michael Angelo, I dissent, and think with astonishment and indignation on the common notion that he equals, and in some respects exceeds Raffaelle. He seems to me to have no sense of moral dignity and loveliness ; and the energy for which he has been so much praised, appears to me to be a certain rude, external, mechanical quality, in comparison with anything possessed by Raffaelle, or even much inferior artists. His famous painting in the Sixtine Chapel seems to me deficient in beauty and majesty, both in the conception and the execution. He has been called the Dante of painting ; but if we find some of the gross and strong outlines which are employed in the most distasteful passages of the "Inferno,' where shall we find *your* Francesca—where the spirit coming over the sea in a boat, like Mars rising from the vapours of the horizon—where Matilda gathering flowers, and all the exquisite tenderness, and sensibility, and ideal beauty, in which Dante excelled all poets except Shakespeare

Shelley applied his axiom, *sweet and strong,* to Art. To Shelley, Michael Angelo seemed the type of strength or horror untempered by beauty ; he only conceived strength either in contrast or in union with grace, as in Leonardo da Vinci's "Medusa," which inspired his beautiful lines begin-

ning: "Her horror and her beauty are divine. . . ."
There is one passage in a curious pamphlet by
Shelley on the Devil, wherein he tries to
account for his marked preference for painters
and poets who have devoted themselves to Beauty
rather than to Horror, to grace rather than to
strength:

Misery and injustice contrive to produce very poetical
effects, because the excellence of poetry consists in its
awakening the sympathy of men, which among persons
influenced by an abject and gloomy superstition, is much
more easily done by images of horror than of beauty. It
often requires a higher degree of skill in a poet to make
beauty, virtue, and harmony poetical, that is, to give them
an idealised and rhythmical analogy with the predominating
emotions of his readers—than to make injustice, deformity,
and discord poetical. There are fewer Raffaelles than
Michael Angelos ; better verses have been written on Hell
than Paradise. How few read the "Purgatorio" or the
"Paradiso" of Dante, in comparison of those who know the
" Inferno " well ! *

Moreover, Michael Angelo did not appear to
him to realise equally with Raffaelle the ideal of
Greek beauty, which is Shelley's standard for all

* "On the Devil and Devils," a very amusing essay
written in the Lucianic manner, in which Shelley criticises
the conflicting opinions on the nature of the Devil, his
attributes, and his place of abode.

the conceptions of Art. The thought of the vanished paintings of Greece, of the mutilations suffered by the masterpieces of modern painters, either from the Vandalism of "restoration" or French bayonets, moves him to gloomy reflections on the fragility and mortality of that fugitive art.

> Sculpture retains its freshness for twenty centuries—the Apollo and the Venus are as they were. But books are perhaps the only productions of man coeval with the human race. Sophocles and Shakespeare can be produced and reproduced for ever. But the paintings of Zeuxis and Apelles are no more, and perhaps they bore the same relation to Homer and Æschylus, that those of Guido and Raffaelle bear to Dante and Petrarch.

From Bologna, Shelley travels slowly to Rome, by way of Rimini, Fano, Foligno, and the Via Flaminia. He follows the course of the Metaurus, the banks of which were the scene of the defeat of Asdrubal, and perceives with astonishment that the sides of the mountain through which the road is carried, yet bear marks of the chisels of the legionaries of Rome. At the romantically situated town of Spoleto, he is full of admiration for a colossal aqueduct, and a castle built by Belisarius or Narses; at Terni, the celebrated cataract of Velino appears to him, after the glaciers of

Montanvert and the source of the Arveiron, one
of the grandest spectacles in the world. At
length he reaches the famous Campagna di Roma ;
he sees the Apennines on the one hand, on the
other St. Peter's and Rome ; " Rome, the capital of
a vanished world ! "

CHAPTER VI.

SHELLEY reached Rome on November 20th, 1818;
on that occasion he did little more than glance at
the Eternal City, but even the superficial inspection
of the miracles of ancient Art produced on him an
impression that exceeded, he says, anything he
had ever experienced in his travels. He saw little
of modern Rome, visiting by preference the ruins
of the Coliseum, which appeared to him as sublime
and as impressive in its present state, as when it
was encrusted with Dorian marble, and ornamented
with columns of Egyptian granite; and the Arch
of Titus, or rather of Constantine, "the Christian
reptile, who had crawled through the blood of his
murdered family to the supreme power." He
wandered in the desert of the ruins of the Forum,

strewn with the wrecks of temples which a great nation once dedicated to the abstractions of the mind ; he rested with pleasure on the green slope of earth beneath the pyramidal tomb of Cestius which is known as the English burial-place, and where his own ashes were soon to rest.

"It is, I think, the most beautiful and solemn cemetery I ever beheld," he writes, as though with a presentiment. "To see the sun shining on its bright grass—fresh when we first visited, with the autumnal dews—and hear the whispering of the wind among the leaves of the trees which have overgrown the tomb of Cestius, and the soil which is stirring in the sun-warm earth, and to mark the tombs, mostly of women and young people who were buried there, one might, if one were to die, desire the sleep they seem to sleep. Such is the human mind ; and so it peoples with its wishes vacancy and oblivion."

He was deeply impressed by the sight of the Coliseum, and here, while Mary sketched the ruined stairs, and little William sported beside her, he began that historical and philosophical romance of which the Coliseum was to be the subject and the title.*

After a week given to the delights of Rome,

---

* A remarkable fragment of this tale, in which Shelley draws his own portrait, has been published by Mr. Forman.

Shelley set out for Naples, where he purposed passing the beginning of the winter. The frantic terrors of a Lombard merchant and a Calabrian priest, supplied the comedy of the journey. They were in mortal fear of being assassinated when travelling, before daylight, through the Pontine Marshes, and trembled at the pistol and the intrepidity of the poet. The first incident he witnessed on arriving at Naples was an assassination, but the beauties of Nature, and the glorious marvels of Art, soon enabled him to forget the hideousness and degradation of man.

He writes to Peacock (December 22nd):

We have a lodging divided from the sea by the royal gardens, and from our windows we see perpetually the blue waters of the bay for ever changing, yet for ever the same, and encompassed by the mountainous island of Capri, the lofty peaks which overhang Salerno, and the woody hill of Posilipo, whose promontories hide from us Misenum, and the lofty isle of Inarime (Ischia), which, with its divided summit, forms the opposite horn of the bay. From the pleasant walks of the garden we see Vesuvius ; a smoke by day and a fire by night is seen upon its summit, and the glassy sea often reflects its light or shadow. The climate is delicious. We sit without a fire with the windows open, and have almost all the productions of an English summer. The weather is usually like what Wordsworth calls " the first fine day of March," sometimes very much warmer, though perhaps it wants that " each minute sweeter than before," which gives an intoxicating sweetness to the awakening of the earth from its winter's sleep in England.

Instead of guide-books, they read " Corinne," Titus Livius, and Winckelmann.

The first excursions were to Baiæ and Vesuvius. On December 8th, Shelley visited with lively emotion those classic spots called by Virgil, *Puteolana et Cumana regna :* Posilipo ; the Bay of Pozzuoli, with its lofty rocks and craggy islets, its arches and portals of precipice, and its enormous caverns, which echoed faintly with the murmur of the languid tide ; the Mare Morto ; the Avernus and cavern of the Sibyl ; in fact, all the scenery of the sixth book of the "Æneid." He was, however, somewhat disappointed to see how these places had fallen from their mythological and Virgilian beauty ; the Elysian Fields having become a vine-yard, the Avernus having lost its deadly and pestilential vapours, and the miserly Acheron, under the name of Fusaro, being now employed for soaking flax, and forming an excellent oyster-bed. The land is covered with tombs and ruins, the whole attraction of the scenery being due to the effect of sea and sky ; "the colours of the water and the air breathe over all things here the radiance of their own beauty." Nevertheless, he admires the cavern of the Sibyl (not Virgil's Sibyl) on Lake Avernus, the ruins of the temple of Pluto, which are reflected in the windless mirror of a lovely basin of water, surrounded by dark and profoundly solitary hills ; and the broken columns of a temple to Serapis at Pozzuoli.

Vesuvius is, next to the glaciers, the most imposing exhibition of the energies of Nature that Shelley had seen. We must quote his exquisite description, which is worthy of a place beside those of Goethe and Châteaubriand :

It has not the immeasurable greatness, the overpowering magnificence, nor above all, the radiant beauty of the glaciers, but it has all their character of tremendous and irresistible strength. From Resina to the hermitage you wind up the mountain, and cross a vast stream of hardened lava, which is an actual image of the waves of the sea, changed into hard black stone by enchantment. The lines of the boiling flood seem to hang in the air, and it is difficult to believe that the billows which seem hurrying down upon you are not actually in motion. This plain was once a sea of liquid fire. From the hermitage we crossed another vast stream of lava, and then went on foot up the cone—this is the only part of the ascent in which there is any difficulty, and that difficulty has been much exaggerated. It is composed of rocks of lava, and declivities of ashes ; by ascending the former and descending the latter, there is very little fatigue. On the summit is a kind of irregular plain, the most horrible chaos that can be imagined, riven into ghastly chasms, and heaped up with tumuli of great stones and cinders, and enormous rocks blackened and calcined, which had been thrown from the volcano upon one another in terrible confusion. In the midst stands the conical hill from which volumes of smoke and the fountains of liquid fire are rolled forth for ever. The mountain is at present in a slight state of eruption; and a thick, heavy white smoke is perpetually rolled out, interrupted by enormous columns of an impenetrable black bituminous vapour, which is hurled up, fold after fold, into the sky with a deep hollow sound, and fiery stones are rained down from its blackness, and a black shower of ashes fell even where we sat. The lava, like the glacier, creeps on perpetually, with a crackling sound as of suppressed fire. There are several springs of lava; and in one place it gushes precipitously over a high crag, rolling down the half-molten rocks, and its own overhanging waves; a cataract of quivering fire. We approached the extremity of one of the rivers of lava; it is about twenty feet in breadth and ten in height; and as the inclined plane was not rapid, its motion was very slow. We saw the masses of its dark exterior surface detach themselves as it moved, and betray the depth of the liquid flame. In the day the fire is but slightly seen; you only observe a tremulous motion in the air, and streams and fountains of white sulphurous smoke.

At length we saw the sun sink between Capreæ and Inarime, and, as the darkness increased, the effect of the fire became more beautiful. We were, as it were, surrounded by streams and cataracts of the red and radiant fire; and in the midst, from the column of bituminous smoke shot up into the air, fell the vast masses of rock, white with the light of their intense heat, leaving behind them, through the dark vapour, trains of splendour. We descended by torchlight, and I

should have enjoyed the scenery on my return, but they conducted me, I know not how, to the hermitage in a state of
intense bodily suffering, the worst effect of which was spoiling
the pleasure of Mary and Claire. Our guides on the occasion
were complete savages. You have no idea of the horrible
cries which they suddenly utter, no one knows why; the
clamour, the vociferation, the tumult. Claire, in her palan-
quin, suffered most from it; and when I had gone on before,
they threatened to leave her in the middle of the road, which
they would have done had not my Italian servant promised
them a beating, after which they became quiet. Nothing,
however, can be more picturesque than the gestures and the
physiognomies of these savage people. And when, in the
darkness of night, they unexpectedly begin to sing in chorus
some fragments of their wild but sweet national music, the
effect is exceedingly fine.

In the intervals between these excursions
Shelley visited the museums of Naples, more
particularly the sculpture galleries, for the collection of paintings, says he, "is sufficiently miserable,"* but: "Such statues! There is a Venus,†
an ideal shape of the most winning loveliness; a

* Shelley excepted from this censure the original studies
by Michael Angelo of the "Day of Judgment," a few
pictures by Raffaelle and his pupils, a "Danaë" of Titian's,
a "Maddelena" by Guido, and some excellent pictures, in
point of execution, by Annibale Caracci; "none others,"
says he, "worth a second look."

† Most likely the Venus of Capua, attributed to Praxiteles,
and the original, it is said, of the Venus of Milo.

Bacchus more sublime than any living being ; * a
Satyr, making love to a youth, in which the living
expression of the sculpture, and the inconceivable
beauty of the form of the youth, overcome one's
repugnance to the subject."

We can easily imagine how deep an impression
on Shelley the ruins of Pompeii must have
produced ; he was astonished, having no conception
that anything so perfect could yet remain.   From
the contemplation of its tombs, its stones, and its
paintings, his mind turned to the consideration of
the human life which once animated this desert of
ruins ; by the aid of its monuments he reconstructs
the spirit and the soul of the ancient city   He
writes :

The houses have only one storey, and the apartments,
though not large, are very lofty. A great advantage results
from this, wholly unknown in our cities. The public buildings, whose ruins are now forests, as it were, of white fluted
columns, and which then supported entablatures loaded with
sculptures, were then seen on all sides over the roofs of the
houses. This was the excellence of the ancients. Their
private expenses were comparatively moderate ; the dwelling
of one of the chief senators of Pompeii is elegant indeed, and
adorned with most beautiful specimens of Art, but small.

---

* Probably the Hermaphrodite Bacchus.

But their public buildings are everywhere marked by the bold and grand designs of an unsparing magnificence. In the little town of Pompeii (it contained about twenty thousand inhabitants) it is wonderful to see the number and the grandeur of their public buildings. Another advantage, too, is that in the present case the glorious scenery around is not shut out, and that, unlike the inhabitants of the Cimmerian ravines of modern cities, the ancient Pompeians could contemplate the clouds and the lamps of Heaven ; could see the moon rise high behind Vesuvius, and the sun set in the sea, tremulous with an atmosphere of golden vapour, between Inarime and Misenum. . . .

At the upper end, supported on an elevated platform, stands the Temple of Jupiter. Under the colonnade of its portico we sate, and pulled out our oranges, and figs, and bread, and medlars (" sorry fare," you will say), and rested to eat. Here was a magnificent spectacle. Above and between the multitudinous shafts of the sun-shining columns was seen the sea, reflecting the purple heaven of noon above it, and supporting, as it were, on its line the dark, lofty mountains of Sorrento, of a blue inexpressibly deep, and tinged towards their summits with streaks of new-fallen snow. Between was one small green island ; to the right were Capreæ, Inarime, Prochyta (Procida), and Misenum. Behind was the single summit of Vesuvius, rolling forth volumes of thick white smoke, whose foam-like column was sometimes darted into the clear dark sky, and fell in little streaks along the wind. Between Vesuvius and the nearer mountains, as through a chasm, was seen the main line of the loftiest Apennines, to the east. The day was radiant and warm. Every now and then we heard the subterranean thunder of Vesuvius ; its distant deep peals seemed to shake the very air and light of day, which interpenetrated our frames with the sullen and tremendous sound. This scene was what the Greeks beheld (Pompeii

was, you know, a Greek city). They lived in harmony with
Nature, and the interstices of their incomparable columns
were portals, as it were, to admit the spirit of beauty which
animates this glorious universe to visit those whom it
inspired. If such is Pompeii, what was Athens? What
scene was exhibited from the Acropolis, the Parthenon, and
the temples of Hercules, and Theseus, and the Winds ;
the islands of the Ægean Sea, the mountains of Argolis, and
the peaks of Pindus and Olympus, and the darkness of the
Bœotian forests interspersed ?

Shelley draws likewise much solemn instruction
from the tombs which rise on either side of the
Consular road, and which resemble "not so much
hiding-places for that which must decay, as volup-
tuous chambers for immortal spirits."

"These tombs," he writes, "are the most impressive
things of all. The wild woods surround them on either
side, and along the broad stones of the paved road which
divides them you hear the late leaves of autumn shiver and
rustle in the stream of the inconstant wind, as it were like
the steps of ghosts. The radiance and magnificence of
these dwellings of the dead, the white freshness of the
scarcely finished marble, the impassioned or imaginative
life of the figures which adorn them, contrast strangely with
the simplicity of the houses of those who were living when
Vesuvius overwhelmed them.

"I have forgotten the amphitheatre, which is of great
magnitude, though much inferior to the Coliseum. I now
understand why the Greeks were such great poets ; and,
above all, I can account, it seems to me, for the harmony,
the unity, the perfection, the uniform excellence of all their

works of Art. They lived in a perpetual commerce with external Nature, and nourished themselves upon the spirit of its forms. Their theatres were all open to the mountains and the sky. Their columns, the ideal types of a sacred forest, with its roof of interwoven tracery, admitted the light and wind ; the odour and the freshness of the country penetrated the cities. Their temples were mostly upaithric ; and the flying clouds, the stars, or the deep sky, were seen above. Oh, but for that series of wretched wars, which terminated in the Roman conquest of the world ; but for the Christian religion, which put the finishing strokes on the ancient system ; but for those changes that conducted Athens to its ruin, to what an eminence might not humanity have arrived ! "

Under the stress of such emotions as these, and the influence of a climate to which he was so unaccustomed, Shelley's strength was soon spent. He felt himself unable to follow up his poetical enterprises. He writes in his letter to Peacock of January 26th, 1819: "Oh, if I had health, and strength, and equal spirits, what boundless intellectual improvement might I not gather in this wonderful country!" He writes but little; and while completing the first act of "Prometheus," conceives the plan of a great moral and political work, in which he will embody the discoveries of all ages, and endeavour to harmonise the contending creeds by which mankind has been ruled. His restless thoughts, beneath the fiery sky of Naples, depress and crush him ; he realises with despair the impotence of his efforts and of his dreams ; he falls into a mental and physical lassitude which is all the harder to bear because he "finds not any heart to share in his emotion." It was at this epoch that he wrote those poems, filled with a deep and intense melancholy, in which he asks from poetry consolation and the power to forget; such as the "Lines on a Faded Violet," the despairing "Sonnet," in which, recalling the enthusiasm with which he had attempted to lift " the painted veil called Life," and his disappointments, having found none to love, nothing earthly capable of satisfying him, he compares himself to

> A splendour among shadows, a bright blot
> Upon this gloomy scene, a Spirit that strove
> For truth, and, like the Preacher, found it not.

But above all, we must read the " Stanzas written in dejection near Naples," if we would form a just idea of Shelley's depression and discouragement at this period. With Shelley, however, despair was never bitter ; it is always mingled with resignation and calm ; there is a smile even in his tears ; he neither curses nor hates.. He has no anger against Destiny who has poured out for him so bitter a cup; he finds a charm even in his melancholy, and like a tired child he could lie down and wait till deathlike sleep might steal upon his senses; he will still bear his life of anguish until he feels his cheek grow cold in the warm air, until he hears the sea breathe o'er his dying brain its last monotony. One cannot refrain, when reading this heart-rending poem, from thinking of Christ's agony in the Garden of Olives. Shelley finds consolation in the idea that mankind will lament him, "for I am one," he says, "whom men love not, and yet regret;" and where shall we find words more touching than these of the poet-lover of humanity who pardons his fellows for having been indifferent to him during life, because he hopes that they will regret him after death? It is as beautiful as the cry of Jesus: "Forgive them, Father! they know not what they do!"

These Neapolitan "Stanzas" are to be compared only with the poem entitled "Misery," which was inspired by similar sentiments. In a fragment written earlier called "Death," he draws Misery as seated near an open grave, and he calls upon his "sweetest friend," to dry her tears and be consoled; now he takes up and develops the same subject. Misery, here, is not only his "sweetest friend," but his sister, his beloved, whom he invites to "the bridal bed, beneath the grave," to caresses and "dreadful transports," which will fade away like a vapour in the sleep that lasts for ever.

Shelley concealed with care these effusions from her who shared his work and pleasure; yet in spite of himself they revealed themselves. He reproached himself for thus betraying the discontent and sadness of his soul, and so unjustly wounding the heart of his beloved Mary, who only, as he said, would have had the right of complaining that she had not been able to extinguish in him even the faculty of describing sorrow. Mary, however, did not complain; but she suffered, and guessed at the secret wound her poet hid from her. "There is one," she writes in her "Biographical Notes," "who looks back with unspeakable regret and gnawing remorse to such periods, fancying that had one been more alive to the nature of his feelings, and more attentive to soothe them, such would not have existed; and yet, enjoying as he seemed to enjoy, the sweet influences of earth and sky, it was difficult to believe that his melancholy was produced by other causes than the continual sufferings which made of him a martyr."

The deep dejection and despair; words so precise as those in the third strophe of the " Stanzas:"

> Alas ! I have nor hope nor health,
> Nor peace within, nor calm around, . . .
> . . . Nor fame, . . . nor love, . . .

would be difficult to explain, as we have already insinuated, without taking into account some extraordinary moral cause, such as that to which Shelley himself attributes them in the narrative given by Medwin of his connection with the beautiful unknown lady who followed him to Naples, and there died.

After having visited the Lago d'Agniano, and the notorious Grotto del Cane, where Shelley would not allow the tortures of the unfortunate dogs when exposed to the fatal vapours of the cave to be exhibited before him; Salerno and its magnificent scenery; Pæstum with its sublime colonnades and ruined temples, which appeared to him " as in the shadow of some half-remembered dream," the poet left Naples at the end of February, 1819, to return to Rome.

He travelled slowly, resting one day at Mola di Gaeta, at the inn called the "Villa di Cicerone," from being built on the ruins of the ancient villa, in the midst of orange and citron groves; and at Terracina, where he admired the high conical crags, the Anxur rocks sung by Horace. At Albano he arrived again in sight of Rome: "Arches after arches in unending lines stretching across the uninhabited wilderness, the blue defined line of the mountains seen between them; masses of nameless ruin standing like rocks out of the plain; and the plain itself, with its billowy and unequal surface, announced the neighbourhood of Rome."

At Rome, Shelley's first enthusiasm for the grand ruins of that vast necropolis awoke anew. He was never tired of revisiting the Coliseum, the monuments of the Forum, the colossal statues of Castor and Pollux, the Arch of Constantine, of which the gigantic bas-reliefs, "expressing that mixture of force and crime which is called a Triumph," gave him the idea of his poem, the "Triumph of Life," which death interrupted.

But the ruins which he takes most pleasure in describing, because they are daily the witnesses of his thought, and in some measure the sources of his inspiration, are the Thermæ of Caracalla. It was here that he composed the greater part of the "Prometheus Unbound," "among the flowery lawns, the copses of odorously blossoming trees which clothe the tortuous labyrinths of this immense platform, and the arches suspended in mid-air which give vertigo."

Modern Rome was far from arousing in Shelley the same interest as ancient Rome. He would have seen modern Italy vanish without any great regret; he was always painfully struck with the contrast between the moral degradation of the people, and the glorious beauty of Nature and Art. He could not endure to see St. Peter's, because of the fettered convicts in parti-coloured clothes who stand in the square, hoeing out the weeds that grow between the stones of the pavement :

Near them, sit or saunter groups of soldiers armed with loaded muskets. The 'iron discord of those innumerable chains clanks up with the sonorous air and produces, contrasted with the musical splashing of the fountains, and the deep azure beauty of the sky, and the magnificence of the architecture around, a conflict of sensations allied to madness.

To the sinister clank of chains must be added the noisy acclamations of "Viva Napoleone!" which greeted the Emperor of Austria and Maria Louisa. Such are men in fair Italy! Idiots and slaves! However, the Romans pleased him much, especially the women, whom he excepts from the prejudiced and unfavourable judgment he passes on the Italians:

The Roman women, though totally devoid of every kind of information, or culture of the imagination, or affections, or understanding — and in this respect a kind of gentle savages — yet contrive to be interesting. Their extreme innocence and *naiveté*, the freedom and gentleness of their manners, the total absence of affectation, makes an intercourse with them very like an intercourse with uncorrupted children, whom they resemble in loveliness as well as simplicity. I have seen two women in society here of the highest beauty; their brows and lips, and the moulding of the face modelled with sculptural exactness, and the dark luxuriance of their hair, floating over their fine complexions—and the lips—you must hear the commonplaces which escape from them before they cease to be dangerous. The only inferior part are the eyes, which, though good and gentle, want the mazy depth of colour behind colour with which the intellectual women of England and of Germany entangle the heart in soul-inwoven labyrinths.

The feeling of contempt which modern Italy

inspired in Shelley, reveals itself in his letters by the curious criticisms he passed on the monuments of Christian and Papal Art. Thus St. Peter's appears to him much inferior in architectural beauty to St. Paul's; while "internally it exhibits littleness on a large scale, and is in every respect opposed to antique taste.* On the other hand the Pantheon, though not a fourth part of the size, is "the visible image of the universe." The idea of magnitude is swallowed up and lost in the perfection of its proportions, as when you regard the unmeasured dome of heaven.

The ceremonies of Holy Week, celebrated in the year 1818 with more than ordinary pomp on account of the presence of the Emperor of Austria, were matters of indifference to Shelley. Nevertheless, on his way home one day from a visit to the Coliseum, he was present at the Washing of the Pilgrims' Feet, and also the distribution of macaroni by the Cardinals to the hungry beggars. On Easter Sunday he admired the

---

* He admits, however, that its colonnade, its palace-like façade, and the rest of the Square form an "architectural combination unequalled in the world."

illuminations of the Cupola and the fireworks at the Castle of St. Angelo, which exhibited an additional set-piece representing the Mausoleum of Hadrian.

Shelley at Rome, as elsewhere, went very little into society. The Italians had no attraction for him; and in Mary Shelley's letters but one single Italian lady is mentioned, the Signora Marianna Dionigi, painter, antiquary, and authoress, at whose *conversazioni* all the authors and artists were to be found. On the other hand Shelley met distinguished fellow-country-men at Rome some, such as Lord Guilford, Sir William Drummond, whom he esteemed highly as a thinker, and Miss Curran, daughter of the Irish Master of the Rolls; this lady had some skill in painting, and becoming a friend of the family, attempted the portraits of Shelley, of Mary, of Claire, and of little William (May, 1819).

Rome was to be for Shelley, as he himself called it, both Paradise and the tomb.

The last moments of his stay in the Eternal City were profoundly saddened by the death of his beloved little William, who was carried off after an illness of a few days (June 7th). Shelley had watched during sixty hours of agony without closing his eyes. "We suffered terrible grief when at Rome," writes Mary, "with regard to our eldest boy, who, for his beauty and promise, was our hearts' idol. We left the capital of the world, impatient to quit for a time scenes too closely connected with his presence and his loss." Shelley was now childless; of his five children not one remained.

This blow struck him so sorely that he thought he would néver recover any cheerfulness again. His grief expressed itself in some pathetic lines to his "Lost William," no longer there to fill the home with his smiles. William was buried in the Protestant cemetery, already so poetically described in the letter to Peacock, and where his father was so soon to join him.

The poet in his grief thought of quitting Rome and Italy, that had robbed him of all he held most dear, and of returning to England. The child's death had had a terrible effect on his health, and the doctors spoke of sending him to Africa or Spain; he decided, however, to remain in Italy, and went with Mary to Leghorn, to seek consolation near their kind friends the Gisbornes.

He took with him, as the most precious result of the inspiration of Rome, the three first acts of his " Prometheus."

CHAPTER VII.

"THE year 1819," says Mr. Dowden, "was Shelley's *annus mirabilis*, and in one year to have created such poems as the ' Prometheus ' and ' The Cenci,' is an achievement without parallel in English poetry since Shakespeare lived and wrote."

The month of June, 1819, found Shelley installed in the Villa Valsovano, between Leghorn and Monte Nero. The villa was a little country house set down in the centre of a grassy farm. A roofed and glazed terrace at the top of the house served Shelley as his study.

He writes to Peacock on July 6th :

I have here a study in a tower, something like Scythrop's,* where I am just beginning to recover the faculties of reading and writing. My health, whenever no Libecchio blows, improves. From my tower I see the sea, with its islands, Gorgona, Capraja, Elba, and Corsica on one side, and the Apennines on the other.

It was in this tower that, within the space of three months, he wrote the tragedy of "The Cenci."

" Shelley had often incited me," Mary writes, "to attempt the writing a tragedy ; he conceived that I possessed some dramatic talent," of which he most erroneously believed himself to be destitute. " He believed that one of the first requisites was the capacity of forming or following up a story or a plot. He fancied himself to be defective in this portion of imagination ; it was that which gave him least pleasure in the writings of others. . . . He asserted that he was too metaphysical and abstract, too fond of the theoretical and the ideal, to succeed as a tragedian.

" The subject he had suggested (to me) for a tragedy was Charles I., and he had written to me, ' Remember, remember Charles I. I have been already imagining how you would conduct some scenes. The second volume of " St. Leon " † begins with the proud and true sentiment,

---

* Scythrop is the hero of Peacock's novel, " Nightmare Abbey," which Shelley had just received and read as a palliative for his melancholy.

† A novel of Godwin's, highly esteemed by Shelley.

"There is nothing which the human mind can conceive which it may not execute." Shakespeare was only a human being.'

"These words were written in 1818, while we were in Lombardy, when he little thought how soon a work of his own would prove a proud comment on the passage he quoted. When in Rome in 1819, a friend put into our hands the old manuscript account of the story of the Cenci. We visited the Colonna and Doria palaces, where the portraits of Beatrice were to be found; and her beauty cast the reflection of its own grace over her appalling story. Shelley's imagination became strongly excited, and he urged the subject to me as one fitted for a tragedy. More than ever I felt my incompetence, but I entreated him to write it instead; and he began, and proceeded swiftly, urged on by intense sympathy with the sufferings of the human beings whose passions, so long cold in the tomb, he revived, and gifted with poetic language. This tragedy is the only one of his works that he communicated to me during its progress. We talked over the arrangement of its scenes together. I speedily saw the great mistake he had made' as to the bent of his genius. . . .

"Shelley wished 'The Cenci' to be acted. He was not a playgoer, being of such fastidious taste that he was easily disgusted by the bad filling-up of the secondary parts. While preparing for our departure from England, however, he saw Miss O'Neil several times. She was then in the zenith of her glory, and Shelley was deeply moved by her impersonation of several parts, and by the graceful sweetness, the intense pathos, and the sublime vehemence of passion she displayed. She was often in his thoughts as he wrote; and when he had finished, he became anxious that his tragedy should be acted, and receive the advantage of having this accomplished actress to fill the part of heroine."

"The Cenci" was, in fact, a strong effort on Shelley's part to leave the poetry of metaphysics and abstractions to which his genius inclined him, and to enter on the field of drama, which is both human and popular. Has he succeeded? It would be the greatest mistake to imagine that in "The Cenci" there is an ordinary tragedy which in any way recalls classical tragedy or historical drama, such as it is in the works of the dramatists who preceded Shelley. His original genius could not restrict itself to a settled conventional form, and in approaching the stage, he was to inaugurate an entirely personal conception of dramatic style, in a work that has nothing in common with any which preceded or followed it.* "The Cenci" stands all alone and separate in the history of the theatre; it has no models, and still less any imitators. Once again, and despite his efforts to forget himself, and think only of the effect he desired to produce, Shelley has created his own image in the

---

* In M. Sarrazin's "Poètes Modernes de l'Angleterre," the remarkable chapter devoted to a critique on "The Cenci" will be read with interest ; also Mr. Swinburne's beautiful preface to Madame Tola Dorian's translation of this tragedy.

person of Beatrice. "It is," as De Quincey has said, "the strife between darkness and light in the story of the Cenci which fascinated Shelley." The two principal characters, the incestuous father and his daughter — the gentle yet indomitable Beatrice—are not so much human beings as living and moving abstractions, ideal and superhuman personifications of the two powers which Shelley delighted to pit against each other in all his poetical works; on one side, in the person of Cenci, the strength and the fatality of evil; on the other, that of Beatrice—as he had already shown in Cythna—of all that is most feeble and fragile, the soul of a young girl, resisting that fatality, and triumphing over it by death and martyrdom. The circumstance of incest was in Shelley's eyes only an accessory circumstance which furnished him with the story, and served to bring out the abuses of domestic tyranny with still greater horror to those prejudiced against social impropriety. The Bible, Greece with the "Œdipus," and Calderon, were his authorities for putting upon the stage an irregularity (punished and expiated by murder) to which he attached in his own mind only a conventional criminality, and a purely poetical value. In one of his letters, he propounds a curious theory on this subject, which proves that he was more engrossed, during the composition of "The Cenci," with Calderon than Mary is willing to admit in the passage cited above. He says, referring to one of the tragedies of this great writer, *Absalom's Hair:* "It is a piece full of the deepest and tenderest touches of nature."

The incest scene of "Amon and Tamar" is perfectly tremendous.* Incest is, like many other incorrect things, a very poetical circumstance. It may be the excess of love or hate. It may be the defiance of everything for the sake of another, which clothes itself in the glory of the highest heroism, or it may be that cynical rage which, confounding the good and the bad in existing opinions, breaks through them for the purpose of rioting in selfishness and antipathy. Calderon, following the Jewish historians, has represented Amon's action in the basest point of view —he is a prejudiced savage acting what he abhors, and abhorring that which is the unwilling party to his crime.

Notwithstanding Peacock's objections to "The Cenci"—he considered the subject too bold, and referred the author to Dryden's "Œdipus," also to the "Mirra" of Alfieri—Shelley, encouraged by his friends at Leghorn, had two hundred and

* A translation of this scene will be found in the Appendix.

fifty copies of the play printed in Italy, and sent one to Peacock that he might offer it to Mr. Harris for Covent Garden. Harris declined it, and would not even offer the rôle of Beatrice to Miss O'Neil, but promised that if the poet would write another tragedy on another subject, he would willingly accept it.

The success of "The Cenci" with the reading public was such as Shelley was little accustomed to. Two editions appeared during his lifetime.

The Shelley Society has made reparation for the error of Mr. Harris and his contemporaries. Under its auspices "The Cenci" was played by the best actors in London in 1886, and an audience composed of the most distinguished persons in art and literature applauded the tragedy, to which the England of 1819 had preferred — to the displeasure of Byron himself — "Marino Faliero."

The delights of Scythrop's tower do not, however, prevent Shelley from casting longing looks towards England. He writes to Peacock on the 22nd August, 1819:

I most devoutly wish that I were living near London. I do not think I shall settle so far off as Richmond; and to inhabit any intermediate spot on the Thames would be to expose myself to the river damps, not to mention that it is not much to my taste. My inclinations point to Hampstead; but I do not know whether I should not make up my mind to something more completely suburban. What are mountains, trees, heaths, or even the glorious or ever beautiful sky, with such sunsets as I have seen at Hampstead, to friends? Social enjoyment in some form or other is the Alpha and Omega of existence. All that I see in Italy — and from my tower window I now see the magnificent peaks of the Apennines half enclosing the plain—is nothing; it dwindles into smoke in the mind, when I think of some familiar forms of scenery, little, perhaps, in themselves, over which old remembrances have thrown a delightful colour. How we prize what we despised when present! So the ghosts of our dead associations rise and haunt us, in revenge for our having let them starve, and abandoned them to perish. . . .

I have been much better these last three weeks. My work on " The Cenci," which was done in two months, was a fine antidote to nervous medicines, and kept up, I think, the pain in my side as sticks do a fire. Since then I have materially improved. I do not walk enough. Claire, who is sometimes my companion, does not dress in exactly the right time. I have no stimulus to walk. Now I go sometimes to Leghorn on business, and that does me good. . . .

I have been reading Calderon in Spanish. A kind of Shakespeare is this Calderon; and I have some thoughts, if I find that I cannot do anything better, of translating some of his plays.

The particular business which took Shelley oftenest to Leghorn was the project of constructing a steamboat, in which Henry Reveley then took a great interest. The poet was ambitious of being the first to put a steamboat on the Mediterranean which should regularly ply between Leghorn, Genoa, and Marseilles, and Shelley devoted all his accustomed energy and enthusiasm to this enterprise; he took the most vivid interest in the designs, and advanced the requisite sums, making over to the young engineer all the profits, and reserving for himself the glory of success—or the shame of failure.

"Well, how goes on all?" he writes on October 28th, to Henry Reveley; "the boilers, the keel of the boat, and the cylinder, and all the other elements of that soul which is to guide our 'monstruo de fuego y agua' over the sea? . . . Your boat will be to the ocean of water what this earth is to the ocean of æther—a prosperous and swift voyager."

Unluckily, a few months later the departure of the Gisbornes for England put a stop to these attractive schemes. Shelley found his only consolation in going to contemplate the steamboat "asleep under the walls," where he was afraid, he said, to waken it, for the same reason that he would have feared to awaken Ariadne after Theseus had left her—unless he himself had been Bacchus.

Soon after (September, 1819), Shelley left the

Villa Valsovano, to the regret of all his Leghorn friends, even of Oscar the house-dog, who was inconsolable at his departure. He was attracted by Florence, the capital of the fine arts, and would have remained there longer only for the wind from the Apennines, which he found both unpleasant and insalubrious. But a great joy came to him at Florence : the birth (November 12th, 1819) of another son, who was christened on January 25th, 1820, receiving the names of Percy Florence.

During his sojourn of a few months at Florence, there was seldom a day in which he did not visit its picture galleries, and especially its sculptures : " There, amid the varied creations of Greek Art, he rested from his most arduous labours. The ' Niobe,' the ' Venus Anadyomene,' the ' Bacchus and Ampelus,' were objects of his most unwearied admiration. I have heard him expatiate on the subject," says Medwin, " with all the eloquence of a poet. He had made ample notes on the wonderful masterpieces of the Gallery, from which he allowed me to make extracts which surpass in eloquence anything that Winckelmann has written on the subject."

Shelley's letters at this period are full of the artistic enthusiasm with which "he drank the spirit" of those marvellous forms of antique sculpture.

"All worldly thoughts and cares," he wrote, "seem to vanish from before the sublime emotions such spectacles create ; and I am deeply impressed with the great difference of happiness enjoyed by those who live at a distance from these incarnations of all that the finest minds have conceived of beauty, and those who can resort to their company at pleasure. What should we think if we were forbidden to read the great writers who have left us their works ? "

It was during that period of mental intoxication, that at Delesert's reading-room in Florence, on one of the early days of October, he came across a late number of the *Quarterly Review*, in which he had been told he should find the famous article on "Laon and Cythna," and be much amused thereby. The grotesque anathemas of the chaste Reviewer did, in fact, move him to convulsive laughter. The article, a very bitter one, was at first attributed by Shelley to Southey, but it was in fact the production of a former Eton schoolfellow, John Taylor Coleridge. From criticism of the author, the Reviewer passed to censure on the man :

He is too young, too ignorant, too vicious, to reform any other world than the little world of his own heart. If we might withdraw the veil of private life, and tell all we know about the writer, it would be indeed a disgusting picture that we should exhibit ; but it would be an unanswerable comment to our text, for it is not easy for those who read only, to conceive how much low selfishness, how much unmanly cruelty, are consistent with the laws of this universal and lawless love.*

Such drivel could not affect Shelley. His was a soul inaccessible to self-love, but full of grief and indignation at the sufferings and wretchedness of his fellow-beings, his fellow countrymen.

He had continued, in Italy, to watch the course of events and politics in England. The news of the " Manchester Massacre " (August 16th, 1819), "that piece of bloodthirsty and murderous oppression," he likens to " the distant thunders of the terrible storm which is approaching. The tyrants here, as in the French Revolution, have first shed blood. May their execrable lessons not be learnt with equal docility. . . . What is to be done ? Something, assuredly."

* Hunt warmly defended his friend in the *Examiner*, and the famous Wilson contributed an article to the January number of *Blackwood's Magazine*, in which he compared the Quarterly Reviewer to a dunce rating a man of genius : "It is impossible to read a page of his 'Revolt of Islam,' without perceiving that in nerve and pith of conception he approaches more nearly to Scott and Byron than any other of their contemporaries."

All that was in his power was to take up the lyre, and in Pindaric odes express his indignation and patriotism. It was now that he wrote his Revolutionary songs — some in burning stanzas and of visionary vengeance, as in the "Mask of Anarchy," the "Ode to Liberty," the "God save the Queen"; others in the form of the bitterest, most withering political satire that ever scourged nations, kings, and Ministers, viz. the admirable Sonnet on "England in 1819"; "Lines written during the Administration of Lord Castlereagh"; "Similes of Two Political Characters," and, above all, his incomparable "Song to the Men of England," the most eloquent and pathetic commentary ever written on the *Sic vos non vobis* of Virgil.

No better idea of the versatility of Shelley's genius can be gained than by comparing these diatribes of Juvenal-like wrath and bitterness, with his masterpieces of humorous and burlesque satire, such as "Peter Bell the Third" and "Swellfoot the Tyrant." "The Cenci" brought us close to the "Œdipus" of Sophocles; but these are near to Aristophanes.

"Peter Bell the Third" is an ideally perfect

satire on literary apostasy, and in particular on the apostasy of Wordsworth.

At the comme ncement of the French Revolution, Wordswort h had been among those Englishman whom the awakening of Liberty had filled with fire and enthusiasm.

He had dreamed of inaugurating a youthful, human, equalising poesy, which should put an end to the reign of the conventional, and the vapidity of traditional and classic poetry, which should force the lowliest and most familiar realities into the mould of verse ; a revolution in both thought and Art analogous to that which Madame de Staël desired for France in 1789. Wordsworth worked all his life long at this revolution, but he soon departed from the generous feelings that had inspired his purpose, and alone could give it warmth, vitality, and durability. He withdrew into himself, and gave up his humanitarian visions ; the triumph of despotic power and the Conservative reaction threw him into the camp of the most determined upholders of established institutions ; and even so far back as 1809 he had become so shameless a pervert as to write his " Pamphlet on the Capitulation of Cintra," in which he reproached Pitt for not making war upon France more vigorously.

In 1818, Wordsworth, who had become the "bard" of the Established Church, published two Addresses to the Liberals of Westmoreland in favour of the Conservatives; thus, by dint of flattery and servility to the reigning power, establishing his claims to the post of Poet Laurcate, in which he, in fact, succeeded Southey in 1843.

Shelley, from his earliest boyhood, had been a passionate admirer of Wordsworth. Many intellectual and literary sympathies attracted him to a school of poetry which was essentially personal, sentimental, and dreamy, and which invested all the phenomena of the universe with meaning; he forgave Wordsworth for what was "drowsy and frowzy" in him, as Byron called it, his puerile inventions, and his dull prosing, for the sake of the moral and emotional idealism through which the solitary poet of Mount Rydal contemplated and vivified Nature. More than one trace may be found in Shelley's works of the influence of that poet who was moved by the humblest flower or blade of grass to "thoughts too deep for tears."

He had at an early period competed with him on his own ground, by treating some of his favourite themes with ingenuousness and simplicity, and while at Geneva had succeeded in imparting to Byron so great an appreciation of a poet whom the haughty author of "English Bards and Scotch Reviewers" had described as "the meanest object of the lowly group," that Wordsworth recognised himself in the third canto of "Childe Harold."

But the greater his admiration and affection for the favoured child of the Muses, the more did Shelley deplore the part taken by him in political matters. In July, 1818, when the Addresses to the Liberals of Westmoreland were published, he wrote in the following unmeasured language to Peacock : " I have been informed of the unfortunate termination of the Westmoreland elections. I wish you had sent me some of the overflowing villainy of those apostates. What a beastly and pitiful wretch, that Wordsworth! That such a man should be such a poet! I can compare him with no one but Simonides, that flatterer of the Sicilian tyrants, and at the same time the most natural and tender of lyric poets."

The satire of " Peter Bell the Third " must have been conceived at this period.

Shelley wanted to prove that the poet capable of abjuring the gods of his youth, and of bowing down before power and public opinion, was condemned to see his sources of inspiration dried up, and to fall into platitudes and dulness.

But Shelley had not waited until those latter days to brand the apostasy of his favourite poet; in 1815, he had bewailed in touching lines the desertion of him whom he calls the " Poet of Nature, . . . a lone star whose light did shine

> On some frail bark in Winter's midnight roar ;
> . . . A rock-built refuge . . .
> Above the blind and battling multitude."

Shelley's reproaches did not reach the ear of the god. Wordsworth had become verbose, oracular, tolerating none lower than himself, scarcely admitting there could be any one higher, and comparing himself to Milton.

He disdained contemporary poets, especially those who dared to stray from the paths newly trodden by him, and he ignored Shelley.

On one occasion, before Trelawney was

personally acquainted with the author of " Queen Mab," he met an English tourist at Geneva, accompanied by his wife and sister, who was bitterly lamenting that Switzerland was becoming a commonplace and civilised country, wherein a lover of Nature could no longer find a solitary spot in which to contemplate at leisure the wild beauty of the scenery.

" Yesterday," he grumbled, "at break of day, I scaled the most rugged height within my reach ; it looked inaccessible ; this pleasant delusion was quickly dispelled ; I was rudely startled out of a deep reverie by the accursed jarring, jingling, and rumbling of a calêche, and harsh voices that drowned the torrent's fall." The grumbling tourist was Wordsworth. Trelawney accosted him, and without further ceremony asked him plainly : " What do you think of Shelley as a poet ? " " Nothing," replied Wordsworth ; then seeing the astonishment of his interlocutor, he continued : " a poet who has not produced a good poem before he is twenty-five, we may conclude cannot, and never will do so." " But ' The Cenci ' ? " " Won't do," he replied, shaking his head, as he got into the carriage ; a rough-coated Scotch terrier followed him. "This hairy fellow is our flea-trap." To the honour of Wordsworth it must be admitted that, at a subsequent period, he overcame his prejudice against Shelley, and rendered him justice, "Peter Bell the Third" notwithstanding.*

Shelley considered "Peter Bell the Third" as merely a slight satire in which, as he says, both lines and language had it their own way. It was hardly finished, when a political incident drew his attention to one of his favourite subjects, that of the Defence of the Liberty of the Press. The publication of the works of the well-known revolutionist, Thomas Paine, and in particular of his "Age of Reason," had been the occasion of one of the most odious persecutions due to the English law of libel, in the beginning of the present century. Carlile, the publisher, was condemned to prison, but continued, from his cell, to appeal to public opinion in the columns

---

* Shelley so designated his poem because it was written after Wordsworth's "Peter Bell," and after a parody thereon, written by J. Hamilton Reynolds, one of the three young poets patronised by Leigh Hunt, and was especially directed against Wordsworth's alleged puerilities and literary fatuity. See Mr. Forman's fine edition.

of the *Republican.* Shelley could not fail to be interested in the fate of so courageous a victim; he took up the defence of Carlile in an eloquent letter intended for the *Examiner.* In that letter he warmly attacks the capricious restrictions imposed on the Press by a power as illusory as it is arbitrary. He names himself, among a constellation of great men and great writers, who, if Law were Justice, would be more rightly prosecuted than a poor bookseller. He claims trial by their peers for Carlile and Paine; a jury composed, not of so-called Christians, but of the philosophers and Deists who are unjustly shielded by their high social position from similar prosecution: such as Sir William Drummond, "the most acute metaphysical critic of the age, a man of profound learning . . . . unblemished integrity of character," and as undisguised an opponent of Christianity as Paine; Godwin, the author of " Political Justice " and the " Enquirer," who has treated Christianity as an "exploded superstition, to which, in the present state of knowledge, it was unworthy . . . . as a moral philosopher, to advert;" and Mr. Burdon, a gentleman of great fortune, who had published

a book " called 'Materials for Thinking,' in which
he plainly avows his disbelief in the divine
authority of the Bible."

Hunt, to whom the letter was addressed
(Nov. 3rd), did not publish it, on account, probably, of its strong language and the high personages attacked by Shelley. The poet acquiesced
without demur in his friend's decision, and set to
work on a political treatise less aggressive in
tone, in which he proposed to include the theory
of every needful reform in Government.* According to Mr. Dowden's analysis of the work,
Shelley, after rapidly sketching the effect of
Reform, the French Revolution, and the eighteenth
century on the "hopes and aspirations of the
human race," passes on to consider the various
reforms necessary to the government of England,

---

* The " Philosophical View of Reform," which was begun
in December, 1819, and in great part finished in May, 1820,
has remained in manuscript. Mr. Forman has published
but two short fragments. Mr. Dowden, who has seen the
manuscript, considers that "it sets forth the writer's opinions
on political subjects with sufficient fulness, and makes us
acquainted with the side of his mind presented to actual
politics as no published writing of Shelley's has done." It
remains for the Shelleyan Society to fill the void by publish-
ing these important passages.

and the possible and desirable mode in which they should take place. The advance of literature in his own country at the beginning of the century, seemed to Shelley to be the prophecy of great social and political change.* One of the principal causes of the social misery in England he held to be the modern device of public credit, by means of which companies and bankers grew rich at the expense of the poor; the increase of the national industry which this system is supposed to effect, ends merely in increasing the misery of the poor and the luxury of the rich; "to make a manufacturer" (an artisan, as we now say) "work sixteen hours where he had only worked eight; to turn children into lifeless and bloodless machines at an age when otherwise they would be at play before the cottage doors of their parents; to augment indefinitely the proportion of those who enjoy the profit of the labour of others . . . to create a new aristocracy of attorneys, excisemen, directors, Government pensioners, usurers, stock-jobbers, who . . . can only eat, and drink, and sleep, and

---

* The passage containing this prophetical view may be found at the close of his " Defence of Poetry."

in the intervals of these actions cringe and lie," without ever exercising the true and noble faculties of the soul, while the poor toiler knows but pain and misery in the present, and has, in the future, only "those gleams of hope which seem to speak to him of Paradise, only to make darkness visible, like the flames of Milton's hell."

"The so-called National Debt is but the debt of the privileged classes and of the tyrants who incurred it in unjust and liberticide wars. The labour which it represents . . . since the commencement of the American war, would, if properly employed, have covered our land with monuments of architecture exceeding the sumptuousness and the beauty of Egypt and Athens; it might have made every peasant's cottage a little paradise of comfort, with every convenience desirable . . . neat tables and chairs, and good beds, and a collection of useful books; and our fleet, manned by sailors well-paid and well-clothed, might have kept watch round this glorious island against the less enlightened nations which assuredly would have envied its prosperity." As a remedy to the then state of things, Shelley proposed that the privileged classes should alone be held legally responsible for the National Debt, and that special tribunals should be created for its liquidation.

As to reform of Parliament and the system of representation, Shelley, in this treatise, is most moderate in his views; universal suffrage, or the admission of women to the rights of suffrage, seem to him dangerous and premature measures.

As he advanced in life, his aversion to violent means and sudden resolves increased.

" The great thing to do," he said, " is to hold the balance between popular impatience and tyrannical obstinacy ; to inculcate with fervour both the right of resistance and the duty of forbearance. You know my principles incite me to take all the good I can get in politics, for ever aspiring to something more. I am one of those whom nothing will fully satisfy, but who are ready to be partially satisfied in all that is practicable. . . . I have a motto on a ring in Italian, ' Il buon tempo verrà.' There is a tide both in public and in private affairs, which awaits both men and nations."

He liked also to quote Rousseau's saying, that he would rather see things remain as they are than shed one drop of blood. He never lost faith in the ultimate triumph of social reform ; but that triumph would be due to a slow and calculated revolution based principally on the moral reform of individuals. It was on this human and philosophic basis that he founded his hopes of the universal regeneration, of the palingenesis of mankind and the world, which he sang with such poetic and sublime fervour in the fourth act of his "Prometheus Unbound."

This, the last supplementary portion, written at Florence in December, 1819, is the culminating point of Shelley's genius as a lyric poet. This grandiose and unique work, which we possess in its entirety, lifts its author at once above every lyric poet of the century.

Shelley was conscious of the value of his "Prometheus," and esteemed it in proportion to the labour it had cost him:

My friends say my "Prometheus" is too wild, ideal, and perplexed with imagery; it may be so. It has no resemblance to the Greek drama; it is original, and cost me severe labour. If that is not durable poetry, tried by the severest test, I do not know what is. It is a lofty subject, not inadequately treated, and should not perish with me.

Shelley's judgment has been confirmed by posterity, and whatever may be the defects of this prodigious work in detail, to us it appears like one of the gigantic Sphinxes of the desert, defying man and time alike. We willingly join in Mr. Rossetti's fine panegyric :

There is, I suppose, no poem comparable, in the fair sense of that word, to "Prometheus Unbound." The immense scale and boundless scope of the conception ; the marble majesty and extramundane passions of the personages ; the sublimity of ethical aspiration ; the radiance of ideal and poetic beauty which saturates every phase of the subject, and (almost, as it were) wraps it from sight at times, and transforms it out of sense into spirit; the rolling river of great sound and lyrical rapture ; form a combination not to be matched elsewhere, and scarcely to encounter competition. There is another source of greatness in this poem neither to be foolishly lauded nor (still less) undervalued. It is this : that "Prometheus Unbound," however remote the foundation of its subject-matter, and unactual its executive treatment, does in reality express the most modern of conceptions, the utmost reach of speculation of a mind which burst up all crusts of custom and prescription like a volcano, and imaged forth a future wherein man should be indeed the autocrat and renovated renovator of his planet. This it is, I apprehend, which places " Prometheus " clearly, instead of disputably at the summit of all latter poetry ; the fact that it embodies, in forms of truly ecstatic beauty, the dominant passion of the dominant intellects of the age, and especially of one of the extremest and highest among them all, the author himself. It is the ideal poem of perpetual and triumphant progression —the Atlantis of Man Emancipated.

Mrs. Shelley has very clearly described in

her notes, the spirit, genesis, and development of this grand composition :

During his travels in Italy (1818–1819), Shelley meditated on the subject of his drama. . . . But though he diversifie his studies, his thoughts centred in the " Prometheus." A last, when at Rome, during a bright and beautiful spring, he gave up his whole time to the composition. . . .

At first he completed the drama in three acts. It was not till several months after, when at Florence, that he conceived that a fourth act, a sort of hymn of rejoicing in fulfilment of the prophecies with regard to Prometheus, ought to be added to complete the composition.

The prominent feature of Shelley's theory of the destiny of the human species was, that evil is not inherent in the system of the creation, but an accident that might be expelled. This also forms a portion of Christianity ; God made earth and man perfect, till he, by his fall,

" Brought death into the world, and all our woe."

Shelley believed that mankind had only to will that there should be no evil, and there would be none. He was attached to this opinion with fervent enthusiasm. That man could be so perfectionised as to be able to expel evil from his own nature, and from the greater part of the creation, was a cardinal point of his system. And the subject he loved best to dwell on was the image of One warring with the Evil Principle, oppressed not only by it, but by all, even the good, who were deluded into considering evil a necessary portion of humanity. A victim full of fortitude and hope, and the spirit of triumph emanating from a reliance in the ultimate omnipotence of good—such he had depicted in his last poem, when he made Laon the enemy and the victim of tyrants. He now took a more idealised image of the same subject.

He followed certain classical authorities in figuring Saturn as the good principle, Jupiter the usurping evil one, and Prometheus the regenerator, who, unable to bring mankind back to primitive innocence, used knowledge as a weapon to defeat evil, by leading mankind beyond the state wherein they are sinless through ignorance, to that in which they are virtuous through wisdom. Jupiter punished the temerity of the Titan by chaining him to a rock of Caucasus, and causing a vulture tó devour his still renewed heart. There was a prophecy afloat in Heaven, portending the fall of Jove, the secret of averting which was known only to Prometheus ; and the god offered freedom from torture on condition of its being communicated to him. According to the mythological story, this referred to the offspring of Thetis, who was destined to be greater than his father. Prometheus at last bought pardon for his crime of enriching mankind with his gifts, by revealing the prophecy. Hercules killed the vulture, and set him free ; and Thetis was married to Peleus, the father of Achilles.

Shelley adapted the catastrophe of this story to his own peculiar views. The son, greater than his father, born of the nuptials of Jupiter and Thetis, was to dethrone evil, and bring back a happier reign than that of Saturn. Prometheus defies the power of his enemy, and endures centuries of torture, till the hour arrives when Jove, blind to the real event, but darkly guessing that some great good to himself will flow, espouses Thetis. At the moment, the Primal Power of the world drives him from his usurpèd throne, and Strength, in the person of Hercules, liberates Humanity, typified in Prometheus, from the tortures generated by evils done or suffered. Asia, one of the Oceanides, is the wife of Prometheus ; she was, according to other mythological interpretations, the same as Venus and Nature. When the Benefactor of

Mankind is liberated, Nature resumes the beauty of her prime, and is united to her husband, the emblem of the human race, in perfect and happy union. In the fourth act, the poet gives further scope to his imagination, and idealises the forms of creation, such as we know them, instead of such as they appeared to the Greeks. Maternal Earth, the mighty parent, is superseded by the Spirit of the Earth—the guide of our planet through the realms of sky—while his fair and weaker companion and attendant, the Spirit of the Moon, receives bliss from the annihilation of evil in the superior sphere.

Shelley develops, more particularly in the lyrics of this drama, his abstruse and imaginative theories with regard to the Creation. It requires a mind as subtle and penetrating as his own to understand the mystic meanings scattered throughout the poem. They elude the ordinary reader by their abstraction and delicacy of distinction, but they are far from vague. It was his design to write prose metaphysical essays on the nature of man, which would have served to explain much of what is obscure in his poetry; a few scattered fragments of observations and remarks alone remain. He considered these philosophical views of mind and nature to be instinct with the intensest spirit of poetry.

More popular poets clothe the ideal with familiar and sensible imagery. Shelley loved to idealise the real—to gift the mechanism of the material universe with a soul and a voice, and to bestow such also on the most delicate and abstract emotions and thoughts of the mind. Sophocles was his great master in this species of imagery. . . . In reading Shelley's poetry we often find similar verses, resembling, but not imitating, the Greek in this species of imagery; for though he adopted the style, he gifted it with that originality of form and colouring which sprang from his own genius. . . .

The tone of the composition [of "Prometheus Unbound"] is calmer and more majestic, the poetry more perfect as a whole, and the imagination displayed at once more pleasingly beautiful, and more varied and daring [than in any of his previous attempts]. . . . Throughout the whole poem there reigns a sort of calm and holy spirit of love ; it soothes the tortured, and is hope to the expectant, until the prophecy is fulfilled, and Love, untainted by any evil, becomes the law of the world.

No ancient myth has, in equal measure to that of Prometheus, awakened in the human soul the longing to lift the thick veil that hides the origin of the world and of the human race. It was very variously interpreted even in the time of the Greeks, by Hesiod and Æschylus, and has become to the modern world a terrible Sphinx, which every soul haunted by the symbolically expressed mysteries of the ancient wisdom has in turn consulted, receiving replies in harmony with its own philosophic convictions, or those of its century. Among all the various interpretations, one seems to have prevailed; that one which makes of Prometheus a personification of good, in the struggle of good and evil, of spirit as against force, of liberty and progress in conflict with tyranny and ignorance—an eternal struggle which seems the very condition of life and being. The Greeks in delivering Prometheus, in order that he may be reconciled with Zeus his eternal enemy, must surely have had some conception of the inherent necessity of things, of the "struggle for life," as it is called by modern science, of life itself consisting in struggle, and of the discord which produces the essential and final harmony of the world. We are inclined to believe that they had; hence we must seek in the third part of the Æschylean trilogy, unhappily lost to us, for the true philosophic and scientific meaning of the mythic Prometheus. Shelley's interpretation is of an opposite character. Being absolutely convinced that with the disappearance of Zeus and all his representatives, a new golden age would be created on earth by the strength of the human will alone, he could not accept a compromise to which the wise temperament of Greece resigned itself, unless he might make the best of it by the aid of his faculties and his genius. Christianity and its ultra-terrestrial utopias had not passed in vain through the mind of the poet. Like the Christian Prometheus, the victim of the Judaic Zeus, he also dreamed of an everlasting Paradise for humanity, but a paradise to be found

on earth purified and regenerated by love.
Christian and Biblical ideas suggested to him the
thought of extending this regeneration not only
to the moral and human world, but also to the
entire universe of suns and spheres, whose destinies,
as in the Mosaic Genesis, seemed linked with that
of humanity itself. This grandiose dream all to
the honour of mind, the only god of this world,
has at any rate given us in the last act, or rather
last chant, of " Prometheus Unbound " the most
sublime hymn ever uttered to the glory of the
eternal harmony of Nature, as apprehended by the
human soul in communion with her.

Michelet, in " La Mer," has written like a poet
of the symphony of worlds of which science is
endeavouring to read the score; of the mathe-
matical relation of the stars between themselves,
which are the harmonic intervals of the celestial
music ; " the earth," he says, " in her tides, greater
and less, speaks to her sisters the planets. Do
they reply ? We must believe they do. From
their fluid elements they too must rise up, conscious
of the impulse of the earth. Mutual attraction,
the bent of each planet to come forth from its

egoism, must be the cause of sublime dialogues in the heavens. Unfortunately the ear of man hears but the least part of these."

Shelley heard one of those dialogues, and has marvellously rendered it for us in the fourth act of his " Prometheus."

CHAPTER VIII.

IT was not without keen regret that Shelley was
forced by the "infernal cold of Florence," to leave
the "fairest of cities beneath the sun," the sculptures he so dearly loved, and the delightful
wooded banks of the Arno, where he studied
Dante, and wrote the last canto of the "Prometheus." He took refuge at Pisa (January 26th,
1820) from the terrible Apennine winds, antici-
pating enjoyment from sky, water, and mountains.
"I must suffer at any rate," he says, "but I expect
to suffer less in a boat than in a carriage."

With the spring there came, in the milder climate of Pisa, the usual improvement in Shelley's health, which was likewise promoted by the wise treatment of the celebrated Dr. Vaccà. "Only for certain moral causes," he "would have been greatly benefited" by his "residence in Italy." Among these moral causes must be reckoned the departure of the Gisbornes for England, the final failure of the steamboat undertaking, the refusal of his tragedy at Covent Garden, his homesick longing for England, and above all, the vexations inflicted on him by Godwin.

It was no slight source of pain to Shelley, that Godwin, after all his sacrifices in the endeavour to serve him, should treat him with so little consideration and friendship. Godwin was on the brink of ruin, and laid the blame of his unfortunate position, which was due to his own carelessness, on his friend and benefactor. Shelley grew weary of flinging money into the Skinner Street abyss:

Except for the *good-will* which this transaction seems to have produced between you and me, this money, for any advantage that it ever conferred on you, might as well have been thrown into the sea. Had I kept in my own hands this £4000 or £5000, and administered it in trust for your perma-

nent advantage, I should have been indeed your benefactor.
. . . Sir Philip Sidney, when dying and consumed with
thirst, gave the helmet of water which was brought to him
to the wounded soldier who stood beside him. It would not
have been generosity, but folly, had he poured it on the
ground, as you would that I should the wrecks of my once
prosperous fortune. . . . If you are sincere on this subject,
why, instead of seeking to plunge one already half-ruined for
your sake into deeper ruin, do you not procure the £400 by
your own active power? A person of your extraordinary
accomplishments might easily obtain from the booksellers,
for the promise of a novel, a sum exceeding this amount.
Your "Answer to Malthus" would sell for at least £400.

Meanwhile some pleasant acquaintances at
Pisa made a break in the clouds. One of the
celebrities of Pisa was Professor Vacca, to whom
the city subsequently raised a monument, designed
by Thorwaldsen, in the Campo Santo. Vacca's
views on philosophy and politics were for the
most part the same as Shelley's; and he did the
latter a great service by inducing him to dispense
with doctors and drugs, and trust to Nature
for a cure.

In addition to this friend there was Lady
Mountcashel, a woman of superior attainments, who
had been the favourite pupil of Mary Wollstonecraft thirty years before, when Mary was governess

in the family of Lord Kingston; and on the occasion of Godwin's visit to Ireland in 1800, Lady Mountcashel had received him with hospitality. She had retained the republican and philosophic principles of her masculine education; her mind was cultivated, her disposition mild, benevolent and imperturbably serene. She had long been separated from her husband, the Earl of Mountcashel, and was living in Italy with Mr. George William Tighe, who, being disgusted with the world, lived apart from it in the company of his books. According to Medwin Lady Mountcashel inspired Shelley with his exquisite poem of the " Sensitive Plant."

Yet, in spite of the charm that the society of friends, so congenial to his intellect, had for Shelley, his heart was in London with the Gisbornes. On May 26th, 1820, he wrote to them :

I am just returned from a visit to Leghorn, Casciano, and the old fortress at Sant' Elmo. . . . Everything seems in excellent order at Casa Ricci—garden, pigeons, tables, chairs, and beds. . . . What a glorious prospect you had from the windows of Sant' Elmo! The enormous chain of the Apennines, with its many-folded ridges, islanded in the misty distance of the air ; the sea, so immensely distant, appearing as if at your feet ; and the prodigious expanse of the plain of Pisa, and the dark green marshes lessened almost to a strip by the height of the blue marshes over-hanging them. Then the wild and unreclaimed fertility of the foreground, and the chestnut-trees, whose vivid foliage made a sort of resting-place to the sense before it darted itself to the jagged horizon of this prospect. I was altogether delighted. I had a respite from my nervous symptoms, which was compensated to me by a violent cold in the head. There was a tradition about you at Sant' Elmo—*an English family that had lived here in the time of the French.*

We go to Bagni next month. . . . I am undergoing a course of the Pisan baths, on which I lay no singular stress —but they soothe. I ought to have peace of mind, leisure, tranquillity ; this I expect soon. Our anxiety about Godwin is very great, and any information that you could give a day or two earlier than he might, respecting any decisive event in his lawsuit, would be a great relief. Your impres-sions about Godwin (I speak especially to Madonna *mia,* who had known him before) will especially interest me. You know that added years only add to my admiration of his intellectual powers, and even the moral resources of his character. . . . To see Hunt is to like him. To know Hogg, if any one can know him, is to know something very unlike and inexpressibly superior, to the great mass of men.

This charming letter was written in Reveley's study, and may serve as a commentary upon the admirable epistle in verse which Shelley addressed shortly afterwards to Maria Gisborne—one of the gems of his familiar poetry in which we knew not whether to admire most the perfection of the descriptions, the exquisite delicacy of the sentiment, or the incomparable wit and humour with which the poet avails himself of the smallest details. All his London friends are named in it with an affectionate regard that does not exclude impartiality or raillery.

It was during his stay at Casa Ricci that, one summer evening wandering with Mary "among the lanes whose myrtle hedges were the bowers of fire-flies," he heard the song of the skylark, and instantly interpreted its ideal impression in one of his most perfect poems :—his salutation to the bird, or rather to the blithe spirit disdainful of earth, whose clear and piercing strain he envies, and would fain learn how to teach the world "such harmonious madness."

The days were spent pleasantly at Pisa in the study of Latin and Greek with Mary, and Shelley rendered into *ottava rima* the Homeric Hymn to Mercury. The playful tone of the free translation struck a new vein of light-hearted inspiration, which soon showed itself in his marvellously fanciful "Witch of Atlas."

The heat of Leghorn in August had forced the Shelleys to remove to the Baths of San Giuliano, near Lucca, and, after an excursion to

Monte San Pellegrino, he wrote in three days that wonderful poem which he describes as entirely fanciful, and, if its merit be measured by the labour it cost, absolutely worthless. In his heart Shelley probably preferred this fanciful improvisation to his more laborious productions such as " The Cenci." It is a fairy tale, but such an one as might be told and heard by pure spirits —a fairy tale, as Mr. Rossetti says, "enchanting and imperishable." We may observe with the same writer that a clue to its meaning is to be found if we understand the Witch to be the Spirit of Beauty, of which all the beauties in the world is but a shadow, "whose words, though too fine to be articulate to mortal ear, fill us with a longing for all high truth ; whose presence, though invisible, quickens within us all hope and joy and love." Here we must pause, nor try to analyse that which refuses to be analysed. Painting alone, and painting by a sylph or an Ariel, could render something of that divine phantasy. " What an admirable subject for Retsch !" says Medwin. " A second ' Midsummer Night's Dream !' " *

It seems incredible that the poet who had just

* Retsch's " Outlines to Shakespeare's Plays."

written the " Witch of Atlas " should be the same
man who, steadily observing the political state of
Europe, suffered no symptom of that awakening of
Liberty among his contemporaries, whose approaching triumph he foresaw, to escape his
notice. The year 1820 seemed to respond to that
presentiment: in the south of Europe the spirit of
revolution was aroused. Spain gave the signal,
and the flame soon spread to the south of Italy, to
Naples, and Sicily. The poet's heart beat in
sympathy with all. " Sicily, like Naples, is free!"
he wrote to Mary (July 23rd) . . . . . " the enthusiasm of the inhabitants was prodigious; the
women fought from the houses, raining down
boiling oil on the assailants." And in September,
" At Naples the Constitutional party have declared to the Austrian Minister that, if the
Emperor should make war upon them, their first
action would be to put to death *all* the members
of the royal family—a necessary and most just
measure, when the forces of the combatants, as
well as the merits of their respective causes, are so
unequal. That kings should be everywhere the
hostages for liberty—nothing more admirable!"
In the fervour of his revolutionary enthusiasm

Shelley wrote the " Ode to Liberty" and the " Ode to Naples " successively.

There are few lyrics so thrilling, so highly charged with passion and enthusiasm, as the " Ode to Liberty," in which Shelley unrolls before our dazzled gaze the history of the victories and defeats of that " virgin huntress swifter than the moon," and " terror of the world's wolves." Athens, Rome, Arminius, Christianity, the Saxon Alfred, Luther, Milton, France in '93, and Napoleon pass in succession before us, leaving the world either luminous or obscure, according as Liberty casts or withholds " the shadow of her coming." A like passion and a like eloquence are breathed in the " Ode to Naples." The poet is still filled with the poetic recollections of Pompeii and Baïæ, of " the unknown graves of the dead kings of melody" (Homer and Virgil). From the splendour of the Elysian shores he rises to the contemplation of the destiny of Naples, of her hoped-for freedom—the signal eagerly awaited by the whole of Italy:

> Didst thou not start to hear Spain's thrilling pæan
>   From land to land re-echoed solemnly,
> Till silence became music? From the Ææan
>   To the cold Alps, eternal Italy

                Starts to hear thine !   The sea
        Which paves the desert streets of Venice laughs
                In light and music ; widowed Genoa wan
        By moonlight spells ancestral epitaphs,
        Murmuring " Where is Doria ? "   Fair Milan,
                Within whose veins long ran
        The viper's palsying venom, lifts her heel
        To bruise his head. . . .

                Florence, beneath the sun,
                Of cities fairest one,
        Blushes within her bower for freedom's expectation ;
                From eyes of quenchless hope
                Rome tears the priestly cope,
        As ruling once by power, so now by admiration—
                An athlete stripped to run
                From a remoter station
        For the high prize lost on Philippi's shore ;
        As then Hope, Truth, and Justice did avail,
                So now may Fraud and Wrong !   Oh, hail !

Austrian bayonets unhappily soon crushed the
Neapolitan revolution. Shelley was deeply affected
by this disaster, and was indignant that his friend
Moore could applaud it in verse unworthy of a
poet and an Irishman.

Should Italy ever commemorate her resurrection to freedom and national life by a monument,
she would be ungrateful indeed did she not place
beside the names of her warrior-heroes that of the
poet who sang so gloriously of her hopes and

electrified her patriotism. When lyrical poetry
attains to such a height and power as his, we may
pronounce it to be, as Shelley himself said, speaking out of the very faith with which he was
inspired, " a prophecy and a cause."

While Shelley was thus pouring forth a flood
of lyrical verse in his most serious and eloquent
vein, the tragi-comedy then being played in
England, with Queen Caroline for its heroine,
afforded him an opportunity of exercising the
kind of talent he had so unexpectedly disclosed
in " Peter Bell the Third "—that faculty of original
and powerful irony, that spirit of comical satire,
burlesque and yet poetical—a mixture hitherto
unknown in the incisiveness of Swift and the
airiness of Aristophanes.

The " Œdipus Tyrannus," like " Peter Bell
the Third," was merely a light and playful improvisation, but it was an improvisation of genius.

One day, while looking at some extracts from
Le Courrier Français, he lighted upon a strange
and astonishing piece of news. Queen Caroline,
on hearing of the death of George III., had
hastened to England. Deserted and dishonoured
by the grotesque King, George IV., the too

notorious Princess was about to claim her rights as wife and queen. The result is well known; the story of the long and shameful suit occupies the whole of the political annals of England, in 1820. Never before had any people offered so odious, repulsive, and ridiculous a spectacle to the world; it alone would have justified all the anathemas heaped by Shelley on the head of Royalty.

Long before this, Shelley had formed his opinion of George IV.; it was that of every thinking Englishman; it was that which Thackeray has emphatically expressed in his "Four Georges," "I do not know that there could be a bitterer satire on English society at that period, than to say it was able to admire George IV."

In common with many others, Shelley had at first been blinded by the farce of Liberalism, acted by the Prince of Wales becoming the friend and disciple of Fox and Sheridan; he had relied for a moment on the hopes raised by a youth who shouted for "Wilkes and Liberty!" But he saw behind the mask, and divined from the conduct of the Regent what the future King of England would be.

In "Swellfoot the Tyrant," we recognise the historic George IV., of the memoirs of the time; the "base fellow" of Lady Hester Stanhope, the hero of the dinner-table, and of dandyism, the inventor of maraschino punch, the fat, crowned fop, exclusively engrossed, amid grave European events, with the cut of a coat, or the seasoning of a dish. All these details, taken from history, are ·invested with heroic and gigantic forms and proportions in Shelley's drama. By a process of poetical hyperbole somewhat analogous to that of Rabelais, George IV. becomes the ideal dandy, glutton, and tyrant; the ungrateful friend of Sheridan and Brummel becomes as Swellfoot (Œdipus) the "Man-Milliner to red Bellona," the dainty epicure is transformed into a Homeric Gargantua, who devours in a single *plat*, devised by his Persian cook, what would suffice to feed a dozen families for a winter or two; the sceptical and fickle Don Juan, whose life has known hardly one real passion except hatred and contempt of his wife, becomes a tragical George Dandin, a victim of the jealous divinity who "waves o'er the couch of wedded kings, the torch of Discord with its fiery hair," the famous green bag laid on the table in the House of Lords, and containing the proofs of the royal adultery, is changed into a terrible invention of Hell, a poison more mortal than death itself "sealed up with the broad seal of Fraud, who is the Devil's Lord High Chancellor," and baptized by "the Primate of all Hell."

In order to idealise Caroline while remaining true to History, Shelley had only to depict her as the credulous and enthusiastic folly of the populace of London saw her. But he was no dupe of the political comedy played round the Queen; he knew very well that the madcap Princess, who seemed all through her life to be bent on the self-destruction of her honour and her reputation, had always been a despised tool in the hands of the Whigs, a puppet of the Opposition which they would fling away on the first change in public opinion. He wrote to Peacock in this sense, July 12th:

Nothing, I think, shows the generous gullibility of the English nation more than their having adopted Her Sacred Majesty as the heroine of the day, in spite of all their prejudices and bigotry. I, for my part, of course wish no harm to happen to her, even if she has, as I firmly believe, amused herself in a manner rather indecorous with any courier or baron. But I cannot help adverting to it as one of the absurdities of royalty, that a vulgar woman, with all those low tastes which prejudice considers as vices, and a person whose habits and manners every one would shun in private life, without any redeeming virtues, should be turned into a heroine because she is a queen, or, as a collateral reason, because her husband is a king ; and he, no less than his Ministers, are so odious that everything, however disgusting, which is opposed to them is admirable.

He was willing to believe in the famous " green bag " :

" I wonder what in the world the Queen has done," he writes at the beginning of this tragic-comedy ; "I should not wonder, after the whispers I have heard, to find that the green bag contained evidence that she had imitated Pasiphaë and that the Committee should recommend to Parliament a Bill to exclude all minotaurs from the succession. What silly stuff is this to employ a great nation about ! I wish the King and the Queen, like Punch and his wife, would fight out their disputes in person."

In the foregoing lines we perceive the first conception and plan of " Swellfoot the Tyrant." Iona Taurina, the Queen, the new Pasiphaë (after long wanderings in all the fabulous countries to which Æschylus sends the unhappy Io), stung and harassed by the same gadfly, returns to Thebes where the husband and wife settle their edifying differences by a solemn and decisive trial.

How did Shelley conceive the idea of the Aristophanic chorus which represents the Theban, that is, the English people? From a mere coincidence.

"We were then" (August, 1820), writes Mrs. Shelley, "at the Baths of San Giuliano ; a friend came to visit us on the day when a fair was held in the square, beneath our windows. Shelley read to us his 'Ode of Liberty' and was riotously accompanied by the grunting of a quantity of pigs brought for sale to the fair. He compared it to the 'Chorus of Frogs' in the satiric drama of *Aristophanes ;* and it being an hour of merriment, and one ludicrous association suggesting another, he imagined a political satirical drama on the circumstances of the day, to which the pigs would serve as chorus ; and *Swellfoot* was begun."

The notion of representing the English people under the form of the most selfish and ease-loving of animals must have amused Shelley. As he makes one of the characters say : "How can I find a more appropriate term," than pig-gishness, "to include religion, morals, peace, and plenty,

> And all that fit Bastia as a nation
> To teach the other nations how to live?'

Had not Burke, that oracle of Anglican cant,

said that an Englishman is, above all, " a religious animal?" Had he not compared Revolutionists to a handful of grasshoppers hidden in the heather, while millions of fine beasts repose in the shade of the British oak, and ruminate in silence? To repair somewhat the irreverence of his first metamorphosis, the poet invented another; the pigs of every caste and kind were transformed at the close of the piece into bulls, the "fine beasts" of Burke, and by a fantastic etymology, the Ionian Minotaur becomes the legendary founder of a people who take pride in their nickname of John Bull.

Shelley could not fail to depict the advisers and ministers of George IV.'s disastrous reign, under hideous and grinning masks. A Wellington, a Castlereagh, an Eldon, a Sidmouth ; each of these courtiers is indelibly branded. Nothing could be more comically strange or more poetically comic,* than the lasting contrast between these modern characters, alike odious and grotesque, and the Greek garments in which they are dressed up, uttering, in the language of gods and Homeric heroes, the most absurd sophistry, the wildest folly ; nothing more irresistibly droll than the mingling of the manners and oddities of modern England, of the John Bull of Arbuthnot, with the most graceful and fantastic traditions of ancient mythology.

The present time, which may be called the age of parody, may bow down before Shelley, and acknowledge in him the Shakespeare of the art.

In July, 1820, Shelley was deeply affected by the receipt of sad news. John Keats was dying of consumption at the age of twenty-five. On June 22nd he had broken a blood-vessel, and the end was near.

On hearing this, Shelley wrote to him from Pisa on July 27th, 1820:

MY DEAR KEATS,

I hear with great pain the dangerous accident you have undergone, and Mr. Gisborne, who gives me the account of it, adds that you continue to wear a consumptive appearance. This consumption is a disease particularly fond of people who write such good verses as you have done, and with the assistance of an English winter it can often indulge its selection. I do not think that young and amiable poets are bound to gratify its taste ; they have entered into no bond with the Muses to that effect. But seriously (for I am joking on what I am very anxious about), I think you would do well to pass the winter in Italy and avoid so tremendous an accident, and if you think it as necessary as I do, so long as you continue to find Pisa or its neighbourhood agreeable to you, Mrs. Shelley unites with myself in urging the request that you would take up your residence with us. You might come by sea to Leghorn (France is not worth seeing, and the sea is particularly good for weak lungs), which is within a few miles of us. You ought, at all events, to see Italy, and your health, which I suggest as a motive, may be an excuse to you. I spare declamation about the statues, and paintings, and ruins, and, what is a greater piece of forbearance, about the mountains and streams, the fields, the colours of the sky, and the sky itself.

I have lately read your "Endymion" again, and even with a new sense of the treasures of poetry it contains, though treasures poured forth with indistinct profusion. This people in general will not endure, and that is the cause of the comparatively few copies which have been sold. I feel persuaded that you are capable of the greatest things, so you but will. I always tell Ollier to send you copies of my books. "Prometheus Unbound," I imagine you will receive nearly at the same time with this letter. "The Cenci" I hope you have already received—it was studiously composed in a different style. . . . In poetry I have sought to avoid system and mannerism. I wish those who excel me in genius would pursue the same plan.

Whether you remain in England, or journey to Italy, believe that you carry with you my anxious wishes for your health, happiness, and success, wherever you are, or whatever you undertake, and that I am, •

Yours sincerely,
P. B. SHELLEY.

Keats answered this affectionate invitation as a friend and as a poet:

HAMPSTEAD, *August* 10*th*, 1820.

MY DEAR SHELLEY,

I am very much gratified that you, in a foreign country, and with a mind almost over-occupied, should write to me in the strain of the letter beside me. If I do not take advantage of your invitation, it will be prevented by a circumstance I have very much at heart to prophesy. There is no doubt that an English winter would put an end to me, and do so in a lingering, hateful manner. Therefore, I must either voyage or journey to Italy, as a soldier marches up to a battery. . . . I am glad you take any pleasure in my poor poem, which I would willingly take the trouble to unwrite, if possible, did I care so much as I have done about reputation. I received a copy of "The Cenci," as from yourself, from Hunt. There is only one part of it I am judge of—the poetry and dramatic effect, which by many spirits nowadays is considered the Mammon. A modern work, it is said, must have a purpose, which may be the god. An artist must serve Mammon ; he must have "self-concentration"--selfishness, perhaps. You, I am sure, will forgive me for sincerely remarking that you might curb your magnanimity, and be more of an artist, and load every rift of your subject with ore. The thought of such discipline must fall like cold chains upon you, who perhaps never sat with your wings furled for six months together. And is not this extraordinary talk for the writer of "Endymion," whose mind was like a pack of scattered cards? I am picked up and sorted to a pip. My imagination is a monastery, and I am its monk. I am in expectation of "Prometheus" every day. Could I have my own wish effected, you would have it still in manuscript, or be but now putting an end to the second act. I remember you

advising me not to publish my first flights, on Hampstead
Heath. I am returning advice upon your hands. Most of
the poems in the volume I send you have been written above
two years, and would never have been published but for
hope of gain ; so you see I am inclined enough to take your
advice now. I must express once more my deep sense of
your kindness, adding my sincere thanks and respects for
Mrs. Shelley. In the hope of soon seeing you,

I remain, most sincerely yours,

JOHN KEATS.

It is very touching to see the rival poets thus
ingenuously communicating to each other their
impressions and their criticisms, and each apparently more anxious for the other's fame than
for his own. The fiery ardour of Shelley forbade
him to follow the counsels of his laborious and
precise friend. He was a worker on an heroic
scale, a painter of frescoes—not a carver or a
miniature-painter. He did not understand the
" Perseus " of Benvenuto Cellini ; according to him
the poet or the artist should not work beyond the
precise moment of inspiration ; the " polissez et
repolissez" of Boileau, and the " slow, dull care" of
Keats, seemed to him absurdity. He deemed the
patient labour of the file incompatible with
strength, naturalness, or effect.

The new collection of poems which Keats had

announced, realised to a certain extent the expectations he had formed on reading "Endymion." Immediately on reading it he wrote to Peacock (November 8th, 1820) :

Among the modern things that have reached me, is a volume of poems by Keats ; in other respects insignificant enough, but containing the fragment of a poem called "Hyperion." I dare say you have not time to read it ; but it is certainly an astonishing piece of writing, and gives me a conception of Keats which I confess I had not before.

In his enthusiastic admiration of that wonderful fragment, indignant at the bitter and unjust review of Keats's earlier poems in the *Quarterly Review*, and exaggerating the effect which must be produced on a sensitive and delicate organisation by such hostile criticism, he writes to the editor of the Review in which the article appeared, as follows :

The wretch who wrote it has doubtless the additional reward of a consciousness of his motives, besides the thirty guineas a sheet, or whatever it is that you pay him. . . . I am not in the habit of permitting myself to be disturbed by what is said or written of me, though I dare say I may be condemned sometimes justly enough. . . . The case is different with the unfortunate subject of this letter, the author of " Endymion " . . . and . . . if it is Mr. Gifford that I am addressing, I am persuaded that in an appeal to his humanity and justice, he will acknowledge the *fas ab hoste doceri.* . . .

Poor Keats was thrown into a dreadful state of mind by this review, which, I am persuaded, was not written with any intention of producing the effect, to which it has at least greatly contributed, of embittering his existence, and inducing a disease from which there are now but faint hopes of his recovery. The first effects are described to me to have resembled insanity, and it was by assiduous watching that he was restrained from effecting purposes of suicide. The agony of his sufferings at length produced the rupture of a blood-vessel in the lungs, and the usual process of consumption appears to have begun. He is coming to pay me a visit in Italy ; but I fear that unless his mind can be kept tranquil, little is to be hoped from the mere influence of climate.

But let me not extort anything from your pity. I have just seen a second volume, published by him evidently in careless despair. . . . Allow me to solicit your especial attention to the fragment of a poem entitled " Hyperion," the composition of which was checked by the Review in question. The great proportion of this piece is surely in the very highest style of poetry.* I speak impartially, for the canons of taste to which Keats has conformed in his other compositions, are the very reverse of my own. I leave you

---

* Byron, who could not forgive Keats for having depreciated Pope, and set himself up as a law-giver in Parnassus while he was as yet but a school-boy poet, and who had bitterly ridiculed him in 1820, made amends for this after the death of the poet. His judgment is inspired by that of Shelley ; he declares Keats to have been a genius of great promise, and says that his fragment, " Hyperion," seems to be directly inspired by the Titans, and is as sublime as Æschylus.

to judge for yourself; it would be an insult to you to suppose that, from motives however honourable, you would lend yourself to a deception of the public.

Shelley, as we see by the foregoing letter, cherished no false hopes concerning Keats's recovery, and it was with no surprise, albeit with keenest sorrow, that a few months later he heard of his death. They had not met again. The author of " Hyperion " died at Rome on February 23rd, 1821, tended by a devoted friend, Mr. Severn, the artist, who watched over him to the last with the truest tenderness. Shelley regretted that he knew of that touching devotion too late to allude to it in the elegy which he consecrated to the memory of his friend. This poem alone, the " Adonais," * would suffice to render the inseparably linked names of Shelley and Keats immortal. We cannot read it without being deeply moved by the melancholy with which Shelley predicts his own fate, and seems to forebode the impending tragedy which is destined to unite him to his friend.

Towards the end of October, 1820, Shelley

'* " Adonais " was not completed until June, 1821.

was driven from the Baths of San Giuliano by an inundation of the canal between the Serchio and the Arno; the water invaded his house, and he returned to Pisa, taking up his winter quarters at Casa Galetti, with Medwin, whom he had not seen since 1813. The latter, after long wanderings, including a voyage to Bombay, where he had bought a copy of "Laon and Cythna" for the price of the paper on which it was printed, had joined his friend in Italy. He has written the most interesting particulars of the literary life of the poet during his residence at Pisa in the winter of 1820–21. He describes him as full of projects of poems, studying Arabic with his cousin, with a view to future travels through Syria and Egypt, delighting more and more in the Greeks and the Spaniards, improvising, for Medwin's benefit, a translation of the "Prometheus" of Æschylus, and luxuriating in the light and perfume of "the golden and starry Autos" of Calderon; purposing to write a version in *terza rima* of Dante's Epic; and reading with admiration Manzoni's "Promessi Sposi." He considered the description of the plague at Milan, to be "far superior to those of De Foe or Thucydides." They also read together

Schiller's tragedy of " Joan of Arc."   The chief merit of this work in Shelley's eyes was that it treated the Christian religion as a mythology, and he said that a hundred years hence it would be more admired than now.

At times, however, in the midst of these pure delights, Shelley would give way to a dark melancholy, " too sacred," says Medwin, " to notice, and which it would have been a vain attempt to dissipate."   At other times, when his features bore the impress of suffering, his spirit was lost in reverie, absorbed in the contemplation of the exterior world, and dissolved, as it were, into Nature.

" More than once," continues Medwin, " I have remarked something of this in Shelley, as we stood watching from my open window in the upper part of the house the sunsets of Pisa, which are gorgeous beyond any I have ever witnessed, when the waters, the sky, and the marble palaces that line the magnificent crescent of the Lung' Arno were glowing with crimson—the river a flood of molten gold—and I seem now to follow its course towards the Ponte al Mare, till the eye rested on the Torre del Fame, that frowned in dark relievo on the horizon. On such occasions, after one of these reveries, he would forget himself, lost in admiration, and exclaim : " What a glorious world ! There is, after all, something worth living for. This makes me retract the wish that I had never been born."

At such times he forgot the bitter thoughts which had made him write: "I am regarded by all who know or hear of me, except, I think, on the whole five individuals, as a rare prodigy of crime and pollution, whose look even might infect. This is a large computation, and I don't think I could mention more than three."

Even in Italy his kind fellow-countrymen missed no opportunity of freshly opening the wound. There is a story that at the Pisa Post Office an English officer said to him, "So you are that damned Atheist Shelley?" and struck him with his cane.

The varied and agreeable social relations formed by Shelley during his second residence at Pisa, were some consolation for the contempt and rudeness of his own countrymen. We find him at Casa Galetti surrounded by such clever and noticeable persons as Pacchiani, Emilia Viviani, Mavrocordato, Taaffe (the translator and commentator of Dante), and Sgricci the improvisatore; there for the first time he enjoyed the society of a chosen and select circle which he was so well fitted to appreciate. Two of his most beautiful works, the " Epipsychidion " and " Hellas," were written under these propitious circumstances.

CHAPTER IX.

SHELLEY IN ITALY — PISA AND RAVENNA — EMILIA VIVIANI AND THE "EPIPSYCHIDION" —"A DEFENCE OF POETRY"—"HELLAS"— "CHARLES I."—1821.

ON March 21st, 1821, Shelley wrote to Peacock: "I have made the acquaintance at Pisa, in an obscure convent, of the only Italian in whom I have ever felt any interest."

This was the young and beautiful Contessina Emilia Viviani, she who inspired the "Epipsychidion." Since the preceding autumn, Shelley had been intimate with a certain Abbé Pacchiani, Professor at the University of Pisa and chaplain in the family of Count Viviani.

Pacchiani was a typical abbé of the eighteenth century, a fit opponent of Voltaire or Diderot.

Medwin gives us an amusing sketch of the man :

Pacchiani was about fifty years of age, somewhat above the common height, with a figure bony and angular, and covered with no more superfluous flesh than a prize-fighter. His face was dark as that of a Moor, his features marked and regular, his eyes black and gloomy. He always reminded me of one of Titian's portraits (his family had been Venetians) stepping out of its frame. Had he lived when Venice was governed by the Tré, he would have made a Loredano, and might have sate to Anne Radcliffe for a Schedoni ; but, to descend to modern times, during the reign of Austrian despotism he was admirably calculated for a spy, or *calderaio*—perhaps he might be one. "*Chi lo sa ?*" Nature certainly never designed him for a divine. As to his religion, it was about on a par with that of Il Abbate Casti (*Casti a non casto*, as *lucus à non lucendo*), of whom he was afterwards a worthy successor, in his native city, Florence. But at Pisa, *Il Signore Professore* was the title by which he was generally known—a professor, like many other professors and lecturers, at least in Italy, who had made a sinecure of his office, that of *belles lettres*, and only mounted the *cathedra* once during the many years that he touched his poor emoluments ; for the Transalpine universities are not quite so richly endowed as our own. Not that this neglect of his duties would have affected his appointment, but, as he told me, he lost it by an irresistible *bon mot*. During one of his midnight orgies, which he was in the habit of celebrating with some of the most dissolute of the students, he was interrogated in the darkness by the patrol in the streets of Pisa, as to who and what he was ; to which questioning he gave the following reply : "Son' un uomo publico, in una strada publica, con una donna publica."

This public avowal cost him his chair. But it gave him *éclat*, and did not lose him his friends, or exclude him from the houses where he was the spiritual guide and confessor. There were, it is true, two reasons why he was tolerated in good society (which Casti says is to be found where he places Don Juan, below)—his pen and his tongue—the dread of both. His epigrams were *sanglantes*, and he gave *sobriquets* the most happy for those who offended him ; as an instance of which, he most happily styled a captain of our Navy *il dolce capitano*—a bye-word that stuck to him through life, and always excited a smile at his expense whenever he appeared. He was a good poet, if one might judge from the quotations he was in the habit of making from his tragedies, which he continually talked about, and which Madame de Staël, who knew him, used to call his *imaginary* ones, for not a line of them was ever published—perhaps written. His talent was conversation—a conversation full of repartee and sparkling with wit ; and his information (he was a man of profound erudition, vast memory, and first-rate talent) made him almost oracular. Shelley, when Pacchiani first became an *habitué* at his house, was charmed with him, and listened with rapt attention to his eloquence, which he compared to that of Coleridge. It was a swarm of ideas singularly extravagant, but which he contrived to weave into his argument with marvellous embroidery. Now he plunged into abysses but to lighten other abysses ; and his words, like a torrent—for there was no stopping him when fairly rushing onwards—carried all before them.

It was this gift of eloquence that made him for a time welcome at Shelley's, where he passed many an evening in the week (I think I see him now, dissecting the snipes with his long, bony, snuffy fingers—for he never in the operation made use of a knife or fork) ; at first I say, for he had in the outset sufficient tact (no one knew mankind better) to keep in the background the revolting vices which were familiar to him and disfigured his character. He had a predilection for our *compatriotes*, with and without the *e*, but particularly patronised the *Belle Inglese*, as he always called English women ; and after the Italian fashion, soon familiarly called Mrs. Shelley, *La Signora Maria*. Wherever he once got the *entrée*, he was a *sine quâ non*, a *fa tout*. He had always some poor devil of low origin to recommend as a master of his language, receiving, under the rose, part of the lesson money. He was never at a loss to find some *Palazzo* to be let, getting a monthly *douceur* out of the rent from the landlord ; for a picture fancier, he had always at hand some mysterious *Marchese* or *Marchesa*, ready to part with a Carlo Dolce, or Andrea del Sarto, or Allori—*originals* of course. He could dilate for hours on the Venus of the Tribune, the Day and Night of Michael Angelo, the Niobe ; knew the history of every painter and painting in the galleries of the Uffizii and Pitti better than Vasari, or his successor Rosini ; in short, he was a *Mezzano, Cicerone, Conosciatore, Dilettante,* and I might add, *Ruffiano*. Mrs. Shelley has sketched him in her "Valperga."

Some years later, Medwin again met with Pacchiani at Florence. He was reduced to abject poverty, had been imprisoned for debt, but was more than ever a *Diavolo incarnato*.

In the course of conversation with Shelley the abbé mentioned to him two young daughters of the Count, who, on their father's second marriage, had been placed in separate convents. He dwelt principally on the elder, Emilia, who for two years had been in the Convent of St. Anna, awaiting a husband who would take her without dowry.

"Poverina," said Pacchiani, "she pines like a bird in a cage—ardently longs to escape from her prison-house—pines with *ennui*, and wanders about the corridors like an unquiet spirit; she sees her young days glide on without an aim or purpose. She was made for love. Yesterday she was watering some flowers in her cell—she has nothing to love but her flowers—'Yes,' said she, addressing them, 'you are born to vegetate, but we thinking beings were made for action—not to be penned up in a corner, or set at a window to bloom and die.'"

Such words as these found a responsive echo in Shelley's heart.

"The next day," continues Medwin, "accompanied by the priest, we came in sight of the gloomy dark convent, whose ruinous and dilapidated condition told too plainly of confiscation and poverty. It was situated in an unfrequented street in the suburbs, not far from the walls. After passing through a gloomy portal, that led to a quadrangle, the area of which was crowded with crosses, memorials, of old monastic times, we were soon in the presence of Emilia. . . .

Emilia was indeed lovely and interesting. Her profuse black hair, tied in the most simple knot, after the manner of a Greek Muse in the Florence gallery, displayed to its full height her brow, fair as that marble of which I speak. She was also about the same height as the antique. Her features possessed a rare faultlessness, and almost Grecian contour, the nose and forehead making a straight line . . . her eyes had the sleepy voluptuousness, if not the colour of Beatrice Cenci's. They had indeed no definite colour, changing with the changing feeling to dark or light as the soul animated them. Her cheek was pale too as marble, owing to her confinement and want of air, and perhaps to thought.

There was a lark in the *parloir* that had lately been caught. "Poor prisoner!" said she, looking at it compassionately, "you will die of grief! How I pity thee! What must thou suffer when thou hearest in the clouds the songs of thy parent birds, or some flocks of thy kind on the wing, in search of other skies, of new fields, of new delights! But, like me, thou wilt be forced to remain here always, to wear out thy miserable existence here. Why can I not release thee? . . ."

Such was the impression of the only visit I paid Emilia; but I saw her some weeks after, at the end of a Carnival, when she had obtained leave to visit Mrs. Shelley, companioned by the abbess. In spite of the Contessina's efforts to assume cheerfulness, one might see she was very, very sad; but she made no complaint. She had grown used to suffering; it had become her element.

Claire and Mary frequently visited her at the convent, and lent her books, such as "Corinne," "La Nouvelle Héloïse," etc. Claire began to teach her English. Shelley often wrote to her, and together with gifts of flowers wet with her tears,* received from her in answer letters full of melancholy and despair. While Mary was for Emilia her "dearest sister," Shelley became the "beloved brother," the "*sensibile* Percy," the "*adorato sposo.*"

On one occasion she writes to him as follows:

This evening I wish to tell you many things, but my vigilant and importunate *Argus* has hindered me from so doing. I will now tell you a part of them. You console me by engaging yourself to effect my liberation. Here I fare ill, both in spirits and health, and suffer very much in every way, so that by taking me from here you would give me a new existence. I leave the *how* to you, who have that experience and that wisdom in which I am wanting. . . . Ah, God pardon my mother! She could make me contented, if not happy, and, on the contrary, it is she who is the chief cause of my misfortunes. I love her still, and wish her every good. I feel that Nature speaks and lives in my heart. Although she forgets that she is my mother, I remember that I am her daughter. . . . You say that my liberation will perhaps *divide* us. O my friend! my soul, my heart can never be parted from my brother, from my dear sisters! My person, once delivered from this prison, will attempt all things in order to follow my heart, and Emilia will seek you everywhere, even to the utmost boundaries of the world. I do not love, nor shall I ever be able to love, any thing or person so much as your family; for it I would abandon everything,

---

* See the exquisite madrigal beginning: "Madonna, wherefore hast thou sent to me, Sweet basil and mignonette?"

and should lose nothing, since in it are included all that can exist of beautiful, virtuous, amiable, *sensibile*, and learned in the world.

Shelley was attracted to Emilia, not only by her sorrows and her beauty, but still more by her charms of intellect and the ideal tendencies of her mind. "She had cultivated her mind," he says, "more than any Italian woman I have met." She read the Italian poets, was herself a writer of verse, and, although ignorant of Plato, had written an "Apostrophe to Love" that has come down to us, and bears witness to her elevation and purity of thought on that subject. This possibly may have given Shelley the first idea of his "Epipsychidion;" and from Emilia he borrowed the words of his epigraph, which is the key to the poem: "L' anima amante si slancia fuori del creato, e si crea nell' infinito un mondo tutto per essa, diverso assai da questo oscuro e pauroso baratro" (the loving soul soars above the visible world, and creates for herself in infinite space a world all her own, and unlike indeed to this dark and dreadful prison).

To see more than a pure platonic affection

in the friendship between Shelley and Emilia, would be wilfully to shut one's eyes against evidence. Mary is too closely interwoven in the "Epipsychidion," as sister to Emilia, for us to suppose for an instant that she could have any cause for jealousy. Shelley himself dismissed any such interpretation of his conduct with contempt. On October 22nd he wrote to J. Gisborne: "The 'Epipsychidion' is a mystery; as to real flesh and blood, you know that I do not deal in those articles; you might as well go to a gin-shop for a leg of mutton, as expect anything human or earthly from me. . . . Some of us have, in a prior existence, been in love with an Antigone, and that makes us find no full content in any mortal tie. . . . I desired Ollier not to circulate this piece except to the initiated (συνετοί), and even they, it seems, are inclined to approximate me to the circle of a servant-girl and her sweetheart. But I intend to write a symposium of my own to set all this right." A little later, in 1822, when his passion for Emilia had passed away, and when, too, that part of himself which is expressed in the

"Epipsychidion" had passed away also, he wrote to Gisborne:

The "Epipsychidion" I cannot look at; the person whom it celebrates was a cloud instead of a Juno; and poor Ixion starts from the Centaur that was the offspring of his own embrace. If you are curious, however, to hear what I am and have been, it will tell you something thereof. It is an idealised history of my life and feelings. I think one is always in love with something or other; the error—and I confess it is not easy for spirits cased in flesh and blood to avoid it—consists of seeking in a mortal image the likeness of what is perhaps eternal.

There can be no mistake, the "Epipsychidion" is to its author merely the history of disappointment in his search for ideal beauty, of which he has caught a glimpse in the created beauty that has at various times detained him in his flight towards the uncreated and the eternal. In Shelley, love, as an emotion of the soul, cannot be satisfied with one object only; everything beautiful in Art, in Nature, in humanity, and especially in woman, is his own; he loves a woman as he loves the sun, the cloud, the song of the lark or nightingale, the "Niobe" or the "Apollo," the "Antigone" of Sophocles, or the "Two Heavenly Lovers" of Calderon. From Harriet

Grove to Emilia Viviani, that which he sings of with rapture, is Love itself; his only Muse, his one God. In order to appreciate the "Epipsychidion," it must be read in the same spirit as the "Vita Nuova" of Dante, or Shakespeare's Sonnets.

The romance of Emilia ends for Shelley as other romances had ended. We have seen the estimation in which he held her, so soon as the commonplace realities of life robbed him of the gracious phantom of his own fascinated imagination.

Mary writes to Mrs. Gisborne on March 7th, 1822 :

Emilia has married Biondi ; we hear that she leads him and his mother (to use a vulgarism) a devil of a life. The conclusion of our friendship (*a la Italiana*) puts me in mind of a nursery rhyme which runs thus :

> As I was going down Cranbourne Lane,
>   Cranbourne Lane was dirty,
> And there I met a pretty maid
>   Who dropt to me a curtsey.
> I gave her cakes, I gave her wine,
>   I gave her sugar-candy ;
> But oh ! the little naughty girl,
>   She asked me for some brandy.

Now turn "Cranbourne Lane" into Pisan acquaintances, which I am sure are dirty enough, and "brandy" into that wherewithal to buy brandy (and that no small sum, *per.*), and you have the whole story of Shelley's Italian Platonics.

Emilia Viviani came to a sad and gloomy end. Medwin thus describes her last days; he had come across Pacchiani several years afterwards in Florence, who one day said to him mysteriously :

"I will introduce you to an old friend—come with me," and he conducted me to a country house in the suburbs. The villa was in great disrepair. The court leading to it, overgrown with weeds, proved that it had been for some years untenanted. An old woman led us through a number of long passages and rooms, many of the windows in which were broken, and let in the cold blasts from "the wind-swept Apennines;" and opening at length a door, ushered us into a chamber, where a small bed and a couple of chairs formed the entire furniture. The couch was covered with white gauze curtains to exclude the gnats; behind them was lying a female form. She immediately recognised me —was probably prepared for my visit—and extended her thin hand to me in greeting. So changed that recumbent figure, that I could scarcely recognise a trace of the once beautiful Emilia. Shelley's evil augury had been fulfilled, she had found in her marriage all that he had predicted ; for six years she led a life of purgatory, and had at length broken the chain with the consent of her father, who had lent her this long disused and dilapidated *campagne.* I might fill many a page by speaking of the tears she shed over the memory of Shelley—but enough—she did not long enjoy her freedom. Shortly after this interview she was confined to her bed ; the seeds of *malaria*, which had been sown in the Maremma, combined with that all-irremediable malady, broken-heartedness, brought on a rapid consumption.

The old-woman, who had been her nurse, made me a long narration of her last moments, as she wept bitterly. I wept too when I thought of Shelley's Psyche, and his "Epipsychidion."

Happily for Shelley, amid all such disappointments in platonic love, "his mistress Urania," as he named poetical inspiration, remained true to him.

A pamphlet by his friend Peacock gave him an opportunity of breaking a lance in her honour early in 1821.

Peacock's article, which appeared in Ollier's *Literary Miscellany*, 1820, was a clever attack on poetry and poets. He gave a rapid sketch of " The Four Ages of Poetry," the age of iron, the age of gold, the age of silver, and the age of brass, which recur in regular succession from the times of Homer to those of Nonnus, and from the times of the Troubadours to those of Wordsworth. He maintained that the poetry of primitive ages (periods during which there are—if we except the priesthood, which always flourishes—only three flourishing trades : those of the king, the thief, and the beggar) was but the hyperbolical panegyric of the exploits and wealth of a restricted number of predominant individuals. The strongest part of the pamphlet was its satire on the modern age of brass—that is, on the contemporary poets, or the Lake School, or "Returners to Nature," as he amusingly dubs them.

The conclusion drawn by Peacock was that poetry is suitable to the childhood of nations, but is not fit for their maturity, and that to treat it seriously is as absurd as for a grown man to rub his gums with a coral, or to be hushed to sleep with the tinkle of silver bells. He made no exception even for moral poetry, which consists, he says, in tearful and egoistical rhapsodies, expressive of the writer's extreme dislike of the world and all it contains.

Such a satire moved Shelley to both indignation and amusement. While sharing to a certain extent Peacock's criticisms on the Bavii and Mævii of the day, he could not admit that poetry herself was responsible for the rhymes of Barry Cornwall, "this stuff in *terza, ottava,* and *tremillesima rima,*" whose earthly baseness had drawn down the lightning of his friend's undiscriminating censure "upon the temple of immortal song" itself.

"Your anathemas against poetry itself," writes Shelley (February 15th, 1821), "excited me to a sacred rage, or *caloëthes* scribendi* of vindicating the insulted Muses. I had the greatest possible desire to break a lance with you within the lists of a magazine, in honour of my mistress, Urania ; but God willed that I should be too lazy, and wrested the victory from your hope ; since first having unhorsed poetry, and the universal sense of the wisest in all ages, an easy conquest would have remained to you in me, the knight of the shield of shadow and the lance of gossamere. Besides, I was at that moment reading Plato's 'Ion,' which I recommend you to reconsider."

An attack of ophthalmia prevented Shelley from immediately setting to work ; but by the month of March, 1821, he had completed the first part of his admirable "Defence of Poetry," which may justly be described as "the song of the swan."

Another lady besides Emilia soon appeared at Pisa to exercise a powerful charm over the poet.

In the beginning of 1821, Shelley made the acquaintance of Edward Williams and his wife. The young couple had come direct from Geneva to Italy for the express purpose of knowing Shelley

---

* *Caloëthes,* the *contrary* of *cacoëthes,* Dowden explains.

personally ; Medwin having described him as a
most marvellous phenomenon. Edward Williams
was the descendant of one of Cromwell's daughters,
and had been a schoolfellow of Shelley at Eton ;
he had served in the navy, and had subsequently
travelled in India with Medwin. He was frank,
loyal, generous, brave, passionately fond of the
sea and of navigation, something of a· poet,
possessed real dramatic talent,* and was therefore
well adapted to win Shelley's affection. Mrs.
Williams realised the feminine ideal he had
essayed to describe in the " Sensitive Plant."
Her sweet and simple nature, the elegance of her
movements, and her gracious manners compensated in Shelley's eyes for any want of literary
culture, while her proficiency in music, her harp
and guitar playing were a new and hitherto
unknown delight to Shelley. He had hardly
known her an hour when he loved her. In several
exquisite little poems† he has expressed his tender

---

* Shelley wrote an epithalamium, to be set to music, for
one of his plays on a subject from Boccaccio.

† See "Lines to Edward Williams," "The Magnetic
Lady to her Patient," "To Jane—The Invitation," "To
Jane—The Recollection," "With a Guitar, to Jane," "To
Jane."

affection for this lady; he compares her to Miranda, and elects himself to be her Ariel. Thenceforth Shelley and Williams were never parted, not even in death.

Among the most frequent guests at the Casa Aulla, was a personage who interested Shelley in more ways than one, but more especially because he represented the sacred cause of freedom for the poet's true mother-country, Greece. He writes to Peacock, on the 21st March, 1821:

We have made a very interesting acquaintance with a Greek Prince, perfectly acquainted with ancient literature, and full of enthusiasm for the liberties and improvement of his country. Mary has been a Greek student for several months, and is reading "Antigone" with our turbaned friend, who, in return, is taught English.

This turbaned friend was Prince Mavrocordato, one of the survivors of the Wallachian insurrection, who had taken refuge in Italy. It was a piece of good fortune for the exiled Greek, and for the cause of Hellenic independence, to meet the poet who was about to take the interests of awakening Greece so warmly to heart, and to sing with heroic enthusiasm and prophetic inspiration, the defeat of the Crescent and the triumph of Hellas.

Shelley knew little of the modern Greeks, except from the historical novel of "Anastasius ;"* he saw in them only the heirs of the Hellenic name and glory, "the descendants of the nation to which we owe our civilisation." He believed that, though degraded by misfortune and slavery, their natural characteristics were a pledge of the future, and doubted not that a change in the political situation would bring about their complete regeneration.

All public attention is now centred on the wonderful revolution in Greece. I dare not, after the events of last winter, hope that slaves can become freemen so cheaply ; yet I know one Greek of the highest qualities, both of courage and conduct—the Prince Mavrocordato—and if the rest be like him, all will go well.

Some months later he was at Leghorn with his friend Trelawney, who took him over the docks, where men of all the nations of the world were congregated together, and showed him the

* "Anastasius ; or, Memoirs of a Greek," written at the end of the eighteenth century. Three vols., 1819 ; by Thomas Hope.

modern Greeks he had just glorified in his "Hellas."

"I hear their shrill nasal voices," said Trelawney, as they approached the Greek vessel they were about to visit, "and should like to know if you can trace in the language or lineaments of these Greeks of the nineteenth century A.D., the faintest resemblance to the lofty and sublime spirits who lived in the fourth century B.C. An English merchant who has dealings with them, told me he thought these modern Greeks were, if judged by their actions, a cross between the Jews and the Gipsies."

Shelley and Trelawney, while thus conversing, had ascended the *San-Spiridione,* where they found the Greeks huddled in little groups on the bridge, shouting, gesticulating, smoking, eating, and playing, like savages. "Does this realise your idea of Hellenism?" asked Trelawney. "No, but it does of Hell," answered Shelley. Still worse was it when he heard Captain Zarita speak; the latter offered them pipes and coffee in his cabin—under a niche with an image of St. Spiridion, before which a lamp burned—and told them he disapproved of war because it interrupted trade. "Come away," said Shelley; "there is not a drop of the old Hellenic blood here. These are not the men to rekindle the ancient Greek fire ; their souls are extinguished by traffic and superstition. Come away!"

It was not possible to Shelley to move among the realities of life without the infliction of constant pain on his own ideal; and he withdrew from the world principally with the object of avoiding a contact involving disenchantment. It may be that we should never have possessed " Hellas," had Shelley spoken with Captain Zarita a few months earlier.

The companionship of Prince Mavrocordato awoke in him all his Greek sympathies. The Prince communicated to him in April the proclamation just issued by his cousin Ypsilanti ; on that day Shelley conceived " Hellas," and ordered two seals to be engraved with the device of a dove with outspread wings surrounded by this motto : " Μάντις ειμ ἔρθλῶν ἀγώνων." The same motto became the epigraph of the drama.

It was fitting that Shelley's last complete work should be a hymn in honour of liberty and of the glorious country of Homer, Æschylus, and Plato. But his enthusiasm for the past did not prevent him from taking a clear view of European politics, and of the action of the great Powers in a conflict involving the destinies of the world. He severely blamed the interested and selfish policy of England; and indicated the only proper course to be taken by a nation regardful of the rights of peoples and of her own dignity: this should be to support the independence of Greece, instead of incurring the indelible stain of a monstrous alliance "with the enemies of domestic happiness, of Christianity, and of civilisation."

One cannot read " Hellas " without being struck with its likeness to the " Persæ " of Æschylus. The dramatic interest is equally simple, grand, and terrible in both. The coming of successive messengers of evil, the evocation of Mahomet II. by Ahasuerus, the despair of Mahmud, the admirable contrast between the choruses of Greek and Turkish slaves—these almost transport us to the stage of Athens. But there is a moral and philosophical atmosphere in Shelley's drama which we do not find in Æschylus, lifting it far above the actual facts on which it is grounded; there is an inspired presentiment of the final triumph of the Hellenic or Promethean spirit over all religious fanaticism and social tyranny. By a marvellous stroke of genius he makes Mahmud himself the mouthpiece of this prophecy ; and in Mahmud is incarnate not only the melancholy belonging to the decline of a great but decaying power, but the deeper and more human melancholy of a mind awakened by adversity to great thoughts on the fragility of human things, and to the revelations of the ever-present, ever-subsisting spirit personified in Ahasuerus.

There is a strange grandeur in this mixture of the real and the ideal, of history and vision, which lifts us far above the narrow scene of action, to the remotest spheres of thought and imagination. All through "Hellas" we feel ourselves in presence of a still higher and vaster conception, which the poet had at first intended to realise, but which he relinquished in order to strike the popular imagination quickly and forcibly. Though "Hellas" did not obtain its rightful meed of fame in London, the poet, had he lived, would have been consoled for the injustice of his fellow-countrymen, by its effect on Lord Byron. "It is impossible to express," says Medwin, "the influence exercised on Byron by that drama, and by Shelley's enthusiasm, when he resolved to devote himself to the cause of Greece." Shelley needed keen intellectual excitement to counteract the moral and physical exhaustion induced at intervals by ill-health and financial difficulties. But the return of fine weather, and the delight of boating, contributed to his rapid restoration. He had now a boat of his own, a boat that held three persons, "a little nautilus-shell," he called it, with which he navigated the rushing Arno, or the Serchio, to the great alarm of Italian onlookers.

This period of tranquillity was only broken by an excursion to Florence, and a short visit to Lord Byron, at Ravenna, in August.

Shelley found him transformed by his passion for the Countess Guiccioli, which had rescued him from the wretched excesses into which he had fallen through pride and indifference rather than from choice, in excellent health, and immersed in politics and literature.

Shelley had barely arrived when Byron hastened to communicate to him a monstrous and shameful story that had been told him by the Hoppners, and which out of hatred to Claire, his former mistress, he was not unwilling to believe. Claire was said to have been Shelley's mistress while at Naples, and to have borne him a child which he had sent to the Foundling Hospital. The authors of the calumny were Shelley's former servants, Elise and Paolo, who thus revenged themselves for their dismissal. Shelley was greatly hurt to think that his highly valued friends the Hoppners could for a moment have believed so shameful a story. He begged his wife to write to the Hoppners, refuting the charge which she "only can effectually rebut." Mary at once wrote as Shelley asked her, a letter full of the most eloquent indignation, as well as the deepest affection for her husband:

That my beloved Shelley should stand thus slandered in your minds—he, the gentlest and most humane of creatures—is more painful to me, oh, far more painful than words can express! Need I say that the union between my husband and myself has ever been undisturbed? Love caused our first imprudence; love which, improved by esteem, a perfect trust one in the other, a confidence and affection which, visited as we have been by severe calamities (have we not lost two children?), has increased daily and knows no bounds.

Shelley handed this letter to Lord Byron, who undertook to forward it to the Hoppners with comments of his own, but he failed to do so, and the letter was found among Byron's papers after his death.

Very different was Shelley's zeal for and in all that concerned his friend. La Guiccioli was desirous of removing to Switzerland in order to extricate herself from the difficulties of her position in Italy, and Shelley, at Byron's request, tasked himself to write her a long letter in Italian advising her to stay where she was; "an odd thing enough for an utter stranger to write on subjects of the utmost delicacy to his friend's mistress," he writes to Mary. "But it seems destined that I am always to have some active part in everybody's affairs whom I approach. I have set down in lame Italian, the strongest reasons I can think of against the Swiss emigration. To tell you the truth, I should be very glad to accept as my fee, his establishment in Tuscany."

Shelley's "lame Italian" was eloquent enough to detain the Countess in Italy, and as a reward for her docility she asks of him a favour: "Do not leave Ravenna without Milord." It was arranged that Byron should join Shelley at Pisa.

During Shelley's stay at Ravenna he visited the

curious antiquities of that ancient city, and "looked with a certain interest at the tomb of Theodoric and the Mausoleum of Galla Placidia ;" but cared little for the beauty of its mosaics and symbolic sculptures.   He wandered through the gloomy pine-forest that separates Ravenna from the sea, wherein Dante meditated, and Byron, at the request of La Guiccioli, composed his "Prophecy of Dante."   Nor did he neglect the tomb of the great Ghibeline.   "I have seen Dante's tomb," he writes to Mary, "and worshipped the sacred spot."

But more than aught else at Ravenna, Lord Byron himself and the progress of his genius was interesting to Shelley.

He has read to me one of the unpublished cantos of "Don Juan," which is astonishingly fine.   It sets him not only above, but far above, all the poets of the day—every word has the stamp of immortality.   I despair of rivalling Lord Byron—as well I may—and there is no other with whom it is worth contending.   This canto (5th) is totally in the style, and sustained with incredible ease and power, of the end of the second canto.   There is not a word which the most rigid asserter of the dignity of human nature could desire to be cancelled.   It fulfils, in a certain degree, what I have long preached of producing—something wholly new and relative to the age, and yet surpassingly beautiful.   It may be vanity, but I think I see the trace of my earnest exhortations to him to create something wholly new.

The unreserved admiration felt by Shelley for Byron, discouraged him, perhaps, more than any other cause from writing. He was bitten by the desire for fame.

" I write nothing," he tells Peacock, "and probably shall write no more. It offends me to see my name classed among those who have no name. . . . I had rather be nothing. . . . And the accursed cause to the downfall of which I dedicated what powers I may have had—flourishes like a cedar, and covers England with its boughs. My motive was never the infirm desire of fame ; and if I should continue an author, I feel that I should desire it. The cup is justly given to one only of an age ; indeed, participation would make it worthless ; and unfortunate they who seek it and find it not."

Yet although Shelley thus allowed himself to be dazzled by the splendour of Byron's genius, he felt that there lay between them an abyss that the most sincere admiration could not bridge. Byron's selfishness and pride closed all the avenues of his heart. And with deep melancholy Shelley says :

Lord Byron and I are excellent friends, and were I reduced to poverty, or were I a writer who had no claims to an higher station than I possess—or did I possess an higher than I deserve—we should appear in all things as such, and I would freely ask him any favour. Such is not now the case. The demon of mistrust and pride lurks between two persons in our situation, poisoning the freedom of our intercourse. This is a tax, and a heavy one, which we must pay for being human. I think the fault is not on my side, nor is it likely, I being the weaker. I hope that in the next world these things will be better managed. What is passing in the heart of another rarely escapes the observation of one who is a strict anatomist of his own.

So just an appreciation of Byron's character, and of the moral obstacles to perfect friendship with him, was due in great measure to the reserve which Shelley had found to be necessary with regard to his friend Leigh Hunt, for whose benefit he had endeavoured, while staying at Ravenna, to promote with Byron's help a periodical to be called *The Liberal.* With Hunt he could speak openly, and in his disappointment at not finding Byron so generous and unselfish as himself he wrote to him as follows :

Particular circumstances, or rather, I should say, particular dispositions in Lord Byron's character, render the close and exclusive intimacy with him in which I find myself intolerable to me. Thus much, my best friend, I will confess and confide to you. No feelings of my own shall injure or interfere with what is now nearest to them— your interest ; and I will take care to preserve the little influence I may have over this Proteus in whom such strange extremes are reconciled.

On October 25th, Shelley left the Baths of San Giuliano, in order to join the Williamses at

Pisa, where he expected Byron. Immediately on arriving, he hired a spacious palazzo, and had it put in readiness for the noble poet. The building, it was said, was partly constructed after designs by Michael Angelo, and was called the Palazzo Lanfranchi; on its front, above a chain such as was worn by captives, were the words "Alla Giornata." La Guiccioli had arrived at Pisa before Byron, and was accompanied by her father and brother; "the lion's jackals," as Shelley called them. Shelley's own residence was on the Lung' Arno; he had taken a few rooms on the upper floor of the Tre Palazzi di Chiesa, from which there was a view of the country and the sea.*

There, among his books, and the clustering plants † he loved to cultivate, and which "for him changed sunny winter into spring," he resumed his tragedy of "Charles I.," which he purposed to make a still more artistic achievement than "The Cenci." Unfortunately, it was never completed.

---

* So says Dowden, but Rabbe says a view "of the *town* and its environs." Dowden says expressly, "*avoiding* the ill odours of the town," etc.

† See his poem entitled "Zucca."

Some considerable fragments, however, remain—entire scenes, truly Shakespearian in spirit. If we may trust Medwin, Shelley threw aside his work from a feeling of disgust, similar to that which prevented Michael Angelo from completing the bust of Brutus in the Florence Gallery, " disgust at treason." He could not forgive the murderers of Charles I., and shrank from painting the hypocritical tyrant Cromwell as a hero.

In Byron's company, Shelley forgot his grievances and his reserve, and abandoned himself to the fascination of a poet whose very faults were attractive, and whose brilliant and paradoxical conversation amused him, and brought his own qualities into play.

The two friends rarely passed a day without meeting, or practising pistol shooting.

A very interesting volume might be made of Shelley's and Byron's conversations as recounted by Medwin and Trelawney. The opposite characters of the two poets are shown in striking contrast ; the one, skipping from subject to subject, touching the surface only, with light banter and love of mystification (Shelley compared him in this to Voltaire) ; the other, serious and earnest,

oracular in speech, and following with contagious
warmth and the most persuasive sincerity the
sublime leadings of his imagination, or the subtlest
turns of the argument; yet able to pass, like
Raffaelle, when occasion served, "from grave to
gay, from lively to severe." Byron read every
day to Shelley what he had composed during
the night: either "Cain," that apocalyptic vision
and new revelation to humanity, or "Heaven and
Earth," one of his most polished productions
(Shelley loved to declaim the choruses of this
work, deeming them models of the lyrical style),
or "The Deformed Transformed," which of all
Byron's works Shelley liked the least. It is said
that Byron, enraged at his criticisms, threw the
manuscript into the fire; but if so, the poem
rose again from its ashes.

The merits of poets, ancient and modern, were
warmly discussed; Shelley enthusiastically de-
fending his favourite poets Dante and Shakespeare
from Byron's narrow and contemptuous criticism.
The dangerous subjects of philosophy and
religious metaphysics were often touched upon;
Byron took pleasure in rousing the irritable sus-
ceptibility of his friend "the Snake," as he called

him, on these points, laughing in his sleeve at the straightforward sincerity of his convictions.

One day in December, 1821, Shelley was informed that a man at Lucca had been condemned to be burnt alive for the crime of sacrilege. "The Spanish woman," as Byron calls her, "who has her petticoats thrown over Lucca, has just condemned a poor devil to the stake for stealing a wafer-box out of a church. Shelley and I were up in arms against this act of piety, and are disturbing everybody to get the sentence changed." In the first burst of indignation, Shelley proposed that Byron, Medwin, and he should rescue the offender at the moment of execution and place him in safety beyond the Tuscan frontier. Byron, less ardent, but more practical, suggested the more prudent proceeding of *representations*. Shelley accordingly wrote on the subject to Lord Guildford, the English Minister at Florence, and prepared a memorial to the Grand Duke. But Lord Guildford's intervention was effectual, and on December 13th Shelley wrote to Lord Byron :

" I hear this morning that the design . . . of burning my fellow-serpent has been abandoned, and that he has been condemned to the galleys."

Shelley had missed a grand opportunity of overturning the idols of the false gods, of extinguishing the flames, and of exclaiming with the hero of " The Revolt of Islam " :

" I am Laon ! "

CHAPTER X.

THE opening of the year 1822 had added to
the little English colony at Pisa a new member,
who very soon became one of Shelley's most
devoted friends and fervent admirers. This was
Edward John Trelawney. He was of a chivalrous
and adventurous nature; noble and generous;
ardent in his admiration of Shelley's intellect
and character; and holding him far superior to
Byron, he became a constant guest at Shelley's
rooms during this the last year of his life, and the
most disinterested and faithful of his biographers.*

"A kind of half-Arab Englishman," says Mrs. Shelley,
" whose life has been as changeful as that of Anastasius,

* " Records of Shelley, Byron, and the Author." London,
1878.

and who recounts the adventures of his youth as eloquently
and well as the imagined Greek. . . . He is six feet high ;
raven-black hair, which curls thickly and shortly like a
Moor's ; dark-gray expressive eyes ; overhanging brows ;
upturned lips, and a smile which expresses good-nature and
kind-heartedness . . . his language, as he relates the events
of his life, energetic and simple, whether the tale be one of
blood and horror or of irresistible comedy. His company is
delightful, for he excites me to think."

Shelley and his friends thought of writing
a play, or at the least a novel, founded on his adventurous life. In the "Fragments of an Un-
finished Drama," we have Trelawney idealised in
the character of the Pirate.

Trelawney gives a most amusing account of his
first interview with Shelley :

It was late when I arrived at Pisa, and after dining I
hurried to the Tre Palazzi on the Lung' Arno, where the
Shelleys and Williamses lived in the same house. The
Williamses received me in their earnest, cordial manner.
We had a great deal to communicate to each other, and
were in loud and animated conversation, when I was rather
put out by observing in the passage near the open door,
opposite to where I sat, a pair of glittering eyes steadily
fixed on mine; it was too dark to make out whom they
belonged to. With the acuteness of a woman Mrs.
Williams's eyes followed the direction of mine, and going to
the doorway she laughingly said : " Come in, Shelley ; it's
only our friend Tre just arrived." Swiftly gliding in, blush-

ing like a girl, a tall thin stripling held out both his hands ; and although I could hardly believe—as I looked at his flushed, feminine, and artless face—that it could be the poet, I returned his warm pressure. After the ordinary greetings and courtesies, he sat down and listened. I was silent from astonishment. Was it possible this mild-looking, beardless boy could be the veritable monster at war with all the world—excommunicated by the Fathers of the Church, deprived of his civil rights by the fiat of a grim Lord Chancellor, discarded by every member of his family, and denounced by the rival sages of our literature as the founder of a Satanic school? I could not believe it ; it must be a hoax.

It is difficult for the present generation even to conceive the acrid bigotry of fifty years ago.

He was habited like a boy, in a black jacket and trousers which he seemed to have outgrown. . . . Mrs. Williams saw my embarrassment, and to relieve me asked Shelley what book he had in his hand? " Calderon's *Magico Prodigioso*. I am translating some passages in it." " Oh! read it to us!" Shoved off from the shore of common-place incidents that could not interest him, and fairly launched on a theme that did, he instantly became ob-livious of everything but the book in his hand. The masterly manner in which he analysed the genius of the author, his lucid interpretation of the story, and the ease with which he translated into our language the most subtle and imaginative passages of the Spanish poet, were marvellous, as was his command of the two languages. After this touch of his quality, I no longer doubted his identity. A dead silence ensued. Looking up, I asked:

"'Where is he?'' Mrs. Williams said : '' Who ? Shelley? Oh! he comes and goes like a spirit, no one knows when or where.''

At the end of 1821, Shelley and Williams had conceived the idea of building a boat according to a model the latter had brought with him from England. Trelawney was consulted, and proposed an American schooner ; but Shelley and Williams persisted in their plan, and the construction of the boat was entrusted to Captain Roberts, a friend of Trelawney's at Genoa. The three friends had discussed it during the night of Jan. 15th, 1822. "Thus on that night," wrote Mrs. Shelley at a later period, "one of gaiety and thoughtlessness —Jane's and my miserable destiny was decided. We then said, laughing each to the other : 'Our husbands decide without asking our consent, or having our concurrence; for to tell you the truth, I hate this boat, though I say nothing.' Said Jane : 'So do I ; but speaking would be useless and only spoil their pleasure !' How well I remember that night! How short-sighted we are! And now that its anniversary is come and gone, methinks I cannot be the wretch I too truly am."

While waiting the arrival of the fatal boat,

Shelley spent his leisure hours in translating from Calderon and Goethe; * he considered the *Magico Prodigioso* and *Faust* to be wonderfully alike, though he admitted the different genius of the two authors. Goethe seemed to him the greater philosopher and Calderon the greater poet.

Two vexatious incidents occurred in March to disturb the calm current of their life at Pisa.

The ground-floor of the building in which the Shelleys dwelt was used on Sundays as an Evangelical chapel, and Mary, out of compliance with public opinion, was occasionally present at the services and sermons. Dr. Nott, the learned editor of the poems of Surrey and Wyatt, was the preacher. On Sunday, March 3rd, Mary received a special invitation requesting her presence, and that morning's discourse consisted of an attack on Atheism, with several direct allusions to Mrs. Shelley, intended to warn her against the baleful influence of her husband's doctrines. The gossips and scandal-mongers were delighted—but Mary

* He found Calderon far less difficult to translate than Goethe; "only Coleridge," he said modestly, " is capable of translating Goethe." *Faust* has, since that time, been frequently translated into French, but never so well as by M. Camille Benoit in a book just published by Lemerre.

bitterly regretted having visited the *piano di sotto,* and longed for the sea-girt isle of which Shelley, sick of the wickedness of men, had spoken to her in his letters from Ravenna.

On another Sunday, March 24th, Byron, Shelley, Count Pietro Gamba, Captain Hay, and Taaffe, the translator of Dante, were returning from their evening ride, when a half-drunken dragoon rode through the midst of the group, jostling against the commentator of the " Divina Commedia." Byron and Shelley set off in pursuit of the ruffian, stopped him, demanded his name and address, and gave him their cards. Sergeant-Major Masi called to the guard, and began slashing right and left with his sword. Shelley was knocked off his horse, and would have been struck, but for the intervention of Captain Hay. Masi fled, and was severely wounded by one of Byron's *sbirri* (" I have some rough fellows in my service," he used to say), and taken to the hospital. This adventure made a great sensation at Pisa, and occasioned the most absurd rumours. At a later period it served the Government as one pretext among others for exiling Count Pietro Gamba.

These untoward incidents, which were made

more annoying through their exaggeration, determined Shelley on removing from Pisa, and seeking a retired spot far from the tongue of gossip and small scandals ; he was further impelled to this course by a desire to break off his superficial intimacy with Byron. He had visited the shores of the Bay of Spezzia a few months before, and had discovered a deserted building, Casa Magni, situated in melancholy solitude between the villages of Lerici and San Terenzo. It was a house of dull and severe aspect, built on cloister-like arches, which gave it the appearance of a convent, sheltered behind by a hill covered with dark forest trees, and overlooking the sea, which washed the very walls of the terrace. "The natives were even wilder than the place. Many a night they passed on the beach singing or rather howling ; the women dancing about among the waves that broke at their feet."

It was in trembling, and with a kind of dumb terror full of forebodings of evil, that Mary took possession of the lonely and comfortless house. "We might have been wrecked," she says, "on one of the South Sea Islands, and have felt no farther from all civilisation ; yet where there is sunshine, comfort becomes luxury, and our own society suffices us."

Shelley's delight was now perfect; he had almost found his solitary isle, and writes to his friend Smith: "As to me, like Anacreon's swallow, I have left my Nile, and have taken up my summer quarters here, in a lonely house close by the sea-side, surrounded by the soft and sublime scenery of the Gulf of Spezzia."

On May 12th, the fatal boat arrived. The inhabitants of Casa Magni were walking after dinner on the terrace when they descried a strange sail rounding the point of Porto Venere; it was the *Don Juan*, as Byron had christened her—a name soon changed by Shelley for that of the *Ariel.*

The enthusiastic poet insisted on trying her the very next day, eagerly seeking opportunities of matching her against the feluccas and other big craft in the bay. Williams, in his curious journal full of Shelley-worship, gives a detailed account of their daily adventurous expeditions to every point on the coast of Spezzia. Their feelings resembled those of Christopher Columbus when discovering the New World.

Our two sailors were in ecstasies over their boat; Williams as jealous of the *Ariel's* reputation as of his wife's; they could not tear themselves away from their plaything, and the Mediterranean soon seemed "too small and calm a lake on which to display her excellence." They dismissed the Genoese sailor engaged by Trelawney, retaining only an inexperienced lad, named Charles Vivian. Williams, who knew something of the sea, instructed Shelley how to handle a boat, "with as much anxiety," says the latter, "as a sparrow's over her cuckoo young."

" It was great fun," writes Trelawney, "to witness Williams teaching the poet how to steer, and other points of seamanship. As usual, Shelley had a book in his hand, saying he could read and steer at the same time, as one was mental, the other mechanical. . . . The boat on one occasion getting, as sailors express it, ' in irons,' Shelley's hat was knocked overboard, and he would probably have followed, if I had not held him. He was so uncommonly awkward, that when they had things ship-shape, Williams, somewhat scandalised at the lubberly manœuvre, blew up the poet for his neglect and inattention to orders. Shelley was, however, so happy, and in such high glee, and the nautical terms so tickled his fancy, that he even put his beloved ' Plato ' in his pocket, and gave his mind up to fun and frolic. ' You will do no good with Shelley,' I said, ' until you heave his books and papers overboard ; shear the wisps of hair that hang over his eyes ; and

plunge his arms up to the elbows in a tar-bucket.' Shelley
was often quite heedless of the boat, so intent was he on
catching images from the ever-changing sea and sky."

As the *Ariel* drew too much water to near
the shore, Williams, with the help of a carpenter,
had constructed a very small boat, of reeds and
tarred canvas, flat-bottomed, and so light as to
be easily carried by one person from the house
to the shore. This fragile toy delighted the poet ;
the slightest movement caused her to capsize, and
more than once Shelley was in real danger. But
he attributed this to the boat's unsteadiness,
rather than to any imprudence of his own. " I
see," he said, "why ships and boats are of the
feminine gender; it is because they are as perfidious
as women." On this subject, Trelawney relates
two anecdotes too characteristic to be omitted :

On a calm sultry evening, Jane was sitting on the sands
before the villa, on the margin of the sea, with her two
infants, and watching for her husband—he was becalmed in
the offing, awaiting the sea-breeze. Shelley came from the
house, dragging the skiff ; after launching her, he said to
Jane : " The sand and air are hot ; let us float on the cool,
calm sea ; there is room, with careful stowage, for us all in
my barge." His flashing eyes and vehement, eager manner
determined on the instant execution of any project that took
his fancy, however perilous. . . . So Jane impulsively and

promptly squatted in the bottom of the frail bark with her babies. She understood that Shelley intended to float on the water near the shore, where the sea is very shallow. A puff of wind, a ripple on the water, an incautious movement, and the tub of a thing must cant over. The poet presently, proud of his freight, triumphantly shoved off from the shore, and, to exhibit his skill as a mariner, rowed round a jutting promontory into deep blue water. There was no eye watching them, no boat within a mile, the shore fast receding, the water deepening, and the poet dreaming. As these dismal facts flashed on Jane's mind, her insane folly in trusting herself to a man of genius, but devoid of judgment, prudence, or skill, dismayed her. After pulling out a long way, the poet rested on his oars, unconscious of her fears, and apparently of where he was, absorbed in a deep reverie. . . . Spellbound with terror, Jane kept her eyes on the awful boatman, lost in his sombre melancholy. She made several remarks, but they met with no response.

Suddenly he raised his head; his brow cleared, and his face brightened as with a bright thought, and he exclaimed joyfully : " Now let us together solve the great mystery." Jane, understanding the danger she would run did she remain silent, or too brusquely rouse the poet from his ecstasy, answered in her usual cheerful voice : " No, thank you, not now ; I should like my dinner first, and so would the children." And seeing the poet shocked by this gross material answer to his sublime proposition, she continued : "And look, the sea-breeze is coming in, and the mist is clearing away ; we ought to go back—they will be anxious about us, and Edward says this boat is not safe." " Safe ! " said the poet ; " I'll go to Leghorn or anywhere in her." " You haven't yet written the words for the Indian air," Jane went on. " Yes, I have," he answered, " long ago. I must write them out again, for I can't read what I compose and write out of doors. You must play the air again, and I'll try and make the thing better."

In the meanwhile Shelley kept on rowing, and regained the shore without accident. Once again the demon of the deep, who watched his prey, had spread his wings and taken flight. Williams and Trelawney, both very anxious, waited for them on the shore. Jane jumped out so hurriedly that the punt and the poet capsized. Williams scolded her for this, telling her that if she had waited an instant he would have hauled up the boat. "No, thank you," she cried, still in excitement. "Oh, you do not know what a dreadful fate I have just escaped. Never will I put my foot in that horrid coffin! Solve the great mystery! Why, he is the greatest of all mysteries! You can form some notion of what other people will do, as they partake of our common nature—not what he will do! He is seeking after what we all avoid—death!" At dinner she ate nothing. "Ah! never put me in a boat with Shelley alone!" she repeated. The poet, hearing his name, glided into the room, with his boyish face and radiant expression. He seized some bread and grapes, which he ate, while he read one of Calderon's dramas.

Another day there was some bustle in the house, as a distinguished stranger from Germany was coming to visit Shelley. The dinner was served without waiting for Shelley, and the stranger was telling them how the German students of English literature considered Shelley as the most philosophical of poets, a writer of transcendent imagination, surpassing all our popular poets in depth of thought and refinement. One of the party remarked that genius purifies ; the naked statues of the Greeks are modest, the draped ones of the moderns are not ; when all at once the ladies hid their faces in their hands in mute despair before a most unexpected apparition. It was Shelley, in the costume of a marine god, dripping with sea-water, his hair full of seaweed. Quite unmoved, he calmly explained his adventure. While taking his customary sea-dip, his skittish skiff had played him one of her usual tricks by upsetting all his clothes in the water, and he could not get to his room without crossing the dining-room, which at that hour was always vacant. A few minutes later he reappeared with a book in his hand, and said triumphantly : " I have recovered this priceless gem from the wreck ! " It was an Æschylus. He then took his place, unconscious of having done anything that could offend.

At the Casa Magni Shelley wrote even less than at Pisa; he gave an explanation of this to Smith, which is already known to us : " I have lived too long near Lord Byron, and the sun has extinguished the glow-worm; for I cannot hope with St. John, that 'the light came into the world, and the world knew it not." In his solitude, he was overcome from time to time by discouragement and melancholy ; and although he had no intention of suicide, he wished to have the possibility of escape at hand. He asked Trelawney to procure prussic acid for him. " My wish was serious," he wrote on June 18th, " and sprang from the desire of avoiding needless suffering. I need not tell you I have no intention of suicide at present, but I confess it would be a comfort to me to hold in my possession that golden key to the chamber of perpetual rest."

These were, however, but passing moods occasioned by despair at the deafness of the world to truths he would fain reveal. Melancholy was banished by the charm of his circle of friends, by Nature, by the sea, and by his boat, which dispersed these importunate clouds as by enchantment. On June 18th, he wrote to Gisborne:

You know my gross ideas of music, and will forgive me when I say that I listen the whole evening on our terrace to the simple melodies with excessive delight. I have a boat here ; it cost me eighty pounds, and reduced me to some difficulty in point of money. However, it is swift and beautiful, and appears quite a vessel. Williams is captain, and we drive along this delightful bay in the evening wind, under the summer moon, until earth appears another world. Jane brings her guitar, and if the past and the future could be obliterated, the present would content me so well that I could say with Faust to the passing moment, "Remain thou, thou art so beautiful !" Claire is with us, and the death of her child * seems to have restored her to tranquillity. Her character is somewhat altered. She is vivacious and talkative, and, though she teazes me sometimes, I like her. . . . Lord Byron, who is at Leghorn, has fitted up a splendid

---

* The little Allegra had just died at the Capuchin convent of Bagnacavallo, in the Romagna, where Byron had placed her.

vessel—a small schooner on the American model—and Trelawney is to be captain. How long the fiery spirit of our pirate will accommodate itself to the caprice of the poet remains to be seen. . . .

I write little now. It is impossible to compose except under the strong excitement of an assurance of finding sympathy in what you write. Imagine Demosthenes reciting a philippic to the waves of the Atlantic. Lord Byron is in this respect fortunate. He touched the chord to which a million hearts responded, and the coarse music which he produced to please them, disciplined him to the perfection to which he now approaches. I do not go on with "Charles I." I feel too little certainty of the future, and too little satisfaction with regard to the past to undertake any subject seriously and deeply. I stand, as it were, upon a precipice, which I have ascended with great, and cannot descend without greater peril, and I am content if the heaven above me is calm for the passing moment. . . . I have read several more of the plays of Calderon. *Los Dos Amantes del Cielo* is the finest, if I except one scene in the *Devocion de la Cruz*. I read Greek, and think about writing. I do not think much of ——— not admiring Metastasio ; the *nil admirari*, however justly applied, seems to me a bad sign in a young person. I had rather a pupil of mine had conceived a frantic passion for Marini himself, than that she had found out the critical defects of the most deficient author. When she becomes of her own accord full of genuine admiration for the finest scene in the " Purgatorio," or the opening of the " Paradiso," or some other neglected piece of excellence, hope great things.

There was but one subject besides literature that never failed to interest Shelley, viz. the triumph of truth and goodness in the

world. As it was his first, so was it his last
passion.

"It seems to me," he wrote to Horace Smith, "that
things have now arrived at such a crisis as requires every
man plainly to utter his sentiments on the inefficacy of the
existing religions, no less than political systems, for restrain-
ing and guiding mankind. Let us see the truth, whatever
that may be. The destiny of man can scarcely be so degraded that he was born only to die; and if such should be the
case, delusions, especially the gross and preposterous ones of
the existing religion, can scarcely be supposed to exalt it.
If every man said what he thought, it could not subsist a day.
But all, more or less, subdue themselves to the element that
surrounds them, and contribute to the evils they lament by
the hypocrisy that springs from them. England appears to
be in a desperate condition; Ireland still worse; and no
class of those who subsist on the public labour will be persuaded that *their* claims on it must be diminished. But the
Government must content itself with less in taxes, the
landholder must submit to receive less rent, and the fund-
holder a diminished interest, or they will all get nothing, or
something worse than nothing. I once thought to study
these affairs, and write or act in them. I am glad that my
good genius said '*refrain*.' I see little public virtue, and I
foresee that the contest will be one of blood and gold; two
elements which, however much to my taste in my pockets
and my veins, I have an objection to out of them. . . . I still
inhabit this divine bay, reading Spanish dramas, and sailing
and listening to the most enchanting music. We have some
friends on a visit to us, and my only regret is that the
summer must ever pass, or that Mary has not the same
predilection for this place that I have, which would induce
me never to shift my quarters."

In this last letter we seem to have Shelley's last will, in a political and religious sense; his thoughts may perhaps be more lucid, wider, purer, and more elevated, but they are essentially the same as in "Queen Mab."

A curious parallel might be drawn between Shelley's first poem and his last, "The Triumph of Life." One is the embryo, the other is the full bloom of his genius.

He had passed from the inspiration of the eighteenth-century philosophers to that of Plato and Dante. The imitation of the "Divina Commedia," even in the rhythm (*rima terza*) is manifest. Virgil, "whose modesty led him to affect to copy others, though he created afresh all that he copied," was no longer the poet's guide in that marvellous vision; but in his place was a genius of later times, a prose-poet, who has also lifted part of the veil of Nature and Futurity—Rousseau. Struck by the strange pageantry of the mysterious chariot and the still more mysterious Shape it bore along, the poet asks its meaning, and a voice answers, "Life!" It is the voice of Rousseau, whom the poet recognises under the fantastic and Dantesque appari-

tion of an old root growing with strange distortion
out of the hill-side. Shelley has never mingled
with more pathetic art the fantastic creations
of his brain and the living realities around him,
incorporated with his dream. The very form is
Dantesque :

> O Heaven, have mercy on such wretchedness !
> That what I thought was an old root which grew
> To strange distortion out of the hill-side,
> Was, indeed, one of those deluded crew,
>
> And that the grass which methought hung so wide,
> And white, was but his thin, discoloured hair ;
> And that the holes it vainly sought to hide
> Were, or had been, eyes.

Then, passing in single file before the poet,
come Napoleon, Voltaire, Frederick, Catherine
and Leopold, Plato, Alexander, and his master
Aristotle, Bacon; the flood of ages and of men,
all the contrasts, all the contradictions, all the
riddles of life. We can only guess what would
have been Shelley's interpretation of those contradictions and riddles by the revelations of his
other poems. The vision breaks off at that
terrible inquiry which sums up all Shelley's
doubts, quests, and aspirations : *" Then what is*

Life?" Death soon solved his doubts by opening to him its infinite horizon of peace and immortality.

He seems to have had a distinct presentiment of approaching death when he penned the following poignant lines (1822) :

> When the lamp is shattered,
>   The light in the dust lies dead ;
> When the cloud is scattered,
>   The rainbow's glory is shed ;
> When the lute is broken,
>   Sweet notes are remembered not;
> When the lips have spoken,
>   Loved accents are soon forgot.

Towards the end of June, 1822, Leigh Hunt, the long-expected friend and guest, at last arrived, accompanied by his wife and seven children. Through Shelley's care, apartments had been prepared for him in Byron's palace at Pisa. So soon as Shelley heard of his friend's arrival at Leghorn, he and Williams put to sea on board the *Ariel*, freshly done up, "to make the port of Leghorn in good style," as Shelley said. Leigh Hunt's eldest son, Thornton Hunt, describes, in his interesting Memoir,* the affec-

* *The Atlantic Monthly*, February, 1863.

tionate emotion with which the friends met again in Italy:

Some years elapsed between the night when I saw Shelley pack up his pistols—which he allowed me to examine—for his departure for the South, and the moment when, after our own arrival in Italy, my attention was again called to his presence, by the shrill sound of his voice as he rushed into my father's arms, which he did with an impetuosity and fervour scarcely to be imagined by any one who did not know the intensity of his feelings, and the deep nature of his affection for that friend. I remember his crying out that he was " so *inexpressibly* delighted ! you cannot think how *inexpressibly* happy it makes me !"

He endeavoured, however, to express his happiness in a piece of verse, the last he ever wrote, which unfortunately has been lost. He accompanied the Hunts to Pisa, in order to see them comfortably settled in the Lanfranchi Palace, and to make final arrangements about the *Liberal*. Byron, meanwhile, had allowed himself to be persuaded by his English friends, Moore in particular, that the projected periodical would be prejudicial both to his fame and his interests; and it was against the grain that he prepared to join in a venture that seemed to Moore to court bankruptcy. Shelley, therefore, found him disinclined to fulfil his engagement, and was deeply disappointed. He was aware that Byron thought too slightingly of Hunt's character as well as of his talents, for any lasting agreement between them ; and as he had not forgiven him his treatment of Claire, neither could he forgive him now for not sharing his own generous feelings towards his friend.

A serious misunderstanding might have arisen between Byron and Shelley, had not the latter been bent on conciliation in the interests of Hunt himself.

But Shelley was acutely sensitive in all that regarded friendship, and his last days were saddened by these difficulties.

A deep melancholy pervades his last letters from Pisa and Leghorn; they seem to forebode the final catastrophe. On July 4th he writes to Jane Williams from Pisa :

You will probably see Williams before I can disentangle myself from the affairs with which I am now surrounded. I return to Leghorn to-night, and shall urge him to sail with the first fair wind without expecting me. I have thus the pleasure of contributing to your happiness when deprived of every other, and of leaving you no other subject of regret, but the absence of one scarcely worth regretting. I fear you are solitary and melancholy at Villa Magni, and, in the

intervals of the greater and more serious distress in which I
am compelled to sympathise here, I figure to myself the
countenance which has been the source of such consolation
to me, shadowed by a veil of sorrow.

How soon those hours past, and how slowly they return,
to pass so soon again, and perhaps for ever, in which we
have lived together so intimately and happily! Adieu, my
dearest friend. I only write these lines for the pleasure of
tracing what will meet your eyes. Mary will tell you all the
news.

PISA, *July 4th*, 1822.

MY DEAREST MARY,

. . . Things are in the worst possible situation with
respect to poor Hunt. I found Marianne in a desperate state
of health, and on our arrival at Pisa, sent for Vaccà. He
decides that her case is hopeless, and that although it will
be lingering, must inevitably end fatally. . . . This intelligence has extinguished the last spark of poor Hunt's spirits,
low enough before. . . . Lord Byron is at this moment on
the point of leaving Tuscany. The Gambas have been exiled,
and he declares his intention of following their fortunes. . . .
Trelawney is here, without instructions, moody and disappointed. But it is the worst for poor Hunt, unless the present
storm should blow over . . . he arrived here, with no other
remnant of his £400 than a debt of sixty crowns. Lord
Byron must of course furnish the requisite funds at present,
as I cannot; but he seems inclined to depart without the
necessary explanations and arrangements due to such a
situation as Hunt's . . . he offers him the copyright of the
'Vision of Judgment' for his first number. This offer, if
sincere, is *more* than enough to set up the journal, a   if
sincere, will set everything right:

· How are you, my best Mary? Write especially how is your health, and how your spirits are, and whether you are not more reconciled to staying at Lerici, at least during the summer. You have no idea how I am hurried and occupied ; I have not a moment's leisure, but will write by next post.

Ever, dearest Mary,
Yours affectionately,
S.

I have found the translation of the symposium.

Jane Williams replied to Shelley's melancholy note by one still more melancholy, in which, after expressing her anxiety at the continued absence of *Neddino* (her husband), she added in a post-script a question to which the event afterwards gave so tragic a reply : " Why do you say you may never enjoy such happy moments again ? Are you going to join your friend Plato ? "

On July 8th, Shelley and Williams decided on leaving Leghorn, and set sail for Lerici. We can have no better informed or more sympathetic narrator of the terrible catastrophe that followed than the widow of the poet.

" Having heard that Hunt had left Genoa," she writes a few days after the event (15th August) to Mrs. Gisborne, "Shelley, Edward, and Captain Roberts departed in our boat for Leghorn to receive him. I was then just better, had

begun to crawl from my bedroom to the terrace ; but bad
spirits succeeded to ill health, and this departure of Shelley's
seemed to add insufferably to my misery. I could not endure
that he should go. I called him back two or three times,
and told him that if I did not see him soon I would go to
Pisa with the child. I cried bitterly when he went away.
They went, and Jane, Claire, and I remained alone with the
children. I could not walk out, and though I gradually
gathered strength, it was slowly, and my ill spirits increased.
In my letters to him I entreated him to return—'the feeling
that some misfortune would happen,' I said, 'haunted me.'
I feared for the child ; for the idea of danger connected with
him never struck me. When Jane and Claire took their
evening walk, I used to patrol the terrace, oppressed with
wretchedness, yet gazing on the most beautiful scene in the
world. . . . I had a letter or two from Shelley mentioning
the difficulties he had in establishing the Hunts, and that he
was unable to fix the time of his return. Thus a week passed.
On Monday, 8th, Jane had a letter from Edward, dated
Saturday ; he said that he waited at Leghorn for Shelley,
who was at Pisa ; that Shelley's return was certain ; 'but,' he
continued, 'if he should not come by Monday, I will come
in a felucca, and you may expect me Tuesday evening at
furthest.'

"This was Monday, the fatal Monday, but with us it
was stormy all day, and we did not at all suppose that
they could put to sea. At twelve at night we had a
thunderstorm. Tuesday it rained all day, and was calm
(the sky wept on their graves). On Wednesday the wind
was fair from Leghorn, and in the evening several feluccas
arrived thence. One brought word that they had sailed
Monday, but we did not believe them. Thursday was
another day of fair wind ; and when twelve at night came,
and we did not see the tall sails of the little boat double the
promontory before us, we began to fear, not the truth, but

some illness—·some disagreeable news for their detention. Jane got so uneasy that she determined to proceed the next day to Leghorn in a boat to see what was the matter. Friday came, and with it a heavy sea and bad wind; Jane, however, resolved to be rowed to Leghorn, since no boat could sail, and busied herself in preparations. I wished her to wait for letters, since Friday was letter-day. She would not, but the sea detained her; the swell rose so that no boat would venture out. At twelve at noon our letters came. There was one from Hunt to Shelley; it said, 'Pray write to tell us how you got home, for they say that you had bad weather after you sailed Monday, and we are anxious.' The paper fell from me; I trembled all over. Jane read it. 'Then it is all over!' she said. 'No, my dear Jane,' I cried, 'it is not all over; but this suspense is dreadful ! Come with me, we will go to Leghorn ; we will post to be swift and learn our fate.' We crossed to Lerici, despair in our hearts. They raised our spirits there by telling us that no accident had been heard of, and that it must have been known, etc. But still our fear was great, and, without resting, we posted to Pisa. It must have been fearful to see us —two poor, wild, aghast creatures—driving (like Matilda) towards the sea to learn if we were to be for ever·doomed to misery. I knew that Hunt was at Pisa at Lord Byron's house, but I thought that Lord Byron was at Leghorn. I settled that we should drive to Casa Lanfranchi, that I should get out and ask the fearful question of Hunt, 'Do you know anything of Shelley?' On entering Pisa the idea of seeing Hunt for the first time for four years under such circumstances, and asking him such a question, was so terrific to me that it was with difficulty that I prevented myself from going into con- vulsions—my struggles were dreadful. They knocked at the door, and some one called out '*chi è ?*' It was the Guiccioli's maid. Lord Byron was at Pisa ; Hunt was in bed ; so I was to see Lord Byron instead of him. This was a great relief to me ; I staggered upstairs ; the Guiccioli came to meet me smiling, while I could hardly say, ' Where is he—*Sapete alcuna cosa di Shelley ?* ' They knew nothing ; he had left Pisa on Sunday ; on Monday he had sailed ; there had been bad weather Monday afternoon ; more they knew not. Both Lord Byron and the lady have told me since that on that terrific evening I looked more like a ghost than a woman. Light seemed to emanate from my features ; my face was very white ; I looked like marble. Alas, I had risen almost from a bed of sickness for this journey. I had travelled all day ; it was now twelve at night, and we, refusing to rest, proceeded to Leghorn ; not in despair, no, for then we must have died, but with sufficient hope to keep up the agitation of the spirits which was all my life. It was past two in the morning when we arrived. They took us to the wrong inn. Neither Trelawney nor Captain Roberts were there, nor did we exactly know where they were, so we were obliged to wait until daylight. We threw ourselves dressed on our beds and slept a little, but at six o'clock we went to one or two inns to ask for one or the other of these gentlemen. We found Roberts at the ' Globe.' He came down to us with a face which seemed to tell us that the worst was true ; and here we learned all that had occurred during the week they had been absent from us, and under what circumstances they had departed on their return. Shelley had passed most of the time at Pisa arranging the affairs of the Hunts and screwing Lord Byron's mind to the sticking-place about the journal. He had found this a difficult task at first, but at length he had succeeded to his heart's content with both points. Mrs. Mason said that she saw him in better health and spirits than she had ever known him, when he took leave of her Sunday, July 7th, his face burnt by the sun, and his heart light that he had succeeded in rendering the Hunts tolerably comfortable. Edward had remained at Leghorn.

On Monday, July 8th, during the morning, they were employed in buying many things, eatables, etc., for our solitude. There had been a thunderstorm early, but about noon the weather was fine, and the wind right fair for Lerici. They were impatient to be gone. Roberts said, 'Stay until to-morrow, to see if the weather is settled'; and Shelley might have stayed, but Edward was in so great an anxiety to reach home—saying they would get there in seven hours with that wind—that they sailed, Shelley being in one of those extravagant fits of good spirits in which you have sometimes seen him. Roberts went out to the end of the mole, and watched them out of sight. They sailed at one, and went off at the rate of about seven knots. About three, Roberts, who was still on the mole, saw wind coming from the gulf, or rather what the Italians call a *temporale*. Anxious to know how the boat would weather the storm, he got leave to go up the tower, and with the glass discovered them about ten miles out at sea, off Via Reggio; they were taking in their topsails. 'The haze of the storm,' he said, 'hid them from me, and I saw them no more. When the storm cleared I looked again, fancying that I should see them on their return to us; but there was no boat on the sea.' This, then, was all we knew; yet we did not despair. They might have been driven over to Corsica, and not knowing the coast, and gone God knows where. Reports favoured this belief. It was even said that they had been seen in the Gulf. We resolved to return with all possible speed. We sent a courier to go from tower to tower along the coast to know if anything had been seen or found, and at 9 a.m. we quitted Leghorn, stopped but one moment at Pisa, and proceeded towards Lerici. When at two miles from Via Reggio, we rode down to that town to know if they knew anything. Here our calamity first began to break on us. A little boat and a water-cask had been found five miles off; they had manufactured a *piccolissima lancia* of thin planks, stitched by a shoemaker, just to let them run on shore without wetting themselves, as our boat drew four feet water. The description of that found tallied with this ; but then this boat was very cumbersome, and in bad weather they might have been easily led to throw it overboard. The cask frightened me most, but the same reason might in some sort be given for that. I must tell you that Jane and I were not now alone : Trelawney accompanied us back to our home. We journeyed on, and reached the Magra about half-past 10 p.m. I cannot describe to you what I felt in the first moment when, fording this river, I felt the water splash about our wheels. I was suffocated, I gasped for breath ; I thought I should have gone into convulsions, and I struggled violently that Jane might not perceive it. Looking down the river, I saw the two great lights burning at the *foce*. A voice from within me seemed to cry aloud, 'That is his grave !' After passing the river I gradually recovered. Arriving at Lerici, we were obliged to cross our little bay in a boat. San Arenzo was illuminated for a festa. What a scene ! The waving sea, the sirocco wind, the lights of the town towards which we rowed, and our own desolate hearts, that coloured all with a shroud. We landed. Nothing had been heard of them. This was Saturday, July 13th. And thus we waited until Thursday, July 25th, thrown about by hope and fear. We sent messengers along the coast towards Genoa, and to Via Reggio. Nothing had been found more than the *lancetta;* reports were brought to us—we hoped—and yet to tell you all the agony we endured during those twelve days, would be to make you conceive a universe of pain—each moment intolerable, and giving place to one still worse. The people of the country, too, added to one's discomfort. They are like wild savages ; on festas the men and women and children in different bands—the sexes always separate—pass the whole night in dancing on the sands close to our door, running into the sea, then back again, and screaming all the time one perpetual air—the most detestable in the world ; then the sirocco perpetually blew, and the sea for ever moaned their dirge. On Thursday, 25th, Trelawney left us to go to Leghorn, to see what was doing or what could be done. On Friday I was very ill, but as evening came on I said to Jane, 'If anything had been found on the coast, Trelawney would have returned to let us know. He has not returned, so I hope.' About seven o'clock p.m. he did return ; all was over, all was quiet now, they had been found washed on shore. Well ! all this was to be endured.

"Well, what more have I to say? The next day we returned to Pisa, and here we are still. Days pass away, one after another, and we live thus. We are all together; we shall quit Italy together. Jane must proceed to London; if letters do not alter my views I shall remain in Paris. Thus we live, seeing the Hunts now and then. Poor Hunt has suffered terribly as you may guess. Lord Byron is very kind to me, and comes with the Guiccioli to see me often. To-day—this day—the sun shining in the sky—they are gone to the desolate sea-coast to perform the last offices to their earthly remains, Hunt, Lord Byron, and Trelawney. The quarantine laws would not permit us to remove them sooner, and now only on condition that we burn them to ashes. That I do not dislike. His rest shall be at Rome beside my child, where one day I also shall join them. 'Adonais' is not Keats's, it is his own elegy—he bids you there go to Rome—I have seen the spot where he now lies— the sticks that mark the spot where the sands cover him— he shall not be there, it is too near Via Reggio—they are now about this fearful office—and I live ! "

The corpse of Shelley had been found on the coast near Via Reggio: the face and hands, and all parts of the body not protected by the clothing, were fleshless.

"The tall, slight figure," writes Trelawney, who was called to identify it, "the jacket, the volume of Æschylus * in one pocket, and Keats's Poems in the other—doubled back as if the reader, in the act of reading, had hastily thrust it away— were all too familiar to me to leave a doubt on my mind that this mutilated corpse was any other than Shelley's. The body of Williams, much more mutilated still, was found on the coast, three miles from that of Shelley. . . . Williams was the only one of the three who could swim, and it is probable he was the last survivor. . . . Shelley always declared that, in case of wreck, he would vanish instantly, and not imperil valuable lives by permitting others to aid in saving his, which he looked upon as valueless. It was not until after three weeks after the wreck of the boat that a third body was found —four miles from the other two. This I concluded to be that of the sailor boy, Charles Vivian.

"I mounted my horse and rode to the Gulf of Spezzia, put up my horse, and walked until I caught sight of the lone house on the sea-shore in which Shelley and Williams had dwelt, and where their widows still lived. . . . As I stood on the threshold of their house, the bearer, or rather confirmer of news, which would rack every fibre of their quivering frames to the utmost, I paused, and looking at the sea, my memory reverted to our joyous parting only a few days before.

"The two families, then, had all been in the verandah,

---

* Mr. Dowden, who has seen the volume at Boscombe Manor, where all the relics of Shelley are collected, by the filial piety of his son, asserts that it is a Sophocles.

overhanging a sea so clear and calm that every star was reflected on the water as if it had been a mirror ; the young mothers singing some merry tune, with the accompaniment of a guitar. Shelley's shrill laugh—I heard it still—rang in my ears, with Williams's friendly hail, the general 'buona notte' of all the joyous party, and the earnest entreaty to me to return as soon as possible, and not to forget the commissions they had severally given me. I was in a small boat beneath them, slowly rowing myself on board the 'Bolivar,' at anchor in the bay, loath to part from what I verily believed to have been at that time, the most united and happiest set of human beings in the whole world. And now by the blow of an idle puff of wind the scene was changed. Such is human happiness.

"My reverie was broken by a shriek from the nurse Caterina, as crossing the hall she saw me in the doorway. After asking her a few questions, I went up the stairs, and, unannounced, entered the room. I neither spoke, nor did they question me. Mrs. Shelley's large gray eyes were fixed on my face. I turned away. Unable to bear this horrid silence, with a convulsive effort she exclaimed, ' Is there no hope ?' I did not answer, but left the room, and sent the servant with the children to them. The next day I prevailed on them to return with me to Pisa."

It was Trelawney, again, who undertook, in conformity with Tuscan law, to burn the bodies. He and Byron consulted together in order to render the cremation a solemn ceremony, recalling as far as possible the ceremonial of ancient times. A funeral oration alone was wanting. "We had lost," says Trelawney, "our Hellenic bard." The body of Edward Williams was burned on August 15th, and that of Shelley on the following day.

Byron assumed a somewhat theatrical and Hamlet-like demeanour on the occasion.

' "When Byron," says Trelawney, "saw the shapeless mass of bones and flesh"—[all that now remained of Williams]—"'Is that a human body?' he exclaimed. 'Why, it is more like the carcass of a sheep, or any other animal, than a man. This is a satire on our pride and folly.' I pointed to the letters E. E. W. on the black silk handkerchief. Byron, looking on, muttered : 'The entrails of a worm hold together longer than the potter's clay of which man is made. Hold ! let me see the jaw,' he added, as they were removing the skull ; 'I can recognise any one by the teeth with whom I have talked. I always watch the lips and mouth ; they tell what the tongue and eyes try to conceal. . . . Don't repeat this with me,' Byron said ; 'let my carcass rot where it falls.'

"The next day Byron and Leigh Hunt arrived in the carriage, attended by soldiers, and the health officer as before. The lonely and grand scenery that surrounded us so exactly harmonised with Shelley's genius that I could imagine his spirit soaring over us. The sea, with the islands of Gorgona, Capraji, and Elba, was before us ; old battlemented watch-towers stretched along the coast, backed by the marble-crested Apennines, glistening in the sun, picturesque from their diversified outlines, and not a human dwelling was in sight. As I thought of the delight Shelley felt in such scenes of loneliness and grandeur, whilst living, I felt we were no better than a herd of wolves or a pack of wild dogs, in tearing out his battered and naked body from the pure yellow sand that lay so lightly over it, to drag him back to the light of day ; but the dead have no voice, nor had I power to check the sacrifice. The work went on silently in the deep and unresisting sand ; not a word was spoken, for the Italians have a touch of sentiment, and their feelings are easily excited into sympathy. Even Byron. was silent and thoughtful. We were startled and drawn together by a dull hollow sound that followed the blow of a mattock ; the iron had struck a skull, and the body was soon uncovered. Lime had been strewn on it ; this, or decomposition, had the effect of staining it of a dark and ghastly indigo colour. Byron asked me to preserve the skull for him ; but remembering that he had formerly used one as a drinking-cup, I was determined Shelley's should not be so profaned. The limbs did not separate from the trunk, as in the case of Williams's body, so that the corpse was removed entire into the furnace. I have taken the precaution of having more and larger pieces of timber, in consequence of my experience of the day before of the difficulty of consuming a corpse in the open air with our apparatus. After the fire was well kindled we repeated the ceremony of the previous day, and more wine was poured over Shelley's dead body than he had consumed during his life. This, with the oil and salt, made the yellow flames glisten and quiver. The heat from the sun and the fire was so intense that the atmosphere was tremulous and wavy. The corpse fell open and the heart was laid bare. The frontal bone of the skull, where it had been struck with the mattock, fell off ; and as the back of the head rested on the red-hot bottom bars of the furnace the brains literally seethed, bubbled, and boiled, as in a cauldron, for a very long time.

"Byron could not face this scene ; he withdrew to the beach, and swam off to the *Bolivar.* Leigh Hunt remained in the carriage. The fire was so fierce as to produce a white heat on the iron, and to reduce its contents to gray ashes.

The only portions that were not consumed were some fragments of bones—the jaw and the skull—but what surprised us all was that the heart remained entire. In snatching this relic from the fiery furnace my hand was severely burnt.

"After cooling the iron machine in the sea, I collected the human ashes and placed them in a box, which I took on board the *Bolivar*. Byron and Hunt retraced their steps to their home, and the officers and soldiers returned to their quarters."

Shelley's ashes were deposited by Trelawney in the English cemetery at Rome, near those of his little son William, and his brother poet John Keats. Leigh Hunt inscribed *cor cordium* on the stone, and Trelawney added the following lines from Ariel's song in the Tempest :

> Nothing of him that doth fade,
> But doth suffer a sea change
> Into something rich and strange.

In the parish church of Christchurch, Hants, there is a monument of melancholy aspect, which recalls alike the image of Christ taken down from the cross and placed in His mother's arms, and that of a mournful, weeping Muse contemplating in silent sorrow the death-disfigured countenance of her dearest votary. This monument by Weeks, erected by filial piety in the shadow of a country church, to Shelley and Mary, awaits the hour when England shall atone for her ingratitude by placing it in Westminster Abbey by the side of the effigies of Milton, Spenser, and Shakespeare.

APPENDIX.

ság# FRAGMENT OF "ST. IRVYNE."

GINOTTI RELATES HIS HISTORY TO WOLFSTEIN.

"FROM my earliest youth, before it was quenched by
complete satiation, *curiosity*, and a desire of unveiling
the latent mysteries of Nature, was the passion by which
all the other emotions of my mind were intellectually
organised. This desire first led me to cultivate, and
with success, the various branches of learning which led
to the gates of wisdom. I then applied myself to the
cultivation of philosophy, and the *éclat* with which I
pursued it, exceeded my most sanguine expectations.
Love I cared not for ; and wondered why men perversely
sought to ally themselves with weakness. Natural
philosophy at last became the peculiar science to which
I directed my eager inquiries ; thence was I led into a
train of labyrinthic meditations. I thought of *death*—I
shuddered when I reflected, and shrank in horror from
the idea, *selfish and self-interested* as I was, of entering a
new existence to which I was a stranger. I must either
dive into the recesses of futurity, or I must not, I cannot die.—' Will not this nature—will not the *matter* of
which it is composed, exist to all eternity? Ah! I

know it will; and, by the exertions of the energies with which Nature has gifted me, well I know it shall.' This was my opinion at that time: I then believed that there existed no God. Ah! at what an exorbitant price have I bought the conviction that there is one!!! Believing that priestcraft and superstition were all the religion which *man* ever practised, it could not be supposed that I thought there existed supernatural beings of any kind. I believed *Nature* to be self-sufficient and excelling; I supposed not, therefore, that there could be anything beyond Nature.

"I was now about seventeen. I had dived into the depths of metaphysical calculations. With sophistical arguments had I convinced myself of the non-existence of a First Cause, and, by every combined modification of the essences of matter, had I apparently proved that no existences could possibly be, unseen by human vision. I had lived, hitherto, completely for myself; I cared not for others; and, had the hand of fate swept from the list of the living every one of my youthful associates, I should have remained immoved and fearless. I had not a friend in the world;—I cared for nothing but *self*. Being fond of calculating the effects of poison, I essayed one, which I had composed, upon a youth who had offended me; he lingered a month, and then expired in agonies the most terrific. It was returning from his funeral, which all the students of the college where I received my education (Salamanca) had attended, that a train of the strangest thought pressed upon my mind. I feared, more than ever, now to die; and although I had no right to form hopes or expectations for longer life than is allotted to the rest of mortals, yet did I think it were possible to protract existence. And why, reasoned I with myself, relapsing into melancholy, why am I to suppose that these muscles or fibres are made of stuff more durable than those of other men? I have no right to suppose otherwise than that, at the end of the time allotted by Nature for the existence of the atoms which compose my being, I must, like all other men, perish, perhaps everlastingly. Here in the bitterness of my heart, I cursed that Nature and chance which I believed in; and, in a paroxysmal frenzy of contending passions, cast myself, in desperation, at the foot of a lofty ash-tree, which reared its fantastic form over a torrent which dashed below.

"It was midnight; far had I wandered from Salamanca; the passions which agitated my brain, almost to delirium, had added strength to my nerves and swiftness to my feet; but after many hours' incessant walking, I began to feel fatigued. No moon was up, nor did one star illume the hemisphere. The sky was veiled by a thick covering of clouds; and, to my heated imagination, the winds, which in stern cadence swept along the night scene, whistled tidings of death and annihilation. I gazed on the torrent foaming beneath my feet; it could scarcely be distinguished through the thickness of the gloom, save at intervals, when the white-crested waves dashed at the base of the bank on which I stood. 'Twas then that I contemplated self-destruction; I had almost plunged into the tide of death, had rushed upon the unknown regions of eternity, when the soft sound of a bell from a neighbouring convent was wafted in the stillness of the night. It struck a chord in unison with my soul; it vibrated on the secret springs of rapture. I thought no more of suicide, but, reseating myself at the root of the ash-tree, burst into a flood of tears. Never had I wept before; the sensation was new to me; it was inexplicably pleasing. I reflected by what rules of science I could account for it; *there* philosophy failed me. I acknowledged its inefficacy, and, almost at *that* instant, allowed the existence of a superior and beneficent *Spirit*, in whose image is made the soul of man; but quickly chasing these ideas, and overcome by excessive and unwonted fatigue of mind and body, I laid my head upon a jutting projection of the tree, and, forgetful of everything around me, sank into a profound and quiet slumber. Quiet, did I say? No—it was not quiet. I dreamed that I stood on the brink of a most terrific precipice, far, far above the clouds, amid whose dark forms, which lowered beneath, was seen the dashing of a stupendous cataract; its roarings were borne to mine ear by the blast of night. Above me rose, fearfully embattled and rugged, fragments of enormous rocks, tinged by the dimly gleaming moon, their loftiness, the grandeur of their misshapen proportions, and their bulk, staggering the imagination; and scarcely could the mind itself scale the vast loftiness of their aërial summits. I saw the dark clouds pass by, borne by the impetuosity of the blast, yet felt no wind myself. Methought darkly gleaming forms rode on their almost palpable prominences.

"Whilst thus I stood gazing on the expansive gulf

which yawned before me, methought a silver sound
stole on the quietude of night. The moon became
as bright as polished silver, and each star sparkled with
scintillations of inexpressible whiteness. Pleasing images
stole imperceptibly upon my senses, when a 'ravishingly
sweet strain of dulcet melody seemed to float around.
Now it was wafted nearer, and now it died away in
tones to melancholy dear. Whilst I thus stood en-
raptured, louder swelled the strain of seraphic harmony ;
it vibrated on my inmost soul, and a mysterious softness
lulled each impetuous passion to repose. I gazed in
eager anticipation of curiosity on the scene before me ;
for a mist of silver radiance rendered every object but
myself imperceptible ; yet was it brilliant as the noon-
day sun. Suddenly, whilst yet the full strain swelled
along the empyrean sky, the mist in one place seemed to
dispart, and, through it, to roll clouds of deepest
crimson. Above them, and seemingly reclining on
the viewless air, was a form of most exact and superior
symmetry. Rays of brilliancy surpassing expression
fell from his burning eye, and the emanations from
his countenance tinted the transparent clouds below
with silver light. The phantasm advanced towards me ;
it seemed then, to my imagination, that his figure was
borne on the sweet strain of music which filled the
circumambient air. In a voice which was fascination
itself, the being addressed me, saying : ' Wilt thou
come with me ? wilt thou be mine ? ' I felt a decided
wish never to be his. ' No, no,' I unhesitatingly cried,
with a feeling which no language can either explain or
describe. No sooner had I uttered these words, than

methought a sensation of deadly horror chilled my sickening frame; an earthquake rocked the precipice beneath my feet; the beautiful being vanished; clouds, as of chaos, rolled around, and from their dark masses flashed incessant meteors. I heard a deafening noise on every side; it appeared like the dissolution of Nature; the blood-red moon, whirled from her sphere, sank beneath the horizon. My neck was grasped firmly, and, turning round in an agony of horror, I beheld a form more hideous than the imagination of man is capable of portraying, whose proportions, gigantic and deformed, were seemingly blackened by the inevasible traces of the thunderbolts of God; yet in its hideous and detestable countenance, though seemingly far different, I thought I could recognise that of the lovely vision. 'Wretch!' it exclaimed, in a voice of exulting thunder, 'saidst thou that thou wouldst not be mine? Ah! thou art mine beyond redemption, and I triumph in the conviction that no power can ever make thee otherwise. Say, art thou willing to be mine?' Saying this, he dragged me to the brink of the precipice; the contemplation of approaching death frenzied my brain to the highest pitch of horror. 'Yes, yes, I am thine,' I exclaimed. No sooner had I pronounced these words, than the visionary scene vanished, and I awoke."

LETTER TO GODWIN ON CLASSICAL EDUCATION.

"You know that in most points I agree with you. As I see you in 'Political Justice,' I agree with you. Your 'Enquirer' is replete with speculations in which I sympathise, yet the arguments there in favour of classical learning failed to remove all my doubts on that point. I am not sufficiently vain and dogmatical to say that *now* I have *no* doubts on the deleteriousness of classical education; but it certainly is my opinion—nor has your last letter sufficed to refute it—that the evils of acquiring Greek and Latin considerably overbalance the benefit. But why, because I think so, should it even be supposed necessary by you to warn me against fearing that *you feel displeasure?* Assure yourself that the picture of you in the retina of my intellect is a standing proof to me, that its original is capable of extending to opinions the most unlimited toleration, and that he will scan with disgust nothing but a defect of the heart. Let Reason, then, be arbiter between us. Yet sometimes I am struck with dismay when I consider that, placed where you are, high up on the craggy mountain of knowledge, you will scarcely condescend to doubt, even sufficiently for the purposes of discussion, although by that doubting, you might fit me for following your footsteps. Yet I will explain my reasons for doubting the efficacy of classical learning, as a means of forwarding the interests of the human race.

"In the first place, I do not perceive how one of the truths of 'Political Justice' rests on the excellence of ancient literature. That Latin and Greek have contributed to form your character, it were idle to dispute, but in how great a degree have they contributed? Are not the reasonings on which your system is founded utterly distinct from and unconnected with the excellence of Greece and Rome? Was not the Government of republican Rome, and most of those of Greece, as oppressive and arbitrary, as liberal of encouragement to monopoly as that of Great Britain is at present? And what do we learn from their poets? As you have yourself acknowledged somewhere, 'they are fit for nothing but the perpetuation of the noxious race of heroes in the world.' Lucretius forms perhaps the single exception. Throughout the whole of their literature runs a vein of thought similar to that which you have so justly censured in Helvetius. Honour— and the opinion either of contemporaries, or more frequently of posterity—is set so much above virtue as, according to the last words of Brutus, to make it nothing but an empty name. Their politics sprang from the same narrow and corrupted source. Witness the interminable aggressions between each other of the states of Greece; the thirst of conquest with which even republican Rome desolated the earth;—they are our masters in politics, because we are so immoral as to prefer self-interest to virtue, and expediency to positive good. You say that words will neither debauch our understandings, nor distort our moral feelings. You say that the time of youth could not be better employed than in the acquisition of classical learning. But *words* are the very things which so eminently contribute to the growth and establishment of prejudice; the learning of *words* before the mind is capable of attaching corresponding ideas to them, is like possessing machinery with the use of which we are so unacquainted as to be in danger of misusing it. But words are merely signs of ideas. How many evils, and how great evils, spring from annexing inadequate and improper ideas to words! The words honour, virtue, duty, goodness, are examples of this remark. Besides, we only want one distinct sign for one idea. Do you not think that there is much more danger of our wanting ideas for the signs of them already made, than of our wanting these signs for inexpressible ideas? I should think that natural philosophy, medicine, astronomy, and above all history, could be sufficient employments for immaturity; employments which would completely fill up the era of tutelage, and render unnecessary all expedients for losing time well, by gaining it safely.

"Of the Latin language as a grammar I think highly. It is a key to the European languages, and we can hardly be said to know our own without first attaining a complete knowledge of it. Still I cannot help considering it as an affair of minor importance, inasmuch as the science of things is superior to the science of words. Nor can I help considering the vindicators of ancient learning—I except you, not from politeness, but because you, unlike them, are willing to subject your opinions to reason—as the vindicators of a literary despotism ; as the tracers of a circle which is intended to shut out from real knowledge, and to which this fictitious knowledge is attached, all who will not support the established systems of politics, religion, and morals. I have as great a contempt for Cobbett as you can have, but it is because he is a dastard and a time-server; he has no humanity, no refinement ; but were he a classical scholar, would he have more? Did Greek and Roman literature refine the soul of Johnson? Does it extend the views of the thousand narrow bigots educated in the very bosom of classicality? But

> '. . . in publica commoda peccem
> Si longo sermone morer tua tempora,'

says Horace at the commencement of his longest letter."

LAST SCENE OF THE FIRST ACT OF "THE HAIR OF ABSALOM," BY CALDERON.

AMON—TAMAR.

Musicians singing behind the scenes.

Tamar.   Eat, Amon, while they sing.

Amon.   I would sooner listen.

Amon and Musicians.   He loveth not, who speaketh not.

Amon.   Be not surprised, divine Tamar, at my boldness, if to-day I violate the laws of modesty and reverence. May this white hand, without changing the lilies into asps, serve as antidote to my poison.

Tamar.   Let go my hand, Amon; it is wrong now to find fault with a mistake.*

Amon.   Were it a mistake, thou wouldst be right, but it is time for my passion to break the chain of my misery.

Amon and Musicians.   For he loveth not, who speaketh not.

Amon.   I am dying for thee, Tamar. My confidence has killed me.

Tamar (aside).   Who could have foreseen this? (*Aloud*).   Consider, Amon.

---

* An allusion to a preceding scene, in which Tamar had consented to act as an imaginary lover, to soothe her brother's distress.

Amon. I will consider nothing.

Tamar. I am thy sister. ·

Amon. True. But if, as the proverb says, " Blood boils without fire," what will blood and fire be together?

Tamar. Our law allows marriage between kindred. Ask my father for me.

Amon. It is late to try persuasion.

Tamar (calling). Hither !   [*A Musician enters.*

Amon. Tamar wishes you to sing.

Tamar. I?

The Musician. We obey.   [*Exit.*

          [*Singing behind the scenes.*

Amon. I must possess thee.—Jonadab, shut the doors at once.

Jonadab (from without). The doors are shut.

Tamar. Think of the risk.

Amon. I fear it not.

Tamar. Father ! Lord ! Absalom !

Amon. Thy sweet harmonious voice is powerless now.

Tamar. Then I will call on Heaven.

Amon. Heaven is slow to answer.

Tamar. Then shall this weapon kill thee. (*She snatches his sword and flies.*) Pursue me not, I have both strength and courage.

Amon. Thou hast wounded me now with my sword, and though this be an omen, I fear nothing. Having spoken, I must needs go on, for assuredly . . .

Amon and Musicians. He loveth not, who speaketh not.

THE END.

CHARLES DICKENS AND EVANS, CRYSTAL PALACE PRESS.